ROCKIN'
FAIRY TALES

Pink Guitars
AND
Falling Stars

*To Stephanie —
Enjoy!
x Leslie
O'Sullivan*

LESLIE O'SULLIVAN

MYSTIC OWL

AN IMPRINT OF CITY OWL PRESS

PINK GUITARS AND FALLING STARS
Rockin' Fairy Tales, Book 1

MYSTIC OWL
A City Owl Press Imprint
www.cityowlpress.com

Cover Design by MiblArt. All stock photos licensed appropriately.

Edited by Lisa Green.

For information on subsidiary rights, please contact the publisher at info@cityowlpress.com.

Print Edition ISBN: 978-1-64898-158-6

Digital Edition ISBN: 978-1-64898-157-9

Printed in the United States of America

To the four notes of my heart song: Melissa, Cameron, Rich, and John

"Love is a smoke made with the fume of sighs.
Being purged, a fire sparkling in lovers' eyes;
Being vex'd a sea nourish'd with lovers' tears."
-Romeo (Act 1 Scene 1)

1

JUMPER

YOU ONLY GET ONE PARACHUTE. THERE'S NO POINT PACKING TWO FOR a B.A.S.E. jump since you'll be pavement art before the second chute blossoms.

"Justin!"

Startled by a bellow from my jump leader/uncle, Timmer MacKenzie, my toe jerks to a stop half an inch above the trigger pedal of my launcher. Is his gray matter shredded, distracting me during a safety check? There's no chute on my back. One accidental tap on the business end of this launcher, and I'll be eye to eye with the flock of seagulls patrolling the Hollywood skies. I retreat onto the non-ballistic end of my perch. Peering over the edge of the Rampion Records Tower, I analyze the antics of the wind.

"Join us," Unc calls, teeth clenched in a P.R. smile. He hosts a cluster of reporters near the center of the circular roof. "Meet the rising star of the Slinging Seven."

Their faces morph into a collective portrait of panic as I leap more dramatically than necessary from launcher to the terra firma of the rooftop. After a salute to the Hollywood sign, a photo op my uncle will appreciate, I join the party. Pre-jump interviews are not my happy place, but keeping a smile on Timmer's face is essential.

He leads our B.A.S.E. jump troop, giving the green light for my carcass to launch off skyscrapers, bridges, and cliffs in a wing suit.

"This Rampion Records Tower may rival Mount Olympus for acceptable jump altitude," Timmer tells the press jam sandwich. "Even so, I believe in enhancing the safety zone for my lads."

I sweep an arm across the roof. "Thus, the launchers."

"Your latest exhibitions of low altitude B.A.S.E. jumps have raised serious concerns," says a fresh-out-of-journalism-school reporter. He rocks a Channel Six pin on the lapel of a blazer clearly tailored for someone else. We get his type all the time: low man on the news roster, usually stuck with covering mudslides or C-list celebrity screw-ups.

I grunt at the question. Timmer's a walking archive of aerodynamics. His B.A.S.E. jump designs adhere to a superhuman canon of safety. Even Unc can't control the wreath of clouds descending on the tower. Humidity makes trickier conditions. My bangs congeal into a sweaty clump. Twenty-three is too young to die when you have plans, and I have plans.

"To you, B.A.S.E. jumping is an extreme sport. To me, it's a science." Timmer slings an arm around my shoulder. "Would I risk my own nephew's life?"

A grandfatherly dude slides square-framed sunglasses to the end of a nose in serious need of a good hair plucking. "Come on, Mr. MacKenzie, that kid can't be eighteen."

I wince at the familiar speculation my youthful image always dredges up. Satan's roadies have prepped a new circle of hell for Timmer's perpetuation of the lie about me being eighteen. My B.A.S.E. jumping talents at twenty-three are PDG – pretty damn great—but a fresh out of high-school dude rocking my moves is prodigy wonder boy territory, great P.R. fodder.

I keep my lip zipped over the deception. I'm not going to lie, it does not suck being a prodigy wonder boy.

Unc spins me to display the product emblems plastered all over my banana-colored wing suit. "Endorsements like these don't come from launching children into the sky. Justin jumps one-hundred percent legally."

The reporter's skepticism settles at the edges of his mouth. Metallic coating on his sunglasses turn my gray eyes silver as I catch my reflection. The gloaming breeze plucks strands of my tawny mane free from the generous layer of product I always apply before a jump. I'll have to retame those suckers to restore my roguishly hot vibe instead of the young and soft look Timmer prefers. I'd give my right nut to have a growth spurt on the spot. Sadly, thanks to MacKenzie short man genes, there probably aren't any in my future.

A gust of wind blows the press a tiptoe closer to the curved edge of the roof. Timmer and I hold our ground with matching "no big thing" expressions.

A babe in a raspberry-colored lady suit pushes toward me, eyes bulging with concern. Twitchy fingers alight on my shoulder. Next to my banana wingsuit, we're a fruit salad. Here comes the *concerned auntie* vibe.

"Justin, why take risks B.A.S.E. jumping with the Slinging Seven Troupe even for someone as enchanting as Zeli?"

I bite back a groan at the mention of the pop queen.

"Is glorifying her platinum record worth your life?"

Truth rumbles in my throat. *Yes, ma'am, B.A.S.E. jumping is worth the moon. It got me to Hollywood, the land of my music dreams. Dreams that will free me from Timmer's whims so I can make my own destiny.*

Timmer's glare scorches a hole in my suit, cueing the trained monkey answer he expects.

I open my arms to the clouds. "Who doesn't want to fly?" Every person on this roof does. I see it in the way their eyes brighten.

My stomach loops into a knot. Unc may piss himself when his prize canary asks to go AWOL. I've jumped off everything Timmer asked of me on our jiggy pathway around the country to make it here. My gaze drifts to the Hollywood Sign as I press toes into the roof of Rampion Records, the touchstone by which all music greatness is measured.

Tonight, this bird will fly off the Rampion Tower. Tomorrow, I dive into the audition for Rampion's annual singing competition, The Summer Number One. It's the U.S. Open of music, amateurs vs. pros, where Rampion Records dangles a chance for nobodies like me to go mic to mic with their current stable of rock stars. According to the Rampion P.R. machine – *Even the little people in this world have a shot at the Summer Number One dream.* This ammie is going to kick some serious pro ass and score a Rampion Records contract. I've got everything I need for the audition: demo tracks, my guitar, ass-hugging black jeans, and a sexy aviator jacket.

For the last five years, in every crappy rent-a-room the Slinging Seven have crashed, I've done dozens of online music courses. I study. I practice. I'm ready.

Unc laughs at one of the reporters he's chatting up, and I see Ma's smile here on the rooftop. Our signature MacKenzie smile packs serious wattage. I should know, I've busted it out often enough to sway, play, and dazzle females of the species.

Once I grab the top spot in the Summer Number One, my pile of gold for winning will be enough to snag my own digs here in L.A., the last place I remember Ma smiling. The cold burn of loneliness flares when I think of her and wonder if she's safe.

Clouds thicken as I watch the sun dip into the Pacific Ocean. I ignore a stitch of concern at the base of my neck as the jump difficulty ticks up a notch and think in my language of future Justin merch.

T-shirt moment: Music Dreams Sucker Punch Death.

Channel Six pushes in front of his colleagues. "Justin, does Zeli have a lock on the top pro spot in the Summer Number One?"

Lady Suit bumps her shoulder into mine. "Is Zeli your dream girl?"

My lips twist into a frown. Zeli is my nightmare.

Timmer digs his fist into my back, my cue to fix my pissy face. I manage to upgrade to a grimace dressed as a smile. By their winks and snickers, the reporters take my tension as embarrassment. I'd like to water cannon them all off the roof. I'm entitled to a dream girl, but it will never be the plastic diva with her bubblegum diluted pop crap. That chickadee is an affront to everything I love about music.

Unc hasn't run out of bluster. "It's an honor for the Slinging Seven to be part of Zeli's platinum record celebration."

My temple throbs. I'm more than half nuts to risk a concrete sandwich for that over-hyped female commodity with a pink guitar.

2

HER

LADY SUIT'S QUESTION MESSES WITH MY HEAD AS TIMMER AND I hustle down the stairs from the roof.

Why take risks B.A.S.E. jumping even for someone as enchanting as Zeli?

Timmer flicks the side of my head. "First you're late–"

I rub the spot he hit. "Don't mess with the guidance system."

Glaring, he extends his middle finger back to the roof. "Then, you pull off that sucking-lemons face in the interview." His nose nearly touches mine. "Next time anyone mentions Zeli, drop to your knees. Worship. She's your goddess. Got it?"

Timmer cups the back of my neck, pressing a finger into an artery. Blood pumps against his touch.

"If we score on tonight's jump, it's the bigs, Super Bowl half-times, inaugurations." He shakes me. "So drop your pissy 'tude."

He releases me from the nerve pinch to scratch stubble on his chin. He zeroes in on mine. "Rock a shave before the jump." He slaps my cheek. "Remember, Baby Face, your job is to make *me* happy. I'm all you've got since my dear sis dumped you on my doorstep to chase her latest Y chromosome."

It's been seven years since she split 'cause Timmer snowed her into believing he offered me a future. Instead, I got indentured servitude.

"I got big dreams for the troupe, J."

Timmer will go supernova when I spill the news of my impending weeklong vacay from the troupe to kick it in the Summer Number One competition.

Unc kicks open the door marked *Floor 33*. He waves a hand over the thumb-sized discs sprinkled all over his yellow jumpsuit and crooks a thumb into the hallway. "Get your twinkle lights pasted on and meet me on the roof in fifteen. Wardrobe is around the bend."

Everything in the Rampion Records Tower is around the bend. The building is a freaking cylinder. My breath catches at the landscape outside the window. On its hillside throne, the Hollywood sign throbs pink through the darkening sky. Pink is Diva Zeli's signature color. Below, pin spots of magenta litter the vast concrete plaza. Light strings, flashing every permutation of pink, run from the Rampion Tower to the rooftops of buildings ringing the circular plaza. Timmer made us memorize which strings were actually zip lines.

Tonight, we'll steer clear of every zip line and light string as we jump through a connect-the-Zeli-dots world. Even the moat flowing around the base of the tower froths with pink Zeli-infected bubbles. The chick does not have enough talent to warrant all this hype. The empress has no clothes.

"Justin time..."

Justin? Wardrobe sings its siren song to me, the lone jumper missing his twinkle dots. The hallway dims as it narrows, walls replacing windows. A door up ahead makes its presence known by the pink glow escaping its edges.

"Our stars crossed just in time..."

I slip into wardrobe and find a wedge-shaped room bathed in twilight. I'm behind a rack of costumes when the door glides shut behind me. Windows bow along the far curvature of the wall. Outside, a flat black surface replicating a vinyl record seems to float in mid-air.

It's one of the iconic licorice discs that skirt each floor of the Rampion Records Tower. The effect is an enormous record stack. The only light comes from a Zeli-pink shine etched in the grooves of the faux vinyl.

A shadow perches on the edge of a bench next to a glass table dead center in the room. Wardrobe's short straw works overtime, waiting to hook me up with twinkle dots.

I'm about to shout "Boo!" when the figure begins to sing.

"To blaze a path across..."

It's the same voice I heard from the hall. Is it in the Rampion employee job description that everyone sings, even wardrobe? My vision adjusts and a beat later, my heart skitters to a full stop.

This is not wardrobe. Across the room sits America's overrated number one pop star.

Zeli.

At least, I think it's Zeli, but the synthesized pop drivel that usually pours from her mouth has changed. This voice rivals dawn birdsong; pure, lovely. And singing my name.

"Just-in."

My jaw sags at a vision so fragile one breath from me will shatter her into Z-pieces. Through closed lids, a single teardrop flows to the tip of her rounded nub of a nose. Does she cry water or rosy pearls? If I captured that tear with the tip of my tongue, would it taste like cotton candy?

The world shifts into soft focus. This can't be over-processed, glam Zeli with magenta lacquered eyelashes stiff enough to dent a door. My sprite vision is too precious to be real. One touch will prove she's an enchantment conjured in place of Rampion's prize pony. Tiptoeing farther into the room, I stretch fingers, expecting the shadow to zap into smoke on contact.

"Just-in."

The richness of her voice draws me in. A flex of my knee, foot off the floor, and–

POW!

A door off to the side bangs open, splattering a cone of yellow light onto a for reals woman. I blow backward, ducking behind costumes. Fate breaks my fall as I land on a soft pile instead of becoming a drumbeat against the tile floor.

Through a space between waves of pink fabric, I see Grant Gothel ooze into the room. *The* Grant Gothel. *The* uber manager. *The* legend. Snagging Gothel's ear is a rocket blast to the music stratosphere. I finger the thumb drive in my pocket with my demo songs. It would be gold to get this into his hands before the Summer Number One audition. I'd take the stage already blipping on *The* star maker's radar.

A rough baritone glides around the walls. "My angel."

Gothel is his own licorice tower with that black suit, hair of glossy tar, olive skin, and eyes that seem to repel light. He opens his arms as if blessing Zeli. A teacup with a curlicue pink Z on its side and greenish steam spiraling into the air rests on one palm. When the queen holds her arms out, Gothel walks into the hug and pats her back. He offers the drink.

She stares with watercolor blue irises set in perfectly round eyes. Wrinkling her pixie nose—that out of nowhere, I imagine dotting with a kiss—she crosses her arms.

"Papa, this platinum record extension is too heavy." Delicate fingers disappear under a silver sack bunched at the nape of her neck. Inside that sack lurks a highway of hair extensions as overexposed as Zeli's music. The shimmery silver case meanders around the room, bulging like a sleeping python with a full belly.

"A quick preshow boost, Angel, will fix you right up. A few tears should do it."

Pain in my jaw tells me to shut my mouth before an ill-timed gurgle gives me away. I've only seen flashes in music vids of those mad extensions that rival Joseph's Coat of Many Colors. Within the sack, rectangle after rectangle of designs string together in a parade long enough to circle this tower. Top designers have contributed to this ungodly mane. Even Peter Max and Andy Warhol tributes are woven into the mess.

She shoots to her feet. "I don't want another boost. I'm done. The platinum record is my last extension. Don't add anymore." Only two stomps away from Gothel, the hair sack snags, jerking Z's head backward. At the same instant, the cushion beneath me strains, trying to slide.

I'm the snag.

3

TRADING RHYMES

BRIDGING INTO A BACK BEND, ALLOWS THE HAIR SACK TO SLITHER FREE beneath me. Zeli stumbles forward as flecks like a Fourth-of-July sparkler burst from one of her extensions to sting my ass.

Gothel's tone of concern is edged with warning. "Careful, Angel." Her campaign to nix new extensions dies as she concentrates on not keeling over.

Light from the doorway catches the curve of a metallic disk peeking out the end of the hair sack near Zeli's slipper. Gothel lifts it, reflection sending a silvery gleam across his skin. "We've come a long way from your first extension." He taps a rainbow rectangle of woven flexi-straws near her shoulder. "First prize on the 'You've Got a Gift' show."

That's where Zeli got her start? Seven years ago, I made it to the second round of auditions for that show when Ma and I lived here in Hollywood. That's when my addiction to make music took wing, only to be clipped when Timmer scooped me up into the jump troupe. Funny thing about addictions, once you get that first taste of the nectar, you forever crave it.

Gothel tilts the disc back to the light. "And now, this beauty."

The extension is an actual platinum record applied onto a square background of twisty white metal.

"This addition ticks your tresses past the nine point eight-million-dollar mark." When he holds it near her cheek, she turns away. Gothel chuckles. "Legend territory."

Zeli clutches her neck. "But Papa–"

Papa?

Sadness in her expression digs at my gut. Gothel crooks a knuckle under her chin with just the right amount of point to hold a dimple smaller than the tip of my pinkie. He lifts Zeli's face. "Let's shoot for ten million, sweets. Five million for each of your dear parents. God rest their souls."

Extensions worth ten million bucks! Obsessed with scoring a better view of Zeli's strands of fortune, I nudge a glitter pink jumpsuit aside. A wisp of daisy yellow hair tickling her jaw line catches my attention. She trains it behind her ear as if hiding what's authentically hers.

"This is your time, my platinum doll."

"I'm so tired, Papa."

"More tears, darling dear. Rampion tea makes pain disappear." Gothel kneels like he's praying and holds the teacup to her lips. She drinks.

His freaky rhyme and tableaux send a chill through me. Light catches twin trickles of tears flowing down Zeli's cheeks.

Gothel reaches inside his jacket and removes a pink glass mini flask. Is this the "boost" he promised? Figures the pop diva runs on her own special brand of vandal fuel.

Instead of offering Zeli a swig, he pulls a stopper from the flask and lays the rim against one cheek and then the other to catch her tears.

She tries to pull away, but his hand cups the back of her neck, holding her in place. Quick little gasps increase her flow of tears. He catches each one as they fall. After a few beats, Gothel raises the pink bottle to the light and swirls the liquid inside.

I swear the flask gives off a faint light.

Satisfied, Gothel throws back the liquid in a long gulp and slides the flask back into his pocket. He threads fingers under the extension closest to Zeli's neck, resting his forehead against hers, and whispers words too quiet to hear.

A golden corona surrounds Zeli's head. A ripple runs the length of the silver sack holding her hair train. From several extensions, sparks like the ones that singed my ass earlier flare. They dance about a foot in the air and then rain down, settling back into place.

A rush of *what the hell* runs up my spine. Why did Gothel toss back a shot of Z's tears? Where'd the freaky glow come from? Whatever this ritual is, it's an eerie brand of weird. It's past time to blow this scene.

Gothel crooks a finger under Zeli's chin, raising her gaze to meet his. "Better?"

With lips pressed tight, Z rolls her neck and nods.

Gothel spreads his arms. "Claim your glory under the stars tonight, my angel with your platinum song and platinum tress."

Zeli stares at him with dead eyes. "Papa Gothel, I need time at the Malibu compound away from the city, the mobs, and cameras."

Again with the Papa?

Gothel tucks the platinum record extension into the end of the hair bag as gently as if it were an egg. "Not this week, Angel. You'll ride this platinum wave into the Summer Number One competition." He snaps his fingers. "I need performance tracks of your new song as soon as you finish it." He pauses. "Do you have a title yet?"

Was that *Just-in* tune she chirped a handful of minutes ago, her Summer Number One song?

"We'll be set to have a million downloads of the new song on Tuneful before you step off that stage. Now finish your tea." Zeli's sigh is the definition of pathetic. "Thirty minutes until go time. Prep Team Z is on their way."

"Yes, Papa."

Grant Gothel follows the path of amber light he brought into the room and snaps the door shut.

Shades of pink twilight swallow us. Zeli rests lips against the rim of her cup, drowning a sob with tea.

Man, that tea smells sweet. I'd like to tickle my vocal cords with it. What did GG call it? Ramp-up tea? Justin wants to ramp up. I stand and take a greedy sniff.

Zeli catches sight of me and leaps to her feet. She screeches like I'm slinging an axe. "Get out. PAPA!"

I trip over the bottom of the costume rack and fly forward, finding balance a hot second before I plow into her. "Whoa, sweetness. I'm not here to mess with you."

She clutches her head. "Hair thief!" She raises a pair of fists with intent to cause damage. "Closer and I'll make your ribs crack."

"Stop screaming or that cute face will go blue."

Zeli circles her fists, searching for an in to deck me. "Don't lay a finger on my extensions."

"I want no part of that crazy hair mess." I shake my head. "Keep your freak show, I've got no intention–" Taking a step back, I fan an arm down her body. "To finger even a single sweet tress."

She's delusional. No thief could bust Rampion security to get up here. Then again, when you've got millions glued to your head, imagining creepers in the dark is not so *out there*.

She zips behind the table, snarling. "You won't get a piece of this either, fool."

Hugging her body, she curls into a ball worthy of an armadillo. I'm not stupid enough to take advantage of our alone time, but that doesn't prevent a Zeli lip lock from ticking onto my mental playlist. Her face pops out of the Z-ball as if she's plugged into my thoughts.

She raises her hands. "Hands here. Raise them up high where I can see."

I brush bangs aside, the portrait of casual. "You're safe, damsel, get a hold of your cool." I jerk my chin her way. "Cut the innocent act. It's clear to me. No way a fast track, rock chick hasn't known–" I throw her an air kiss. "Tune-piping Romeo love of her own."

She stretches to her full height, not enough to hit the five foot mark, and plants hands on hips. "Jacklick."

After flashing my best stink-eye, I head for the hallway before her insults bait me into action I'll regret. The *smack* of her hand against the table makes me jump.

"You're leaving?"

I flick my wrist. "You ain't nothing but a wrong turn." I almost clear the doorway of the twilight room when she giggles. I whip around. "What? I'm not the big bad wolf anymore?"

She abandons her table fortress and rakes a finger up and down my wingsuit. The silver bag glides after her. "Big bads don't wear bananas."

I cringe.

Realization dawns in her eyes. "Oh, you're one of my lucky stars." She claps.

"What?"

"Seven lucky stars, falling from the sky for my concert?"

"Maybe."

"If not, you're rocking a wack look." Zeli smiles, easy with me now that she's defined my place in her kingdom.

Don't count me out. I can rock a threat, babe. I'm tempted to grab her and plant a kiss on that laughing mouth. I feel my face flush Zeli pink. Stealing a taste of Z-lip is not worth summoning Gothel and screwing my chances at the Summer Number One audition.

To my surprise, she strolls over and dances a finger across my shoulder. "What's it like to B.A.S.E. jump? Terrifying or Heaven?"

The touch renders me momentarily mute.

Her fingers pop off my shoulder like I'm a hot stove. "I don't want anyone jumping for me to be afraid."

The slightest sensation lingers from our contact. Does rock chick Zeli honestly care how Justin MacKenzie feels flying off her tower? Is this chick nice? For reals, nice? Heavenly tea breath wafts from her lips. An urge for a softer kind of kissing sneaks up on me. Kisses that whisper, not shout.

I match her finger dance and dab a touch on her shoulder close enough to feel the warm skin of her neck. "Nice of you to care." If I slide my hand around the back of her neck, pull her in...

Downshift. This is freakin' Zeli. Boundaries, Justin. "Your drink smells amazing."

Mention of her tea flips a switch, and she breaks contact, snatching the teacup to cradle against her chest. "Don't touch it." Z downs the rest of the tea in one gulp. The swallow appears to temper her prickly 'tude. Peeking at me through the handle, a smile tricks up the right side of her lip. "You could lick the cup."

Tempting. That smell and a taste of Zeli on the rim...

She wiggles the cup, taunting me as she moves in close. With my pinkie, I catch the tiny drop of tea clinging to the corner of her mouth. The touch releases a mew from Zeli's lips that sends ripples of heat through my body. The aroma of the tea rides the air between us, acting like a magnet. My prize of that single drop forgotten, I lean in to taste tea straight from her lips. She closes her eyes, and a delicate pink tongue dampens her perfect bow mouth with an invitation.

I have no respect for this babe but being in her presence fizzles my brain as effectively as a line of whisky shots. Mind and body turn stone stupid. A strain against the crotch of my wingsuit slams me back to my senses.

Retreat, Justin.

I force my right boot and then my left back to create distance from the tea and this chickadee. "I'm sure you have enough cup lickers in your life."

Zeli's eyes snap open. She smashes the teacup onto the glass tabletop hard enough to break off the handle.

"You got that right, jumper."

Sass and salt are not what I expect. Perhaps, this chick has more shades than I gave her credit for. Who is Zeli?

My cell rises from the dead in my pocket. It's Timmer.

Justin WTF

"I'm out," I say. Z's face rocks disappointment. "Got this jump thing."

"I got this singing thing." Her smile glows sweeter than pop-babe Zeli's smile. She's sweeter. "Goodbye, star."

"Goodbye, Zeli." I back out of the twilight room away from tea and temptation.

She snaps her fingers and points at me. "Be careful."

I take her instruction to heart. With the possibility of the Summer Number One in my future and another chance to see Zeli, I'll rock the best jump of my life tonight, no mistakes.

4

TWINKLE TWINKLE

T<small>HE ROOF OF THE</small> R<small>AMPION</small> T<small>OWER HOSTS THE NIGHT'S CHILL.</small> W<small>HILE</small> Timmer recites tonight's B.A.S.E. jump formation for the millionth time, I rip and stick the Velcro that anchors a thumb-sized switch to my sleeve. One squeeze and the dots plastered all over my suit twinkle. I'll be a sparkling banana. The Velcro rhythm underscores my mental replay of Zeli's unexpected combination of sweetness and spunk. I barely touched her, and she's plastered on my psyche.

What if I'd stepped in it and kissed her? Invited that perfect little pink tongue to rock a taste of me. And that tea, I'll take a gallon.

Timmer smacks my shoulder. "Is your head in the game, Justin?"

"Nowhere else."

"What the piss took you so long?"

Do I confess my royal encounter or hope Timmer never finds out? "I skipped into the wrong room and ran into Zeli."

Timmer waves his hand. "No big. While we worked the press, the lads got their five seconds of meet and greet with Miss Z." He slaps the twinkle light disk over his heart. "Did she feed you the *seven lucky stars* line?"

My gut deflates. So much for the connection I imagined between Z and me. Shitiot, Justin. Nothing is for reals in the Rampion Tower.

Timmer laughs at my scowl. "You fell for her script." He snorts. "Chick is a concoction, dash of voice, pinch of cutesy face, and that ungodly hair."

I puff air. "No falling here."

"You've seen the Zeli-Telly show. She dials up her lucky star number on a new dumbass every week and gives them a pink guitar." I follow his eye line to a pile of pink guitars stacked at the bottom of our equipment rack.

One Z-tear, a whiff of tea, and I caved without even my own pink guitar to show for it. Her lucky star, my ass. I shine on my own, baby.

The wind knocks me into Timmer. "Load up your ballast, J."

A bucket full of oval sandbags the size of zucchinis skids to my feet. I fill the slots in my wingsuit with ballast since my puny ass is easy prey for rapacious winds.

The Hollywood Sign flashes pink-white-pink-white. At the base of the hills, Hollywood Boulevard radiates an electric blur. One in a long line of Ma's boyfriends was a DJ, Freddie Belarus, Feisty B. He'd pieced together a recording studio in a room of his apartment that overlooked Hollywood and Vine. He made music, staring down on the land of dreams. Freddie said I have a voice that calls to people. He'd take me to music stores, pop headphones on my noggin, and encourage me to sing along with the sample tunes. People always came to listen. Their reactions proved I've got the goods.

Feisty B. stoked my hunger to take music further. It killed me when Rhona MacKenzie pulled her signature boyfriend bail on him. At least I left with a half-decent demo of my original tunes, Feisty's old laptop, and upgraded strings for my guitar.

Timmer calls to the Slinging Seven. "Ready, lads?" He glares at the wind. "Keep a fix on those zip lines."

There's no way to miss the biggest line that stretches from the top floor of Rampion Records to a rooftop across the plaza. I've seen videos of Gothel riding that line like Tinkerbelle in a black suit spewing P.R. The line itself is surrounded by a larger spiral track to hold the light show that accompanies the big man's ride above his kingdom. Pink lights along the top allow us to spot it in the dark. Luckily, it's on the opposite side of the tower from the stage complex set up for her royal pinkness.

The lads and I hoof it to the launchers spread around the rooftop. Seven exits, jumping off points, seven souls poised to tempt the void between life and death, our spirit dance. Off to the west the inky expanse of the Pacific holds its breath. Below, leering up at me is the shadowy maw between the lights of Hollywood Boulevard and Rampion Plaza. That's vandal territory, home of druggies, thuggies, and freaks, the last stretch of Hollywood to risk as a landing pad.

Timmer whistles the ready cue. I position my foot over the trigger and give my chute straps a final tug. The notes of Zeli's song, "Stars and Fireflies," bounce off the Hollywood hills. Platinum, my ass. Her ballad is tin. She squeaks like a rat sensing cheese. Why does she spew this tripe instead of the delish voice I heard in the twilight room? Z hits a crescendo. It's go time.

Every light around the plaza dies. The light strings that crisscrossed the plaza drop until they are faint twinkling lines of pink dripping down the sides of the Rampion Tower, out of our way.

My foot drops onto the launch trigger. I'm star bound, blasting into the night twice as high as the rest of the troupe. The world is black except for a waxing sliver of moon, pink spotlights on a bubblegum diva, and seven yellow stars falling from a Zeli sky. Moisture-sucking drafts rip into my nose. The sound of Zeli wailing her song punches through the air.

"Stars. Fireflies."

I squeeze the switch to activate the twinkle dots. Strobing lights swarm over me like carnivorous gnats. Wind sings a sibilant tune, trying to flip my eyelids inside out. I rescue my goggles before they peel off into space. The Hollywood Sign twinkles with the same pinpricks of light that blink off every inch of the Slinging Seven.

"Stars. Fireflies."

I'm dropping too fast. I shoot my arms to the side. The wingsuit tames the wind and I curve under the moon, every cell in my body harmonizing with the air around me in a rarefied state of alive.

Screw death.

Screw life.

The in-between and freaking bliss is all there is.

Come back from the trance, Justin. Engage your routine. Between Zeli's screeches and a let up in the wind, the first glitzy banana comes into view.

Target.

I head in his direction. In two beats, I'm spiraling around Timmer. One down. I'll pass them all, wickets in my celestial game of croquet. I head to the next lad in the chain. Round and round the plaza I twirl, weaving a path in the air.

MacKenzie Magic.

One by one, platinum-colored chutes deploy. Each jumper flares and then descends, glittering fog seeking the stage. Mania from the crowd pierces the wind. They chant for me, the last of the seven stars, to open my chute.

"Se-ven."

Milk it, J. Scare the shit out of them and draw Gothel's attention to my star shine. By the time I join him on stage for the Slinging Seven's bow, Grant Gothel will beg for the demo of this starlight personified. Down I drop, soaking in the spotlight. Chute in ten, nine...

I see Zeli.

It's not the woman I fix on who sways in a sea of color on an outdoor stage encased in a carapace of silver trusses. It's her extensions. Lights chase across the river of hair that's blasted free from the silver sack and snakes from the stage halfway around the base of the Rampion Tower.

Every ten steps, a chickadee in a pink-sparkle cat suit tosses the hair, spins underneath and catches it, prancing in unison to the beat of Zeli's tune. Along extension row, patterns mutate into color bands, swirls, patchwork, madras, metallics, bizarre colored animal prints, and more.

The hair maidens finally dance the end of Zeli's outrageous mane onto the stage. Grant Gothel raises the new platinum extension above his head. Its image fills the massive Jumbotron screens flanking the stage while voices from the people crammed together on the plaza erupt in adoration for their pink pop queen.

I sync my breath and heart back into a workable duet. There's a sudden key change to the crowd's song. In a beat, the source of their freak out is easy to I.D.

Me.

My trajectory aims straight for their heads. I've dipped too close without opening my chute.

Poptastic Zeli and her fireflies are not worth dying for. I flick the release of my chute. A gust of wind jerks me toward the moon.

The plaza screams in appreciation, swaying to and fro. They chant, "Jum-per."

Spotlights find me. I wave, feeling the love. *Remember me, Justin the Jumper who makes your heart go pumper.*

My own pulse hiccups when I calculate the cost of my late chute. I'm off target. It'll take mad skills to achieve the original landing point. Before a course correction is possible, more wind fills my canopy, zipping me away from the concert. As I head to the fringe of the crowd, I catch sight of Timmer and the lads hitting the target zone in front of the stage.

Unc searches the night until he finds me. He flashes me the touchdown signal at a point past the crowd. Spotlights abandon me.

Grant Gothel waves Zeli's platinum record extension in time to the next song. The Slinging Seven stand on stage with Z, twinkling and waving while I bobble under the masters of chute and wind.

The chance to press my demo into Gothel's palm withers under a pink star.

5

STAMPEDE

My throat cinches tight enough to kill breath as I maneuver alongside the grandstands at the edge of the plaza. The original landing target is lost. New plan: I'll touch down, ditch the chute, and dash up one of the aisles to the stage.

Timmer and the lads along with thousands on the plaza fist pump to Zeli's music while minions dance the highway of hair onstage. Each time an extension is featured under the center spotlight, the audience screams and stomps, turning the plaza into a huge echo chamber.

Gothel whips the crowd into a bigger frenzy while Z's fabulocks sway, the current of a river.

My belly shreds and braids itself back together. Those extensions are a soul-sucking gimmick, a shackle to fame. I can testify that Zeli has no love for that last extension. Someone should lop them all off and free the chickadee.

I position my body to land and curse over going momentarily soft. Zeli's hair train must be a ruse. Chick probably unhooks it every night as soon as she's out of fan view. The wind centers me above the grandstands as Zeli's pop noise comes to an end.

My last hope to take the stage dies.

Pink fireworks light the sky. Rock babe sweeps into a ballerina bow. She freezes halfway down, catching sight of me.

"There he is!" Z hoots, clapping pop diva palms. "The last jumper." In a synchronous wave, the multi-headed crowd beast turns my way. Zeli chirps into her mic. "My luckiest star."

Luckiest, my ass. I'm not today's pink guitar poster boy, woman. I'm Justin MacKenzie who out sings you any day ending in y.

The crowd resumes their earlier chant. "Jump-er."

I smile, savoring my resurrection of fame. After I nail my audition and take the Summer Number One stage forty-eight hours from now, I'd like to hit replay on this level of love.

My scrutiny flicks from the crowd to a hubbub up front. Before Gothel can stop her, Zeli taps down the steps leading offstage. She sprints along the red-carpet aisle cut through the center of the plaza. Behind her, a circus comes to town. Hair maidens trip over one another to keep extensions off the ground. Chasing after them is a black current of bouncers in high-end suits, Gothel goons.

Zeli pours on steam, powering through the audience well ahead of the Rampion muscle on her tail.

"Holy pink hell," I swear as her target become clear. She heads for the piece of real estate directly below me.

I wave her off, but the crowd envelops her. My heart pummels ribs. What chance does her petite frame have against this fanatical blitz?

Her head and body are jerked backward as hands grab at her hair. Pieces of her extensions rise to the surface of the mob and flow away in every direction. Her so-called, beloved fans tear Zeli's trademark tail to bits.

I forget to breathe, willing the Gothel goons to halt the mauling and get Zeli back onstage. Why did Z run to me? My notion of a bubblegum witch with a *look-at-me* mane shifts back to the weepy chick begging to see the beach, one who cares if Justin MacKenzie makes it back to Earth. A babe to kiss with gentle lips.

This is no time for my brain to reprogram its Zeli file. Below, the scene goes from manic to mad. Compliments of relentless updrafts, I'm well above the mob. Not for long. I point my wingsuit to where human carrion birds pick at Z's hair.

"Get your hands off her." Yanking the ballast out of my right sleeve, I heave it into the thick ring of bodies surrounding Z. I rocket every sand sausage out of my wingsuit until my banana skin is empty of everything but me.

Without the extra weight, wind spits me sideways. Eardrum-splitting sirens pierce the plaza. Another black wave of thugs-in-suits pours over the bridge that spans the moat surrounding the Rampion tower to chase down the stolen extensions. Through every speaker, Gothel's warnings drone a dissonant chord.

If I try to touch down into the chaos, my chute strings will strangle me or some other fool. Managing to steer both wingsuit and the chute canopy snapping over my head away from the war zone, I target free space in front of the ring of palm trees lining the tower moat.

Zeli's dash is my fault. My shitiocy lured her offstage. She reached out to me and fell into a viper's nest. I sneak a peek to see if she's okay.

That single moment of distraction destroys my hope for a clear landing. Ducking my face into the crook of an elbow, I crash through layers of palm fronds. My hand slaps the chute release, so the lines don't turn noose on me. I freefall the last ten feet like a marble through a milkshake.

Go limp, Justin. A relaxed body breaks into fewer pieces. I splash into the moat before I pull a deep breath. Sucking water was not part of my scenario, but sucking I am. My arms flail, attempting to set a course for oxygen.

Flail. Kick.

My face breaks water long enough to gulp air. I go under and up again. A wave gushes into my mouth. I spit out the over-chlorinated soup of the Rampion moat.

Flail. Kick. Choke.

A chunk of frothy pink foam overtakes me. I'm a wad of drowning bubble gum. Underwater jets zip me around the moat. Through the pink filter of water, the gargantuan Rampion record stack wavers above. I'll drown staring at my dream. Maybe Zeli will get a new banana colored extension to remember her not-so-lucky star.

I kick toward the side of the moat closest to the tower. My hands meet nothing but slick. There's no scrabbling up the three feet of black tile between the surface of the water and dry land.

My lungs are one click shy of bursting as I approach the bridge spanning the moat in front of the main entrance to the tower. The water pulls me, too strong to fight. This is it. In two beats, I'll be a bug on a black tile windshield.

Under the bridge, a circle of light comes into view. It's a tunnel, a tunnel with handholds. I kick through the water toward the opening and manage to grab a metal handle.

I *am* a lucky star.

Pulling along the series of handles, I slide up and out of the short tunnel onto a concrete floor. The *whoosh* of the moat rises behind me.

Streams of pink goo splutter from my nostrils, and chlorine singes my sinuses. I'm a fish flapping on the sidewalk. I flip onto my knees and puke pink. Raspberry tinted bubbles pop all around me.

The room reeks of berry smell from Zeli bubbles. I blink until my vision clears to register this place as a maintenance dock. Pool skimmer nets and long handled scrub brushes hang on the wall next to a row of chlorine canisters.

The twinkle dots left on my wingsuit short out one by one, a series of tiny taser stings. I smack at them and go rigid when I feel the thumb drive in my pocket.

My demo can't be ruined.

I unzip and retrieve the night's single miracle. Thanks to the lining of my suit pocket and a plastic snack bag, the thumb drive is dry.

"Halle–fucking–lujah."

I've got to find Timmer. The wingsuit sopped up enough water to make slogging across the dock heavy business. I aim for a door at the end of the room. The hands I lay on the crash bar are dyed pink. Even my cuticles scream Zeli.

Why is that woman stuck to the inside of my brain like a crinkled piece of tape impossible to shake off a finger? It's her secret voice. That rich, gorgeous sound she's hiding away pulls me into its orbit.

"Don't be squashed, Pop Queen."

I crack the door and peek into a utilitarian space. No glitz, glam, or sign of the Z-riot here. My heart sloshes along with my steps. I drew Zeli off her safe perch. If she's hurt, Gothel will plaster my face on a Rampion wanted poster. That'll munch my shot at making it into his Summer Number One.

Outside the dock, bluish, concrete walls wrap around a ring-shaped maintenance corridor that loops in a tighter curve than the business hallways of the tower. Not far from the door, I find a service elevator. The Slinging Seven will be up on floor 33 in wardrobe, shedding twinkle dots and banana skins.

There's a cramp in my chest from the combo of swallowing moat water and fear of facing Timmer.

He'll be glad I'm alive so he can kill me.

6

PINK GUITAR

INSIDE THE ELEVATOR, THE SKELETAL HAND OF PANIC JABS A BONY finger between my eyes. I'm freaked that Rampion's diva may be damaged goods because I blew off Timmer's order to land. Double freaked my shitiocy may have blown my chance at the Summer Number One.

I run hands through gummy hair. "Ugh." My effort yields another layer of pink under my nails.

That last glimpse of Zeli was ten shades of ugly. A quick peek into her ready room, the twilight room where we met, should answer my million-dollar question.

"Are you okay, Z?" I whisper to myself.

The service elevator doors open onto floor thirty-three. It lands me in a circular maintenance corridor matching the one I left below. Nearby is a serious metal door, the barricade between the music maker's realm and the worker bees. Holding my breath, I start to ease it open, but pull back. I should go straight to wardrobe, not Zeli's ready room. Why am I busting this risky move? After kicking me in the ass, Timmer can report whether Zeli is shredded or whole.

"Lucky star." I gag, remembering Z's cornball line, but my skin prickles with a *need to know* sensation. I peek into the dead hallway. The windows overlooking the Hollywood sign are in front of me. That means the door to Zeli's ready room is on the right.

Her door slams open. I ditch back down my rabbit hole, listening.

"Give her time to cry it out. I need her tears," says Gothel.

I open the door a hair width to spy.

"No one steps into that room without my say. Got it, Mange?"

Silhouetted in front of the windows, Gothel talks to six and a half feet of buzz cut and muscle that must be Mange. Grant Gothel has his own Frankenstein monster on payroll. One sleeve of Mange's suit is pushed up to show a forearm as wide as my thigh and hairier than my head. The light grooves in the disk of the vinyl skirt outside have shifted from pink to electric blue, bathing the faces of both men in a corpselike glow.

Mange grunts. "Yessir."

I jump when Gothel slams the flat of his hands against the window. The rattle reverberates to the roots of my teeth. "Six months ago, Zeli's name alone would have crammed that plaza. I'm out a wad of cash, bankrolling bodies to fill it tonight."

Bankrolling? My eyebrows go north. Gothel paid those fools to worship his pink goddess?

Gothel spits air through his teeth as they pass me. Hopefully, Mange will stand guard near the elevators instead of coming back this way.

I wait until the sound of their voices fade to tiptoe to Zeli's closed door. Not a speck of light spills from underneath, but Z's sobs do. They mush my bones. She deserves comfort not abandonment after being ripped apart.

I've got my answer. Gothel goons plucked her from the mob in time. The smart move is to split and leave Z's waterworks behind. Only I can't. A pink puddle drips around my feet from the wingsuit. Who's crying on the other side of this door, soft Zeli with a delish voice that sang my name and lit me up, or spoiled, diva Zeli?

I nudge the door open. The room is trashed. Chunks of extensions are slung in piles against walls, disconnected, ripped off her head. She leans on the windowsill, staring at the Hollywood sign. Without the pink light show splattering its letters, the sign is as white as the sack of a dress Zeli wears. There's only enough of her mane left to tickle the back of her knees.

I gasp. What else do you do in the presence of a train wreck?

"Totally hideous," she whispers, grabbing at her raggedy hair. "Don't turn on the light, Papa Gothel."

"Not Papa."

Zeli whips around. A hand sweeps to her mouth. It's her turn. Gasp for a gasp. "You," she says, lowering the pink flask half-filled with her tears in the other hand.

My hands ball into fists. "What got into your head, diving into that mob?"

Zeli sets the flask on the windowsill and glides across the room, her gaze glued to my fists, until we stand toe to toe. I wait for a slap.

She raises sapphire eyes to me. "You didn't crash."

"Give me credit."

Zeli rests a hand against my cheek. It's toasty, reminding me how cold and clammy I am. "I thought I killed you." She holds my face in both hands, sending tingles up and down every inch of my skin.

This is a danger zone.

"I begged to have jumpers fall from the stars at my concert tonight. You're so beautiful and free."

I pull away before my arms go rogue and clutch her against my sloshy suit. "Whatever Zeli wants, Zeli gets." I catch a glimpse of the pink flask on the sill. I've half a notion to quiz her on the freaky tear boost ritual I witnessed between Gothel and her, but I zip my lip.

Hurt seeps across her face. "What crawled up your banana suit?"

It's time to fade out. I never should have come. Every brain cell screams this babe is nothing but grief. I pivot and beeline for the door.

Her voice stops me. "Why did you come to find me?"

I turn. "I thought I killed you."

She violates my personal space again, closer this time. Her body heat sneaks through my suit. It ups my wattage, raising toasty little ripples across my skin.

I could play on her guilt. Ask her to introduce me to GG. I'd be a shitiot to ignore these go signs from her. I'll give her a sweet treat kiss and earn a big fat hello to Grant Gothel. The night will not be a total loss.

I draw a line up her arm with my finger. "That would have blown your celebration."

She watches my hand and then copies the same move on my arm. "Big time."

I fall a little deeper into those round blue peepers. Taking a risk, I slide one hand down to her hip, and give the tiniest tug to pull her closer, testing.

Again, she studies my move. In imitation, she crosses her arm over mine to find my hip bone. Am I giving a seduction tutorial?

This close, the living-doll vibe of her Rampion packaging melts away. She's a petite mini-human, but definitely a woman. Without stage make-up, I see the slightest puff under her eyes. I've always thought of Zeli as a perpetual teen, but she's a good five years into her career. If memory serves, her majesty had a mega-blast for her sweet sixteen right around the time she caught fire. That puts her close to my age.

T-shirt moment: No Cradle Robbing Here.

The hand on my hip trembles. *Nervous, are we?* I've got to keep the pace slow. The better teacher I am here, the bigger the payoff, a meet-up with the G-man.

I capture her shaky fingers and guide them to my neck. For once in my life, I don't curse my own paltry height. Z and I fit together to rock a perfect kissing angle.

My next move brings her body to mine. That shapeless white dress hides a far less than shapeless body.

"You're soggy," she whispers.

The damp chill of my wingsuit brings her nipples to attention. I sway side to side rubbing ever so slightly to encourage her excitement. There's a spark almost as strong as the twinkle dots shorting out against my chest from our contact. Restraint is off the menu when a breathy gasp floats from her lips. My hands slip to the small of her back and smash those sweet breasts with their perfect cherry toppings flush against my chest.

Zeli tenses in my embrace but doesn't pull away. Instead, she wiggles her hips as she fits herself to me. I didn't teach her that. She's freestyling. It takes all my willpower to keep my hands from vacating her hips to pay her unexpectedly full breasts the attention they deserve.

"Thank you for not dying."

This woman is not supposed to melt so perfectly in my arms. This is Zeli, the poster woman of low-quality pop crap. The safest move is to check this kiss off my list, grab the favor of a Gothel intro from her, and split.

I lower my lips to hers, pausing at first contact in case she freaks. No sign of freakage, so I whisper against her mouth. "You're welcome."

The heat of her breath flowing over my lips zips my self-control to its limits. I force my mouth to move against hers in practiced moves. I'm leading this dance. Oh, so gently, I taste that pouty bottom lip with the tip of my tongue. To my delight, the faintest flavor of tea greets me.

Following my lead, Zeli's own soft tongue explores the curve of my top lip.

With painstaking slowness, I deepen the kiss, attempting to stay detached. Every layer I taste is sweeter than the last. Her mouth is warm and wet as she continues to match me move for move.

Such a good student.

My mind spins toward other warm and wet parts of Zeli.

Such a bad teacher.

Zeli pours a low melodic moan over my lips. It's the sumptuous voice that first drew me to its mysterious owner. The sound undoes me. Now, I'm the one mimicking her hip wiggles as I mash her against my second crotch seam compromise of the day. Damn this wingsuit. There's not a lot of give to accommodate the part of me that's enjoying our kiss more than good sense dictates.

This woman I'm programmed to detest whips me into a whirlwind of lust. I sink into a pink fantasy with a babe who's not who she's supposed to be. Zeli is talented and sweet, and shockingly seductive.

Sink with me, Zeli.

This time when she shimmies against my body, I whisper her name. "Zeli."

I guide her backward toward the glass table. My fingers slip under the straps of that white dress. I'll lay her down and peel it to her waist so I can taste and tease those fantastic breasts.

She threads her fingers in my hair and pulls my mouth harder against hers, groaning, "Jumper."

I can't wait for the table. My hands travel up to the sides of her breasts. She sucks my bottom lip into that deliciously toasty mouth. My star pupil matches me moan for moan as her body slides against mine with renewed force, causing enough friction to light up the entire Rampion Tower. Her dress, damp from my wingsuit, makes my targets easy to spot. My thumbs sneak across her breasts toward tight round nipples.

My first stroke across those beauties brings a moan so adorable I smile against Z's lips. The second earns me a two-handed smack to the chest that sends me stumbling backwards. I crash through the clothes on the costume rack, ass over noggin to the floor.

"I'm so sorry," says Zeli. "I can't get carried away."

I push up off the floor. "I take that as a compliment." Gothel keeps a tight rein on this chickadee with gilded locks and gilded keys. How much life has Zeli only glimpsed out her window instead of experiencing?

"There are too many people around," she sputters.

She comes off so sweet, so inexperienced, and so tempting. Not what I'd expect from a pop star of her age and notoriety. Based on her participation, I'm guessing it's lack of opportunity, not willingness that's to blame. Will our brief connection be enough to get me an intro to the big man?

Running steps head our way.

"Shit," Zeli gasps.

The volume of approaching footfalls sets my heart beating an unpleasant riff.

Z snatches something behind her and swings it through the air toward me.

It's a fucking pink guitar.

My hand flies up to protect my face. *Damn it, Justin.* You couldn't leave it at a basic kiss? The price of my roving hands will be pink splinters embedded in my scalp.

Instead of clocking me with the guitar, Zeli snugs it against her body like a shield. As lights blaze on, I leap to my feet.

Grant Gothel fills the doorway. The rock god I planned to dazzle is poised to fillet me.

Zeli shoves the guitar against my chest. "Take this guitar with my love and song." She shines, a moonbeam with suspiciously ragged breathing.

To my horror, I see the evidence of my stubble rub as a red rash across Zeli's soft cheeks. Based on his own swarthy facial shadow, Gothel has reddened plenty cheeks in his day. He'll read Zeli's tainted skin as my confession.

The pink stain down the front of her dress is my death sentence.

Gothel snatches a fistful of wingsuit. He looms over me with gemstone green eyes. I wince at the pink liquid dripping between his fingers. "Who the hell are you?"

"It's cool, Papa. This jumper was late to the party. I owe him swag." Zeli strolls to the window showing the room her back. Stunted hair swishes side to side like this is all dull business.

Gothel burns. He tosses me to the ground and charges Zeli, digging claws into her upper arm to swing her around. He scrutinizes the pink streak down the front of her white dress.

Gothel shakes her, his voice dropping an octave. "You turned skank for this miniscule lump of scat?"

The alarm on her face rockets me to Gothel. "Let her go, man. It wasn't like that."

His foot cranks a round kick to my chest that sends me flying. I flip up to my feet, but Gothel's on me. He closes fingers around my neck. Heat from his grip crawls up my skin like I'm too close to a flame. What the hell? The dude burns me. He flings me at Mange who crunches me into a head lock. I can't twist to check on Z.

Behind me, Gothel's roar ripples air. "Vacate my tower, asshole, or I'll launch you out this window without a chute."

BANISHED

MANGE HEAVES ME OUT THE DOUBLE GLASS DOORS OF THE LOBBY. ON the pinnacle of the concrete bridge that curves over the moat, Timmer stands, head lowered, ear pressed against his cell. The rest of the troupe clusters across the bridge.

The hand clutching Unc's cell drops. He shoots me a venomous glare and crosses the bridge onto the plaza.

I jog after him. No one in the troupe meets my gaze. One by one, they sling their Zeli pink guitars over a shoulder and retreat in a line, a firing squad ready to turn and shoot.

T-shirt moment: Death by Pink Guitars.

Shadows digest the Slinging Seven. My troupe. My family.

Timmer's fists clench and open in rhythm while we pass the crews transforming Zeli's stage for the launch of the Summer Number One amateur performances that begin the day after tomorrow. Jumbotron monitors the size of buildings rise from pockets in the concrete on either side of a stage populated with LED projection panels.

Timmer's disconnect flashes warnings from one nerve to another. The moment we enter a dark patch on the outskirts of the plaza, knuckles smash my cheekbone.

· Seconds after I slam onto sidewalk, the body of his pink guitar explodes on the ground next to me. I shield my face to keep pink lacquered shards from skewering my eyes.

Despite a skull that may or may not be cracked, I scramble to my feet. A warm finger of blood trickles down the icy skin of my jaw.

I jump back when Timmer drops the neck of the slaughtered guitar and raises a fist.

"You lost me the bigs." His face is steel hate.

"What?" Fear crawls up my legs like fire ants.

"Gothel is blackballing us." Heat from his noxious glare could singe eyelashes. "You ruined me. What possessed you to drag Rampion's cash crop to the slaughter?"

I raise both arms in surrender. "Zeli dumped herself into the mob scene."

"When she saw you hang like a wad of shit in the sky."

"Timmer, fizz down. The woman is crazy."

When I reach out to grab his arm, he snaps his elbow into my jaw sending me back to the ground. I want to crawl away, but I have to ride this out. Let him blow.

Timmer kicks chunks of pink guitar across the ground. "Whatever went down between you and Zeli screwed the troupe. We're dead."

My blood freezes.

"Gothel vows we'll never book another gig."

"He can't do that."

"He already did. Gothel killed the NYC jump off Lady Liberty on the Fourth of July, and our manager is too freakin' intimidated to book us anywhere else." Timmer rushes me until we're nose to nose. "I changed this whole sport, worked up the B.A.S.E. jumping food chain for two years to score that New York jump. You annihilated our future in two minutes."

"Gothel can't screw the NYC gig. It's solid."

He snorts. "Shitiot, Gothel is Zeus. No one messes with him."

The thought I've ruined the Slinging Seven's future crumbles my insides. "I'll take the blame."

"Damn straight. You're out of the troupe."

Above me, Timmer's scattered hair glows blue from Rampion Tower backlight. He's cover art for my funeral album. I brace for a boot in the ribs. Instead, my uncle drops a wad of cash at my feet.

"Here's your last cut. Don't show your face around the troupe ever again."

Heat streaks up my spine. Timmer keeps walking. "Unc, wait. Where am I supposed to go?" I grab the cash and start after him.

His voice bleeds into the night. "Figure it out, jacklick."

"What the hell, Timmer. I'm your star, your family."

"Don't you get it? I'm the last of your family so now you've got none. Rhona never wanted you, and your father was nothing but a skid mark. At least I got some use out of your pain in the ass carcass."

Timmer's digs are a stick in the eye.

Before I call him a liar, wind whips the cash from my hand. I chase it down and cram bills into pockets. When I look up, Timmer is gone.

Tears sting my raw cheekbone. I trip. Concrete slashes through the fabric of my suit, bloodying my knees. Crawling to a square of grass in the courtyard between buildings, I flop onto my back and will the moon to pull me into the sky.

I'm a shitiot, supposing I could dance into Hollywood and conquer the Summer Number One with Timmer's okay. Or believing Gothel would open his arms to welcome me into his stable of stars. I am a fucking man-boy, who allowed Unc to run my life for the last seven years while I played jumper and buried my head in a music pipe dream.

Pain cuts past the physical to what's left of my soul. Banishment sinks in. Across the plaza, The Rampion Tower laughs as its lights blink out floor by floor from the bottom up until only a thin cobalt light rims the edge of each vinyl in the stack.

My shitstorm is Zeli's fault. Her brainless dash into the crowd cost me everything.

A surge of adrenaline launches me to my feet. The diva is probably in the tower getting a massage and sipping Rampion tea while they glue her extensions back together. I try to erase the taste of her kiss and the feel of her body against mine that turned my brain to sawdust. Zeli, the musical hack, was supposed to be my entre to Gothel, not my downfall.

Why does she have to be so complicated?

The intensity of the Zeli contradictions zipping through my thoughts clench my jaw tight enough to send lightning bolts through my temples.

My heart pounds, increasing the pain in every spot Timmer hit me. I've got to focus on the Summer Number One. I pat my pocket, demo tracks, check. The wad of cash from my cut covers the entry fee. I can't piss the rest away. It's all I have.

I need a guitar for the audition. I lock my sites on the Rampion Records Tower. I've got to get back into the twilight room and snag a pink one. My throat turns to sandpaper at the possibility of seeing or hearing Zeli, but I refuse to blow my shot at the Summer Number One because the woman scrambles my brain.

8

THE DARK TOWER

I crouch next to the moat ready to dive in. The tower grins, a neon skeleton daring me to crawl between its bones. My teeth clack in four/four time. As I check for Gothel goons, a hiss above me shifts my focus to the sky. Dark blots drift through the blue glow of the tower–B.A.S.E. jumpers.

Chutes bloom, each a pearl, stealing a moonbeam to carry with them to Earth. A quartet of jumpers are mist personified as they thread between the light strings and zip lines. Their jump is mad beauty, free of show biz stink. Four feathers float to Earth. They're freaking poetry.

The shush of the moat masks flapping chutes as four shadows tame their lines. An ache inside me yearns to jump and feel the wind, the chute, the moonlight. The bliss of a jump like their's could reset this shitty night.

There was no poetry in my last jump, a dive bomb over a plaza full of crazies, losing their sanity for a pop queen with a freak zone of hair.

The jumpers' breaths fog the night as they land nearby. All four mark me as I step from the shadow.

I point to the moon. "Your jump...beautiful."

"Stolen peace, little brother," says a dude double my height with panther black curls as dark as his skin. Fingers born to pack chutes lift my arm to examine the drooping wing of my suit. "You jumped for Zeli."

"It's the twirler," says the lone woman in the group. "Impressive."

"Thanks." My insides hollow out. I was prepared to trade B.A.S.E. jumping for music. Seeing the grace these folks etched in the sky reignites the urge to jump for the moment, for the peace not the flash. Tears prick the corners of my eyes. Will I ever jump again?

The jumpers peel away except for Panther Curls. He squeezes my shoulder with those chute-packing fingers. "Next time you jump." He thumps a fist over his heart. "Jump for this. Not the spotlight." With a nod, he heads into the shadows.

I can't lose this connection to be part of a jump like the one I just witnessed. "Hey."

Panther Curls turns back. I sweep my hand to the sky. "Any room for another bird in your troupe?"

"We're no troupe. Just four breaths in a whisper." He stares me down, assessing my street value. He aims a finger at the flat chrome rooftop of a tower across the plaza from Rampion Records opposite the side with the stage complex. "Up there the night after the Summer Number One disappears. Pull down some sky with us at midnight."

He flicks a business card at me, *Singen Mot, C.P.A* "What's your name? I'll leave it at the desk."

"Justin MacKenzie. I'll be there."

He flicks two fingers in farewell.

"Wait." I glance at his card. "Singen Mot, where do I score jump gear around here?" He tilts his head, studying me with intensity that makes me stammer. "I need a new rig."

Finally, he points toward the Hollywood Sign. "On the boule-

vard find Fedele Costumes next to Leeni's Hair For Days. Show
Santino your jump license and my card. He'll set you up."

My heart deflates. Everything I own, including my license, and
I.D. are with Timmer. I've let him pull my strings long past time I
should have been taking responsibility for myself. Shit, he controls
the little I do have in my bank accounts. He'll keep it as blood money
I owe him for wrecking the troupe's future. I'll never see a cent of it.

"Go home, man." Singen Mot scans the plaza, jerking a thumb
to the sinking moon. "Vandals will be creeping out of their holes
soon."

I throw a salute and round the tower, acting as if I have a home
to go to. Vandals, the sideshow of criminals that prowl Hollywood
in the quiet of the night, are the least of my worries.

Alone in the shadows, the gravity of how screwed I am hits
hard. Tonight's gig was my chance to meet Gothel. If he recognizes
me at the Summer Number One audition tomorrow, he'll rip out
my vocal cords before I sing a note.

I tuck Mot's card in the sandwich bag next to my thumb drive
and wad of cash.

The moat twirls between the tower and me, lulling stars to
sleep. The water is clear, not a drop of Zeli pink left. After a check
for roving guards, I slip under the bridge and into the moat.

When the initial shock of the freezing dunk subsides, I appreciate the way water soothes the bruises and welts from Timmer's
fists.

I grasp the handholds in the service tunnel and flop onto the
familiar concrete of the maintenance dock. Back inside the belly of
the beast, rage revs and blood simmers, threatening to boil. The
calm I leached from the encounter with the jumpers settles into
memory as I storm the door.

The service elevator is too big a risk. Gothel goons might use it.

By the time I hike up a mountain of stairs and reach the metal
door with 33 stenciled in black spray paint above the crash bar,

exhaustion bitch slaps determination. I slump against the door, waiting for my breath to lose the timbre of a death rattle.

When I crack the door to check out the main hallway, a cacophony explodes from the direction of Zeli's ready room. My stomach sours. The diva's after party is in full swing.

Of course, Gothel still pampers his pet. Vilify me – worship her.

T-shirt moment: Jacklicks Die Young.

I hum an A, my calming note, and stalk through the fluorescent glow seeping down concrete walls of this utilitarian circle. Up ahead, the party soundtrack spills through a vent the size of a jumbo doggie door near the ceiling. Wicked slashes of light cut between slats, plastering hot white rectangles against the inner wall of my sanctuary.

A voice so rough it makes my own vocal cords ache, rolls through the vent. "It's the last one, Z. Don't fade out on us."

Ribbons of despair twist through Zeli's voice on the other side of the wall. "I can't take anymore."

Even though I know it's best to shed soft feelings for Zeli, the ribbons strangle me.

Tucked against the concrete wall is an old school, wooden road box as tall as my shoulder. *Gossamer Curtain – Zeli Press Room* is scrawled in black marker on a piece of duct tape. I lift the lid to find swaths of sheer gold fabric piled inside. Wheels complain when I shove the road box under the vent but not loud enough to interrupt the doings in the ready room. After scrambling to the top of the box, it takes my vision a sec to adjust to the glare. There's no calling it a twilight room anymore. It's high noon.

Piles of violated hair have disappeared. Zeli's restored tsunami of extensions wrap around the room in concentric circles suspended from the ceiling by silver cables. Eye-popping patterns form the top layer of the hair parade. Stretching below them is Zeli's real hair. A river of gold flows beneath the length of her extensions. Wherever light catches waves of honey, they shine in gentle contrast to the blasts of design the world sees attached to her head.

It's a crime to hide such treasure.

Crisscrossing the underside of Z's natural locks beneath the extensions is a delicate metal framework made of silver wires thinner than strands of yarn. Figures weave the wiry skeleton through her real tresses and into her multimillion-dollar monstrosity. The metallic highway all but disappears.

All Gothel's horses and all Gothel's men weave Zeli's ticket to fame together again.

A chick in a lab coat with the biceps of a wrestler waves a tablet along the hair. As she passes each extension, a new pattern fills her screen.

"Hold up." She rescans a section. "Damn it, Cordel. The chartreuse zebra stripe comes ahead of paw prints in the African span."

Cordel, the human version of a locust with an updo, grinds fists into her bloodshot eyes. "Fizz down, Deb. It goes A to Z. Paw then zebra."

Deb slides her finger across the tablet and blurry images of Zeli's extensions fly by. "You're right. We're good." She snaps her fingers. "Someone, bring me an espresso."

Where's Z in this mess? I slide to the other end of the vent for a better view. My gaze travels along Zeli's extensions of rainbow swirls, gray and black fleur de lis, and a seashell collage before I find her. My intestines tie a knot around my stomach.

"The fuck!"

I drop down in case my outburst draws attention to the vent. Inching my way back up, I zoom in on the petite figure slumped over a chair back. Mange, with his buzz cut and scarred face presses a teacup to her lips.

Zeli shakes her head side to side, refusing the cup. When the creep forces her mouth open to pour liquid down her throat, I nearly shout her name.

Her face is moon glow pale as she chokes on the tea. "Stop. The wires will add too much weight. Even with Papa's boost, I won't be able to handle them."

Mange flicks a hand. "Gothel's orders. Drink your tea."

Reflected in the window, tears run down the soft cheeks I rubbed raw with my kiss.

Cordel pats the first extension behind the crown of Zeli's head. Wires droop against the back of the diva's neck. "Your extensions rock a sweet metal skeleton now," says Cordel, a cruel pitch to her voice. "They're impossible to rip apart." She flicks the wire frame with a sparkly fingernail. "See, thin as thread but strong as steel. There's a slight loss of twist and flex when you move them, but you'll barely notice." The chick is all business – no compassion.

Mange isn't Frankenstein's monster, Zeli is. Instead of bolts coming out of her neck, her royal pinkness is hard wired to Rampion Records.

"Last one," says Deb. Her commando arms flex as she lifts the platinum record extension in front of Zeli's nose. "It's worth a little extra oomph to reattach this beauty."

Zeli cries out, grabbing the back of her neck.

With a sympathetic smile, Deb weaves a series of wiry metal inserts from the platinum record extension into its neighbor.

My fingers, white from gripping the slats of the vent, go numb. Zeli's cry echoes inside my heart, bruising every chamber. I stare at the horror below. My crappy life is fairy heaven compared to the insanity Gothel's tribe unleashes on Zeli, all for hair.

The next voice curls my windpipe into a bendy straw.

"Thank you, all," purrs Gothel. "Excellent work."

The room clears faster than a picnic in a rainstorm except for two of the weavers. Gothel strolls up to Zeli. He brandishes what looks like a vest make of silver lace and lovingly helps Zeli into it. The remaining weavers snug in behind to twist the trailing wires from Z's first extension into the vest before they too leave.

Gently Gothel closes the clasps on the front of the thin metal vest. "We'll boost you more often, and the vest will handle the extra strain on your pretty little neck." He taps a finger on her nose. "You'll be in top form when you meet the Summer One crowd and gift them with your opus."

His mood suddenly darkens. A dangerous growl leaks from his lips. "My investment will not be vandalized again."

Zeli clasps hands over her heart. She's on the brink of hyperventilating. "The vest is too tight, I can't breathe."

Again, Gothel collects her tears in his vandal flask, and drinks. He lays hands on Zeli's shoulders. "Easy fix, Angel." An eerie amber light rises from his fingertips, meandering onto the lacy metal of vest until the whole thing glows. "Tell me when it feels right."

Zeli wriggles in the vest, tugging at the bottom as she finds the right fit. "Enough." His finger beams turn her face as red as a beach day sunburn. Threads of wavering light bleed back into Gothel's fingers, coursing through him from fingertip to wrist for a couple of beats before they fade.

I must be losing my freakin' mind if I believe I just saw Gothel generate a power surge to fit Zeli into that vest. My hand clutches my neck where Gothel grabbed me. It's tender. The asshole did scorch me with his freaky fire fingers. Now, the bastard and his dark crew have shackled Zeli to those godawful extensions.

He steps back, admiring his work. "You'll get used to the new support."

Zeli's voice is razor sharp. "I don't want to get used to it." She tries to undo the clasps, but her hands slip. Fingernails rake across Gothel's arm, leaving a long red welt.

When he drags a finger through the tears dripping below Zeli's closed eyelids, she jerks her head away. Light catches the golden beads of Zeli's tears that shine on Gothel's fingertip. "Quid pro quo, Angel." He rubs the droplets over the mark Zeli slashed into his forearm.

The red welt on Gothel's arm disappears.

9

GOTHEL'S SWEET RIDE

GOTHEL'S VANISHING WOUND HITS MY LIMIT. I JUMP TO THE FLOOR.
The scene repeats in my head as I try to make sense of Gothel's tear
harvesting and fire fingers. Everything around me is a dingy blur as
I pace the maintenance ring.

Ten steps. "Jesus, Zeli. Why do you submit to that man? Are you
really nothing but a singing automaton?" Twenty steps. "A soulless
creature willing to feed the fame beast anything?" Thirty steps.
"Needy pop star addicted to the love of your fans." Forty steps. "Or
a lost soul, left with nothing but your music?"

Like me.

I cease my manic march. Aren't we a pathetic pair of bookends
who've let others control our lives?

At least she still has Gothel. I growl to the dimness. "There's no
one to bring me tea and put my pieces back together."

A line of Zelies spins through my brain. *Pop Zeli. Quiet Zeli.
Spoiled Zeli. Sweet Zeli. Brave Zeli. Tortured Zeli. Cocky Zeli.*

I've met them all tonight. I scratch my scalp until it burns.
Whoever Z is, she's been consumed by the fame beast.

My pacing brings me back to the road box and the vent to Zeli's
ready room. This tower is circles within circles. Its outer walls,

inner walls, and hidden corridors are for humans unworthy of the spotlight. The gods and goddesses of music enjoy black lacquer, metal, and marble to reflect their greatness while secrets fester behind the shine.

The door to the corridor squeals open, and I duck out of sight. The woman who twinkle dotted me earlier shoves in a wardrobe rack and then splits.

Priority one: regroup, get a guitar, and find somewhere to crash and hide. Make a plan. I'm all about the plan. There's only one change maker in my future, and that's me. I will climb out of this hole and into the Summer Number One. Hope lights a fire in my belly.

"Will you know me, Gothel?" The twilight room was still in twilight when he caught me. It's not like we had an in-depth convo. He snarled and tossed me.

I check out the newly arrived costume rack. It's draped with jeans, leather jackets, and a tangle of sneakers at its base. I rifle through clothing as the rough sketch of a plan emerges.

"Hide the jumper."

I'll take a shot at the Summer Number One with an alias, someone other than Justin MacKenzie.

I grip the pole of the costume rack. I can't give up music without a fight or abandon songs yet to be written. I refuse to forsake my dream of the life I know in my soul I'm meant to live.

Renewed commitment simmers in my marrow. My dreams are not delusions. I have talent.

After peeling off my damp banana skin, I score jeans from the rack. A cardboard box on the bottom is filled with a stack of Gigabyte staff t-shirts with upcoming concert dates silk-screened across the back. I use one tee to scrape off the last bits of pink still clinging to my skin and claim a size small to wear.

"Justin MacKenzie, Gigabyte roadie." A new backstory seeps into my brain. "I'm the dude who works for the band, and then bam! His own turn in the spotlight comes."

Even though the world is pelting me with crap, I intend to set it spinning back my way. I won't be a Zeli. No one is going to lord it over me the way Gothel has that chickadee in a pinch. Music will be my joy. I'll craft the life I want with the contest winnings.

Fatigue knocks me harder than Timmer's right hook as I tie the laces on a pair of black, leather, high top sneakers.

Like a head of wilted lettuce, I sit head to knees with my back against the road box to wait for my chance to grab a guitar from the ready room. In the still of the night, truth has a way of making itself known. My mind drifts back to the Zeli I traded rhymes with, the Zeli who didn't want me to be afraid of a jump, and the Zeli with a body designed to fit mine. I remember the Zeli who responded to my touch and gifted back what she received, the Zeli that broke past my defenses to spark feelings. Above the rest, I feel the Zeli with a voice as radiant as sunset. That is the Zeli I kissed.

I scrub hands across my face. Don't look back. Zeli chose this life.

A while later, I heave my carcass back to the top of the road box. Every creak cracks the silence like cannon fire. Through the vent, I confirm twilight has returned to the ready room. Off in a corner sits the cart with pink guitars. My fingers quiver to strum and pick.

"Okay, Z, I'll accept a swag guitar with your love and song."

Since Zeli's been trundled off for the night, the door to the twilight room is unlocked. Toll the bell – all is well as I stroll across the room. Cupping the neck of a holy pink acoustic relic, I smooth my fingers over the strings.

Next to the cart, a spiral staircase climbs a good twenty feet in the air to double doors. Ah, here's the gateway to Zeli's private royal dressing room. I'm tempted to wash lingering pink off my skin in her majesty's shower. If the Rampion Tower is as dormant as it seems, a five-minute dunk won't blip on anyone's radar.

I'm about to hop onto the first step when my luck runs out. The doors at the top of the spiral stairs bang open. Buttery light spills into the room. I squeeze my body behind the steps.

Above me a familiar bird chirps, Zeli.

"Papa Gothel–" Her voice breaks. "Please take me home to the beach."

Does the dude ever leave her alone? Summoning shallow breaths, I will myself not to twitch.

"Absolutely not. Your crowd diving stunt cost me a chunk of change. Correction – cost you."

Her voice is ragged. "How could my fans shred my hair? I thought they loved me." Sobs rise like a drum solo. A wave of tears will break over the stairs any second and wash me into the middle of the room. Gothel will need a keg to catch them all.

"Grow up, Rapunzel. Fans care more about stealing a piece of your extensions than kissing you on the cheek."

Rap – who?

"You hit the Summer Number One stage in five days. I'm not taking any risks."

There's a stomp on the floor above my head, and Zeli belts a take-charge note. "Amateurs sing first. I can chill at home before I need to come back into town."

I'm impressed. After what the woman suffered tonight, she's still spunky.

Gothel's chuckle raises goosebumps along my arms.

"This is now home."

On the wall across the room, figures dance like shadow puppets. Zeli surges down the steps, but Gothel's shape wraps around her like a death shroud. There's a thunk from above. Zeli's cry is laced with pain. He didn't – he wouldn't hurt her?

"Put the kettle on, Rapunzel, and play the game you were bred to play. More tears, darling dear, Rampion tea makes pain disappear."

There's that creepy ass rhyming again, and who is Rapunzel?

"Finish your new opus for the Summer Number One. It better shine platinum. I expect to hear it soon."

Zeli's weeping trickles to my ears.

"Enough dramatics. Get off the floor."

Did she fall or did he push her? Between the steps, I make out a loop of extensions hanging over the top rail. Footsteps too heavy to be Zeli's ring against steel as Gothel's dark spirit descends halfway down the spiral.

"Mange!"

I drop flat behind the lowest turn of the spiral as Mange throws the hall door open. Ape man must have come on duty seconds after I grabbed a guitar. The shakes hit me again and not from the cold. If they catch me, dental records will be all that's left to I.D. Justin MacKenzie.

"Roll it away," says Gothel. His smile catches the yellow light of the archway. "We don't want my angel..." He snaps his teeth toward Zeli like a cobra targeting prey. "Getting into more trouble."

Mange sneers. "On it, boss."

I play a lethal game of twist and bend to stay in hiding as Mange releases clamps on either side of the spiral stairway and rolls it just beyond leaping distance from the double doors.

Gothel's form fills the doorway, a statue of ink blocking the light. A whimpering Zeli as limp as dishtowels in a fridge handle is draped over his arm. Gothel reels in the dangling extensions. In a sinister duet, he slams the double doors while Mange does the same to the twilight room door.

A rush of stupid urges me to fly up and snatch Zeli from Gothel's claws. She's in this mess because of me. The rush of smarts right behind it stops me.

"Damn you, Zeli," I whisper to my prison walls. Do I owe her a rescue? She's the reason I'm on this trajectory of disaster. Even so, the woman has churned my feelings into froth.

I take a tentative step out from behind the stairs, but a teeth-cracking squeal behind the doors above sends me scurrying blindly back into hiding. The sound settles into a dull rumble.

Hope flickers in my chest. Is that an elevator? Maybe there's a way to light foot it into Z's dressing room while all is quiet, grab the elevator, and get me the hell out of here.

I slither up the spiral, listening at every step. I don't hear anything until I'm arm's distance from the double doors. A gold plaque on the wall reads, *Penthouse 33 $^{1/3}$*.

"Listen for the cue: Rapunzel, Rapunzel let down your hair."

"Yes, Papa." Zeli's voice is flat.

"Keep a three-extension distance," says Gothel. "The track will pull every hair from your head if you get too close."

Track?

Gothel's voice drones a low baritone. "Not one word about your isolation. After your mob dive, we don't need more bad press. We'll roll the stairs back in place when you need to leave for recording sessions and stage time. Mark my words, any more trouble from you, and I'll auction off every one of your extensions."

"Yesssss, Papa." Zeli pops the Ps in Papa, scorching the air.

"Don't test me, Rapunzel."

Again, with the Rapunzel.

I stretch out on my stomach far enough to see through an inch wide space at the bottom of the double doors into the room. I've seen *out there* stuff, playing hobo with Ma and travelling with the Slinging Seven, but the scene before me shaves the cat.

Thirty steps across a mansion in the sky, Zeli stands in front of a floor to ceiling glass window at least twenty feet wide that yawns open to the night. Beyond the window, a pulsing blue line stretches from the tower all the way to the chrome top building where I'm set to meet up with Singen Mot and his jump crew after the Summer Number One.

I'm looking at the mother of all zip lines. Just outside the window GG looks like he's levitating snugged into a customized zip line harness. He and his rig glow electric blue from the light of one of the tower discs. His arms extend upward clasping lines between the harness and the cable as if he's controlling the canopy in a B.A.S.E. jump.

Zeli's extensions jump out the sill to catch onto the huge spiral surrounding the zip line. This is the line I've seen Gothel ride in Rampion videos. Now, instead of sliding through the usual tunnel of twinkle lights, he's surrounded by Zeli's extensions as they spool into the night, pulling Gothel in the zip line rig. Design after design leave the window to encase GG and flutter above the plaza.

Other videos flip through my mental playlist. I have seen this before in videos too. The spiral is how they display Zeli's locks to the public. Shitiot me, I thought her color blocks were detachable, and this bizarre highway was nothing more than a P.R. laundry line for the pop queen's fans.

Protruding from the wall next to the window is a handle fashioned to resemble a gilded sword covered in pink jewels. Z's fingers wrap around the hilt while her hair spirals up from a pile between her feet and the window. She's careful to stay out of the direct line between her extensions and the mechanism making this freak show possible.

Zeli's extensions deliver the fiendish specter of Gothel to Singen's rooftop. I can just make out Gothel pulling himself through a frame that serves as his landing station. When his voice rises from a cell on the floor next to Z, I freeze.

"Full stop, Angel." Zeli grasps the sword handle and jerks it parallel to the floor. The unearthly conveyor belt squeals to a stop. "Nicely done, Rapunzel. Pity you can't try my private skyway."

She snatches the cell, covering the mic and whispers, "Crash and burn."

Even in this freaky reality, I'm impressed by her sizzle.

Gothel's voice slinks through the cell. "Goodnight, my angel."

Zeli flings the phone to the carpet, clutches the sword beneath its pink, jewel encrusted pommel and wrestles it into the up position. Extensions reverse, snaking back across the cable into the tower. Colors pile into a mound on the floor inside the window. The final piece, her platinum record extension, is attached to the zip line harness with wicked hooks.

It takes Z a couple of tries to yank the harness free from Gothel's chariot track. She holds the platinum record up to her face.

Ugh, is she gonna kiss the thing? Why not go straight to the source and kiss Gothel's ass?

Instead of a lip smack, Zeli whacks the extension against the wall and heaves the slightly dented disk to the carpet.

There may be hope for this diva yet. My wish that the mechanical clank and purr I heard was an elevator dies an ugly death. It was GG's zippy line. If Mange is stationed at the twilight room door, I'm sealed in this tower as tight as Zeli.

10

JUST IN TIME

ZELI SQUEALS AND DELIVERS A DIRECT KICK TO THE WINDOW. FOR AN ass-clenching second, images of her falling through shattered glass spill across my brain, and I reach for her. She growls and pivots, only to have a slipper tangle in a curl of extensions. Miss Z ass plants on a pile of hair.

As she turns my way, I imitate an ice sculpture. If my eyeballs are spotted under the door, her screaming will screw me.

Collapsing onto one of two strawberry and white striped couches long enough to accommodate a giraffe lying on its side, Zeli raises both arms. "Speak to me, stars."

My angle allows me to follow her eyeline to a spider web pattern of crystal teardrops, hanging inches below a ceiling covered in pink velvet. A single strand of that web must be worth enough to buy me a house in the Hollywood Hills, with a pool.

The velvet is too dark to call pink. It's fuchsia colored like the flowers Ma used to call *dancing ladies.* She swore fuchsia blooms carried the same luck as shooting stars.

I take in the rest of Zeli's digs. It's three hundred and sixty degrees of curved windows broken up by an occasional expanse of solid wall decorated with album covers, gold records, or framed concert photos. The sights I saw from the roof are visible through her circle of glass. A black marble slab with writhing pink veins in the center of the penthouse supplies the back wall to a kitchen sculpted from stainless steel.

My stomach growls at the sight of the fridge. I wonder if her pinkness stocks frozen pizza and beer.

A second black marble wall curves toward the center of the room, blocking a portion of the windows. Through a half open door in its middle, I spot the royal bedchamber.

The tiniest bubble of a sob brings my sightseeing tour to an end.

Zeli's face is hidden beneath crossed arms, but the trembling of thin shoulders is clear. Her sobfest gut punches me. I wiggle away from the door and climb halfway down the spiral before dropping onto a step.

Zeli is screwing with my mind. I'm pissed she shredded my life, but the version of this woman with a kickass voice and enough nerve to stand up to Gothel is deep under my skin. Who is Zeli? Construct or actual person?

Rubbing thumbs into my temples, I admit she's stuck in my head.

Rapunzel.

Gothel called her Rapunzel.

Ra-pun-zel – Rapunzeli - Zeli.

Why dump Rapunzel for Zeli? Rapunzel is lyrical. The shortened, bubblegum version of the name reeks of Gothel's publicity machine.

"Ra-pun-zel." I whisper-sing her name using a minor third. Then I start on a high note and change keys to craft a different chord. "Ra-pun-zel." It's a musical name. Unlike Justin. Every third dude on the planet is named Justin. I need a musical name. At least three syllables.

What would she do if I show up on her doorstep again? Does she blame me for her new metal ponytail? If anyone scored a worse night than me, it's Z-girl. What a pair of losers under a loser moon.

Reality check: Zeli and I have nothing in common. She's riding a supersonic career. All I have is a soggy wad of bills and a road box.

Her voice startles me. "Just in time."

It's the same tune she was singing when I first stumbled into her presence.

"Our stars crossed just in time."

Her jukebox voice is once again replaced with a beautiful sound. I sneak back to the top of the stairs and listen.

"To blaze a path across the moon drenched sky."

I could listen to this Zeli forever.

"My heart wept. Reaching deep for hope, to search beyond the clouds for lover's eyes."

What is this song? Not her usual drowning in syrup, pop ballad. This sound, these words, they're climbing into my soul. I feel this song.

Son of a bitch. Zeli is dialing in her tune for the Summer Number One. I want a song this intense. I need it as my ticket to climb to the top of the Rampion Tower instead of being slowly digested in its belly.

"Two hearts met just in time."

Just in time. Just-in time. Justin Time.

My musical name. Thank you, Zeli. Now give me your song. I listen. I learn. Gluing every nuance, every chord to my brain. If this is the song slated to zip Queen Zeli to first place in the Summer Number One, then it should do the same for me.

Amateurs battle it out first. I vow to be among the two hundred ammies that make the cut tomorrow. I'll perform the song days before Z and her hair step onto the stage. I quietly sing with Queen Zeli, taking ownership of her song, the tune to put King Justin on the throne.

The fame beast nuzzles its head against my ankles while my conscience whacks me in the head. Stealing Zeli's song is a nasty kick when she's already down.

How far down can someone living under a diamond ceiling fall?

I can't do this. She doesn't deserve it. I shake off the swirl of feelings this woman has sparked in me and cue self-preservation, mold guilt into purpose. I'm as good a singer as Zeli–better than that bubble gum voice she uses in public. I deserve a shot. Z must have a thousand tunes brewing under those extensions. She won't miss this one.

Here's another Quid Pro Quo, Z. You crapped on my life by diving into a mob, and now I'm crapping on yours by stealing this song. Call it my revenge. We'll be even.

I drop my head into my hands. If my reasoning is so damn logical, why is confusion about doing this pinging wrong in my brain?

Gothel told her to write him a "new" opus that he expects to hear soon. He hasn't heard this song yet. A feeling deep in my soul tells me this song is a Zeli hit, a platinum ticket even though it's so unlike her usual pop queen fare. Would Gothel even green light a song this far out of her lane?

I have no guarantee my original song is in this league. My chance of scoring in the Summer Number One with a song this good rocks. If I beat Zeli to the musical punch, this song will be mine.

Time to blow this pop stand. I slink down the stairs and tippy toe to the hallway door.

"Mange, Mange go away. Chap my ass another day." I plaster my ear to metal and hear nothing. I try a tentative rap on the door and prepare to bolt back to the shadows.

My tune sensitive ears hear nothing.

I note the rack of pink guitars. In what universe did I think this would work? I blame Timmer's fist to the head for my damaged logic. If I snag one of these, I'll have to sand off the finish to de-

Zelify it. I don't have time to manage that before the audition. Gothel's no shitiot. He'll connect the dots between Justin the Jumper and Justin the singer if I stroll into the audition with a Zeli pink guitar strapped to my back. Scoring an instrument for cheaps up on Hollywood Boulevard is the better move.

Cracking the door confirms I'm in the clear. I glance back at the double doors of Zeli's digs. Not only am I stealing her song, I'm leaving the woman trapped in the tower.

If we use her locks to lower her into the ready room with me, we could zip away together. I almost laugh at my own stupidity. It's impossible to spring her unless I chop off that damn highway of hair. A rescue attempt with *doomed to fail* written all over it is a lose/lose for both of us. I'll forfeit her song and my shot at success, and who knows what Gothel will do to Z. I've got to get my head on straight.

Her voice floats on the other side of the double doors. "Destiny drew your kiss to touch my wishing lips. Magic chased the dark to light our way."

I lay a finger to where Zeli's sweet lips touched mine. Her song is my way to breathe life back into my odds for the Summer Number One. It's not just my revenge, it's possibility.

Her voice thrums through the door. "Two hearts met just in time."

Jus-tin Time.

Ra-pun-zel.

I can be a chord too.

"We banished loneliness found love to stay."

Sing it again, Zeli. Say goodbye to your song. It's mine now. Thank you. I'm a grateful thief.

I slip out the door, down the hallway, back to the service ring, and into my road box to crash for a few hours.

Her voice reaches me.

"Goodnight, Zeli." I relive our kiss and the unexpected feelings it woke inside me. "Someday, I do hope you'll forgive me for stealing your song." A hope that I have a sneaking suspicion is going to stick around.

Her gorgeous voice sings me to sleep as I settle into a bed of gossamer.

11

SANTINO

DEEP SLEEP ON INDUSTRIAL GRADE GOSSAMER FABRIC PROVES impossible with hooks and other curtain hardware finding a thousand ways to dig into your hide. After an extended session of doze and poke, I abandon the road box.

The Summer Number One audition is today.

"It's ducks in a row time." My ducks are all over the pond.

My cell didn't survive moatageddan last night so the only way to get the latest on the audition is to show up on the plaza.

I climb down thirty-three floors and sing my penance in a low voice, "Just in time. I stole your song just in time." It doesn't relieve my lingering guilt. I still feel like a thieving asshat.

By the time I hit the plaza, the line for the Summer Number One amateur auditions already circles partway around the tower. I thought I had a couple of hours to suit up. A time bomb ticks in my gut. I'm not ready. This Gigabyte roadie tee is no costume, and I still need to score a guitar.

When I hail a Zeli wannabe with raspberry sparkled eyelids and a couple yards of rainbow extensions, unpleasant memories of the pop star on house arrest flash through my mind.

"What number are you?"

She holds out a forearm with double sevens written in black ink. "Lucky seventy-seven."

Panic circles my chest. This may be the end of the line now, but a steady trickle of people wind their way in this direction. Only the first two hundred amateurs who pass the judges' muster will get into the contest.

I've been sloppy. Even though most of the yahoos at the audition don't make it in, I'm dangerously late to the party.

I finger the thumb drive in my pocket. I've got demo tracks, but I can't jump in line looking like a roadie. I need to radiate an artist vibe. Talent plus image scores an invite to this party.

The stage complex has doubled in size since last night. Reflective black metal curtains cordon off a backstage area to the right of the performance space. Jumbotrons flanking the stage already broadcast audition requirements. A quick read confirms I'm down two essentials, a costume for my *look* and an instrument.

What is my *look*? Do I go heartthrob or edgy? Eyeliner, yea or nay?

Just in time, Our stars crossed just in time.

The tune buzzes through me, and in a blink, she's back in my head.

Zeli.

Rapunzel.

I smack both cheeks to focus.

I'll hit the place on Hollywood Boulevard Singen Mot said I could score jump gear. *Fiddling Costumes?*

Past grandstands at the outer edge of the Rampion Plaza, I dip into an alley that shoots straight from the plaza to Hollywood Boulevard. I navigate between walls that haven't felt the business end of a paintbrush since before I was born. Bars cover ground level windows. That's Hollywood, from glam to glum in an eye blink.

Near the boulevard, an old-style Hollywood hotel blocks the morning sun. Rows of twisted iron balcony rails grace cream colored stucco walls all the way to a framework on the roof where immense letters spell out *Hotel Caliwood*. On the other side of a cinderblock wall is a garden gushing with palms and bougainvillea.

I bow to this stucco gentleman, a living piece of Hollywood history. When my first single drops, I'm totally having my launch party here.

The second my high tops hit the Hollywood Walk of Fame; a superhero impersonator snaps his cape at me. "Want a picture?"

I dodge a chick holding a huge placard that reads, *GO TO HOLLYWOOD – GO TO HELL.*

As the crowds thin, it's as if I cross into a different city. Sidewalk cracks create an obstacle course alongside overflowing, public garbage cans. In a recessed doorway, a for reals vandal sits on the highest of three steps. Aren't these folks supposed to climb back into their hidey holes by breakfast?

I nearly collide with a clown in a rainbow wig and a red bulb nose twirling a sign in the shape of an arrow. His arrow is my X marks the spot: *FEDELE COSTUMES.*

The clown's phone buzzes. "Chill, Santino. I'm half a block away."

Santino. That's the dude Singen Mot told me to find.

I trail the clown to Fedele Costumes. Above the double glass doors, turquoise and pink neon letters flash *Open Late*. The place is epic, the size of a gym. It's Halloween on hyperdrive. Reapers, sexy pirates, and every animal in the jungle score a place in this ocean of racks. Rubber masks line the back wall just below the ceiling. The blank eyeholes of Lincoln and Nixon join werewolves and blood elves to pass judgment on all who enter.

Past a selection of gorilla suits are rows of leather jackets, pants, and a color palette of silky shirts. Perfect building blocks for my *look*.

Who is Justin Time? I'm seeing an amalgam, *this* plus *that* with a dash of *what*. When you mix all colors together, they make black.

I'll rock the Summer Number One in black. Not Goth black – super-star black. Thief black. I'm stealing Zeli's song, might as well look the part. Justin Time steals from the rich and sings for the poor.

Nothing hits the right note until I come face to face with a tailored black coverall. I pinch the nylon with its barely detectable dark grey pin stripes.

"Hello, Justin Time."

One step back and those vertical lines give the suit a shimmer. It's got a jumper vibe without being a wingsuit. The cut is tight enough to accentuate my assets. I won't be a rubber stamp of every other ammie in skinny jeans, a neon shirt, or torn leather. My *look* is a slick echo of a B.A.S.E. jump suit.

Doubt comes a knocking. Is it *too* jumper? Will the association trigger Gothel's recognition? No paranoia allowed. Why should Gothel make a connection between a pink stained banana and Justin Time?

I've nailed my brand.

"Need help?"

Behind me, a guy in a baseball cap who can't be more than half a handful of years older than me hooks an elbow over the end of a rack. Wavy brown hair, like sand in shadow, runs wild on his head. The logo on his cap matches the Fedele Costumes sign above the door. On the breast pocket of his denim button down, *Santino* flashes across an LED nametag.

"I'll take this, and Singen Mot said you'd hook me up with B.A.S.E. jump gear. Rig, wingsuit, chute, the works." I pull Panther Curls' card out of my pocket to show him.

Santino chuckles. "Singen is messing with you. I don't sell jump equipment to kids."

"I'm a short twenty-three."

"Sure, you are." He shakes his head, disappearing behind a stand of feathers and iridescent scarves.

Grabbing my costume, I follow him.

The clown pushes through the racks. "Tino, did you text the new passwords to *Blitz*?" he asks.

"No, I don't want them screwing up the website again."

Blitz! That's top of the indie, A-list music venues in Hollywood. Feisty B. used to sub for their D.J. He swore it was the best gig in town.

Santino waves an invisible paintbrush through the air. "That website is my art."

Websites? Clubs? Interesting. I could use the down low on local haunts. Open mic nights–talent contests. This Santino dude can hook me up with more than a costume and a rig.

The clown gives the surrender sign. "You call them."

Santino texts while he briefs the clown. "Robbie, plant yourself closer to the Caliwood today. Work the Summer Number One audition crowd."

I tap a toe on linoleum. How can I convince Mr. Costume to hook me up with jump gear?

Strolling past leather pants in red, turquoise, and even skull patterns, I attempt to reengage. "What club should I hit tonight?"

Santino stops texting and raises an eyebrow.

"You were talking to the clown about clubs," I prompt.

He shakes bangs out of his eyes. "Already swapping your epic B.A.S.E. jumping career for rock? Look, short twenty-three, your browsing window is closed. Buy or fly."

Slinging Seven Justin MacKenzie will have to rise from the dead long enough to get Santino to take me seriously. "Catch the Zeli gig last night?"

"Who didn't?" He squints at me. "Oh, I get it. You want to rock the sky like the baby jumper." He returns to texting.

I wince at the name. Even my fake eighteen doesn't deserve *Baby Jumper*. "I already rocked that sky. Figure eights around other jumpers. Flat spins. Full body twirls. Late chute."

His finger freezes over the cell as his eyebrows stretch toward his hairline. "No way you're the banana shrimp who started the riot on the plaza."

"Don't blame Zeli's nut brain dash on me."

Santino gapes as I shake Singen's card at him. His eyes are the color of cinnamon floating in hot milk. "Let me wrap my head around this. That was you – in the wingsuit?"

I hold my arms out to the sides and bow. "Justin."

He slides the phone into his pocket, so his hands are free to flap and twirl. "Those were righteous moves."

This Santino appreciates talent. My throat clenches, remembering the lack of a B.A.S.E. Guild license in my bag of tricks, and then unclenches. I'd never have been allowed to jump at Zeli's gig without being certified. Toes crossed he won't ask for proof. "You'll hook me up?"

"You're an artist, man. It'll be an honor." He waves his hand for me to follow. We thread our way between racks of wizard's robes and tutus. "Equipment's in the back. Wow, I can't believe you're standing in my shop."

A freaky demon clown clock watches us from the wall. Bees swarm my gut. I've got to make this sale quick and get in that Summer Number One line before too many fools snag the spots.

12

YOUR NUMBER'S UP

My new guitar bounces against the parachute pack between my shoulder blades as I jog toward the plaza. Even though the instrument is a piece of crap, it took a lot of convincing, and by that, I mean cash, to get the chick singing for her supper in front of the falafel stand to part with it. At least it's black. Goes with my brand.

With twenty-five plus pounds of B.A.S.E. equipment on my back, I skid to the end of the audition line. Sweat pours down my sides in twin waterfalls. I attempt to tune the guitar. Its G string breaks. Lovely. I poke the chick in front of me. "Do you have extra guitar strings?"

She clicks her tongue. "No."

"Have they assigned numbers this far down the line yet?"

She bites her lip. "Shit ones. I'm four hundred seventeen."

Nausea wrings out my stomach as the line continues to grow behind me.

A boulder with legs in a black suit strides down the line. "Arm." When I pull up a sleeve, he scribbles 418 on my forearm with a fat marker.

My odds are lousy, but if the goon is still inking arms, the amateur quota isn't filled. I tap Snarly Girl again. "How many ammies are in?"

She snaps her jaw. "They'll pass the number down the line." Sure enough, the number sixteen is whispered from person to person.

"They've only taken sixteen?"

She flicks her head around so fast; the blunt end of her cerulean hair scratches my cheek. "Sixteen spaces LEFT, jacklick."

This is bleak. The line picks up speed as singers are cast aside like gum wrappers. Finally, I'm close enough to watch the audition routine. Each ammie steps into a circle taped on the ground and sings about sixteen bars of the same song until they cut them off.

I reopen my dialogue with Lady Blue Hair. "What's up with that tune?"

"Stop messing with me."

"No, really."

She blows hot breath across my face. "Scope out the Summer Number One app."

"No Internet."

My lack of preparedness slithers around my neck like a snake, tightening my throat when I need it to be loose, ready to sing. "The tune?"

"It's the last minute twist Grant Gothel always adds on audition eve. Last year you had to rock at least a yard of extensions. This year, it's the song. Blow a single note of his required ditty, and your demo won't see the light."

Gothel's curve ball isn't a death knell like extensions would have been. I pick up tunes quicker than a lightning strike. Tuning out background noise, I focus on the handful of ammies in front of me who quietly practice the song.

I internalize the rhythm, the lyrics.

A good ole boy who looks like he just left the football field to pose in front of an American flag steps into the do or die audition circle. When a judge gives him the nod, he kills on the violin, giving Gothel's surprise tune new life with his strings and voice.

Now that I've got the tune down, possible variations fly through my head. I have to own this song the Justin way.

Time stops while a table of judges, split fifty/fifty dudes and chicks, don headsets to listen to the quarterback's demo. Time only starts up again when he high fives the line of judges then disappears behind the black barriers next to the stage.

Lady Blue Hair punches her thigh with a fist. "They took him."

The hushed tally rolls down the line. "One."

The girl behind me wails. We move into the shadow of the tower, and I shiver. There's one space left. Every person on this plaza would sell their soul for it. Why in the hell do I think I'm entitled to it? Because life screwed me? No, because this is my art, and it's time to fashion my life around it.

Ego whispers in my ear. *You're freaking good, Justin. They'll throw open the door of Rampion Records and beg you to enter.*

Nerves smack down my ego. Faces around me in line radiate a different truth. An arrogant prick like me with zip-wah music credits hasn't earned the right to be in this line. A spot in the Summer Number One is to every artist on this plaza what B.A.S.E. jumping off the Statue of Liberty is to Timmer.

The bigs.

A brother/sister duo steps into the circle. They get the "buh-bye" after six bars. The next guy cracks on the high note.

That single spot in the Summer Number One remains open. For the first time, I truly accept the depth of commitment and honor I owe to this opportunity. If fate has mercy, it will search my heart to find the oath scratched across its surface. I vow to be the man to earn this.

A first step would be not to steal Zeli's song.

Will my own song give me as strong a showing in The Summer Number One? It's solid. It's original. Does it have the same level of zing and soul? Maybe, but Zeli's song isn't a question mark, it's a guarantee.

Just in Time will give me the chance I need. I move closer to the audition circle. Closing my eyes, I hum to coax a locked-up larynx back into singing mode.

"Ahem, ahem." The twenty-something ammie in front of Lady Blue Hair nails the rock star look. His throat clearing is bad news.

The judges, headphones wrapped around necks like scarves in a snowstorm, make slashing signs across their throats, and the ammie is led away.

"Oh my God," hisses Lady Blue and grabs my shoulders. "I'm up." Into the circle she goes, strangling her guitar. Her smile shows an unappealing amount of gums. When she shakes her hips and screams, "Are you ready to rock?" the judges look pained. Lady Blue doesn't sing. She talks Gothel's tune to a rhythm, emoting like a middle schooler doing Shakespeare. Her buh-bye comes fast and furious.

The circle that's rejected over two hundred ammies awaits. I set down the chute pack, and my foot touches sacred ground.

The Rampion gatekeeper grunts, "Sing." He flips through papers on his clipboard, not glancing up. The firing squad of judges chat with one another. They've clearly hit burnout. No one even bothers to start the backing track.

I adjust my guitar and bust out the required tune.

Two bars in, gatekeeper, a tall dude in jeans and a Rampion Records polo, breaks eye contact with his clipboard. Three more bars, and the judges check me out. Despite the missing string, I've got an acoustic syncopation going with kicky riffs and punctuated vibrato as I sing. Someone starts the music. I meld with the track instantly. They let me finish all sixteen bars.

"This isn't happening," erupts from the line behind me.

Judges give the high sign. Gatekeeper plugs my thumb drive into their system. It's not *Just in Time* gold, but it proves I've got the goods. The judges don headphones, entering the zone while they listen to my track. Heads bop, and a lip or two curls up. One by one they lower headphones and nod.

Gatekeeper snaps a blue band around my wrist. "Number two hundred."

The judges are up and stretching. A line of Gothel goons materializes from behind the stage. Weeping and wailing explode across the plaza as Rampion muscle breaks up the line of *out of luck* auditioners.

Gatekeeper whisks me behind partitions and deposits my sloshing heart in front of a desk. "Two zero zero," he says, shoving me into a folding chair. "Kaydance will take it from here."

The glare from the woman behind the desk attempts to burn a third eye into my forehead. This Kaydance mingles adorable with terrifying. Sitting tall, her height gives Gothel goons a run for their money. Her features are model perfect, a pleasing blend of round and angular. The arm of a black foil blazer stretches across the table and aims a copper fingernail at my jugular. "Name."

"Justin Time." Before typing it into her laptop, she peers at me over hexagonal glasses that match her nails. "Spelled just like it sounds."

She blows coffee scented air from her lips. "Song?" Caution pricks my insides, telling me not to say *Just in Time*. Hey Gothel–Justin Time is singing *Just in Time*. I run lyrics through my head.

Ourstarscrossedjustintimetoblazeapathacrossthemoondrenchedsky

"Stars Crossed."

The glasses come all the way off. They match thin copper dots on her foil jacket. "Super yawn title." Her sarcasm takes a bite out of my confidence. "*Heard this before* songs never win. Pull an original tune out of your ass."

"It's original."

She shakes her head. "It better be." Her extensions, strands of polished pennies, tinkle. "Stars Crossed by Justin Time." After entering the info on her computer, fingers pinch the air. "Entrance fee. Five hundred."

I peel five hundred dollar bills off my wad. After paying Santino and buying the guitar, my nest egg that seemed adequate last night looks pitiful.

Her lips purse when I hand it over. "No plastic?"

I imagine her fingernails hovering over the lever of a secret trap door. "I'm a cash guy."

She chews the stem of her glasses. "Misssster Time." Her expression bubbles with disgust as she snaps a small white plastic disc onto my wristband. "You'll find registration requirements and your contest verification in this QR code. You'll have to upload I.D., your music tracks, links to your media pages, and your publicity packet." She sets her glasses next to the tablet. "Anything doesn't check out, you're history."

"Ye of little faith."

Kaydance drops the cash on her keyboard. "You've got a ridiculous name and a potentially forgettable tune, Mr. End of the Line." She stands, glasses back on and studies me. "My advice, blast yourself on every social media platform before tomorrow. You'd better have a sweet presence. It's all about bodies in the plaza screaming your name when the music starts."

I lap up the drip of advice. "Will do."

She softens. "You get that ammies never win, right? Time for a good cry into your pillow, boyfriend."

As I watch the copper threads in her jacket pick up rays of the sun, Kaydance's message sinks in. Being number two hundred isn't enough to make music dreams come true. In her eyes, I'm nothing but a five-hundred-dollar pile of Rampion roadkill.

13

SKY SONG

MY VICTORY CURDLES. YES, I'M THE TWO HUNDREDTH AMATEUR IN the Summer Number One, but every conduit to announce my presence to the world is jacked up. My phone is trashed. Timmer has my laptop. Without a lick of self-promo, who will be left on the plaza to hear me sing after a hundred and ninety-nine others?

My buddy guilt hip checks me. If I win with my own composition, victory is legit mine. Will making it to the top with Zeli's song taste anything but bitter? There may still be time to update Kaydance with a different song title. The clock is ticking.

I tune out guilt's naggy voice and concentrate on the list I need to accomplish for any chance to stay in this competition. "Verified I.D., bulletproof registration, *Just in Time* backing tracks, web presence and social media, audience, fans, worshippers." All the above need access to the almighty Internet, and I've lost my key.

T-shirt moment: Magic and Miracles Accepted Here.

"How's this working for you, Justin Time?" I groan. Justin Time. God, the name is as plastic as Zeli. I'm saddled with it until I can become the artist formerly known as Justin Time.

The sky shifts from cornflower to a bleeding watercolor of cherry and grape lollipop stripes followed by a wash of black licorice. I watch the crew put finishing touches on the stage complex for the first day of the amateur showdown tomorrow.

Kaydance's sneer is etched on my retinas. I punch the parachute pack. I'll show her. Music is my gateway to a solid life. I pinch the bridge of my nose. My shot may be weak, but at least I have one. I will survive the three days of amateur competition to face the pros.

I thumb through my wad of bills. "Two hundred, fifty, sixty." It's not enough to buy a laptop and fake I.D. What was I thinking, wasting precious funds on jump gear? I'll return it to Santino and get my money back. Maybe he has a lead on where to score a previously enjoyed laptop and a phone for cheeps.

I chew what's left of my fingernails. Success is based on fan votes. Half the ammies are eliminated on day one and then half of those are D.O.A. by day two. Of the fifty left standing on day three, only twenty survive to duke it out with Rampion pros on the first pro/am night. Ammies and pros are wheedled down from there until the final night where it's Rampion's top five chart toppers versus five of us plebians.

"I've gotta survive." If not, my new address will be a storm drain on Hollywood Boulevard.

Slipping into my pack, I cut around the back of the tower away from the stage. "Fedele Costumes or bust." That's when I hear her voice.

"Stars and Fireflies."

The inky sky matches the backlit silhouette high above in the open window of floor 33 $^{1/3}$, Zeli's penthouse. She calls to the stars with golden notes, not a hint of her usual jukebox tripe.

She calls to me. Yesterday, I was her falling star.

An urge to sail through the sky punches my solarplexis. One last jump. Once I sell the gear back to Santino, my days as stardust are over. B.A.S.E. jumping has been my life from boy to man. After the last twenty-four hours, I need this jump to fit me back into my own skin.

The jump isn't mine alone. I'll jump for Zeli again, this time for the for reals woman I've blown my chance to ever know. It'll be my goodbye to the memory of our single kiss, and the way it turned me inside out. If she hears me sing her stolen song, a chasm too deep to cross will exist between us.

Singen Mot's building is out for a jump point since my name probably won't make it to the front desk until it's closer to the night I'm slated to join his group. A noisy throng of lads pour over the bridge toward the double glass doors of Rampion's lobby, a throng I know from music videos, Gigabyte.

I snatch the roadie tee from my pack and yank it over the jumpsuit. After a thirty count for the band to make it to the elevators, I trace their footsteps through the doors.

The guard's 'don't waste my time' scowl is the only greeting I get.

"Gigabyte." I point to the tee.

He squints. "Nice try. You ain't in Gigabyte."

"Someday, man. I tune their strings." I wiggle my fingers. "These make instruments sing like angels."

He rests his chin on a finger tipi. "Never seen you before."

"You never looked low enough."

He laughs. I raise my Summer Number One wristband and spin it. "I'm back late from dinner, and we're laying down Summer Number One tracks tonight. Cut me a break. I'm history if I don't get up there."

I lock my molars.

Finally, he flicks his hand toward the elevators. "Studio A."

I shake my thumb and pinkie at him to say thanks.

"Hey, Gigger. I'm pulling for the Bytes this year. If anyone can beat Zeli, it's you folks."

He doesn't even mention the possibility an ammie might upset the pros for the top spot. Watch and learn.

"I'll tell the team."

Clouds circle the tower again. I strip off the roadie tee and stretch my arms wide, a creature of the sky about to be reborn. This jump will kill pathetic, abandoned Justin MacKenzie, and send Justin Time soaring.

After swapping jumpsuit for wingsuit and triple checking my rig, I clutch the rail that runs around the edge of the roof. The launchers from last night are gone, but there's no wind to screw with me. Below, on the west side of the plaza, the Summer Number One stage is deserted. By the time the tower lights dim to neon blue, I've mapped an exit point and a landing target that steers clear of the killer zip line Gothel rode out of Zeli's penthouse.

The rising moon and empty plaza throw me a thumbs up. Its's go time.

A familiar, teeth aching squeal rolls through the air. I drop to my stomach and peer over the edge of the roof. Not far below, Gothel slinks across the sky within a multicolored highway of extensions. They unspool along the line until GG lands at his station on the flat-topped roof of Singen Mot's building. After he extracts himself from the rig, his voice carries through the still night air in stereo from the far rooftop and the cell underneath me in Zeli's open window, "Goodnight, my angel."

Angel, my ass. "Goodnight, my mountain of cash," I mutter. I picture Z pulling on the golden lever, calling her endless strands home. Hot spikes run up my back, remembering Gothel's roughness with her.

I wait until Gothel strolls around the curve of the tower. And then I wait some more until the faint hum of Zeli's hair returning to her window is silent and the plaza regains its stillness.

The whole time I think about damn Zeli. Is she real or a Rampion creation? Her pink glow clings to me like an invisible stain. No matter how I try to resist, the woman loiters near my heart. Playing the fame game got her plunked in the tower, but I know how wrong smells. She and Gothel are all wrong.

I smack my cheeks with chilly palms. "Focus on the jump." I thump a fist over my heart. "I'm jumping for this, Singen Mot."

Using handholds, I climb the sculpture of a giant record needle that leans over the edge of the tower to buy another hundred feet. The Hollywood Sign accepts my salute. Take off in five, four, three, two...

I'm a falling star, soaked in bliss. The pilot chute is free and then my canopy awakens. The chute lines obey my touch. Every vessel thrums with the thrill of the jump.

It is unfettered joy.

Using a zigzag pattern prolongs my fall. I present an offering to the night in a song. "Just in time. Our stars crossed just in time to blaze a path across the moon drenched sky."

The lights of Hollywood Boulevard are my audience. The song grows big enough to fill the sky.

"My heart wept. Reaching deep for hope."

A hint of breeze prophesizes triumph with its gentle kiss. No one will beat me. Justin Time will grab the Summer Number One victory with this song.

"To search beyond the clouds–"

"Clouds–"

I snap my mouth closed. My notes aren't alone.

"For lover's eyes." Zeli, a speck in the dark, sings out the open window. Reflections from one of her metallic extensions wrap around her legs like glittering mist. She shares the night song with me.

I sing to the pop star and the stars above. "Destiny–"

She picks it up. "Drew your kiss to touch my wishing lips."

It's the woman with the luscious voice, a secret Zeli. Warmth radiates from my heart to my fingertips, and I cross into undiscovered land. Oh, that I were breath drifting across those dear lips so that I might touch them again. Honeyed notes pull me deeper, and I can't imagine life without them.

I answer. "Magic chased the dark to light our way."

We sing together.

"Two hearts met just in time, and now our lives entwine. We banished loneliness, found love to stay."

Our voices blend as if they've never been apart. We are the essence of music; harmony, synergy, grace. Our notes are quicksilver shining beneath the moon, the sweet song of lovers who've shared but a single kiss.

It isn't her song anymore or the one I stole.

It's our song.

My feet tap onto pavement. I hear her. Not Zeli with blocks of extensions that lives in a pink bubble. Not Pop Queen Zeli dripping with Gothel's sugar coating.

Not Zeli at all.

I've found Rapunzel.

14

VANDALIZED

OUR DUET UNZIPS MY SOUL AND GIVES ZELI AN ALL-ACCESS PASS TO places inside me marked off limits, my vulnerability, my heart.

Her voice, Rapunzel's perfect notes, blaze against my emotional fortress until it melts into the earth. Singing with another is a truth teller. Our song speaks of a connection greater than the sum of who we are apart.

Zeli had to feel it too. But what if she thought I was just a dream?

It takes every drop of willpower not to fling my chute into the moat so I'm free to storm the tower and throw myself at her feet to beg another kiss. My shell of resisting her cracks into fragments never to be reassembled.

Did my heart understand love before now?

Oh, Rapunzel, I've never heard true beauty until tonight.

Thoughts tumble, shatter, and then reform. The Summer Number One isn't just about winning. Victory will be the ladder to reach my awakened heart.

Rapunzel.

Every ounce of my being screams, "Climb!" The cinder of regret

I felt leaving her in the tower last night blazes into a promise to free her.

Our song is power, the guarantee I need to enter her world. My choice is irrevocable. I must sing *Just in Time* in The Summer Number One to reach Zeli.

To Zeli, the voice that fell through the night and twined with hers is a mystery. I must scale the tower to show her our duet wasn't a dream. It's proof magic and hope still flourish under the Hollywood Sign.

I scramble to repack my gear. My gaze flicks to the rooftop where I left my poor excuse for a guitar hidden. I need to zip up to retrieve it and hit Fedele Costumes before closing time. I can't lose my footing on the first rung to Zeli. I need a refund from Santino to buy my way back onto the Internet and conjure an online presence before I take the stage tomorrow.

If I'm cut from the Summer Number One, my path to Zeli disappears. I won't let that happen. I will not abandon magic and the chance to sweep her from that tower.

After the notes of our song found one another under the stars, I know in my heart walking away from Rapunzel is impossible. She's my best chance to fill the negative space gouged into my spirit by a life that's treated me as an afterthought.

One kiss and our song in the dark have forever changed me.

My new best friend at the Rampion guard desk waves me in, and I retrieve the sum total of my belongings from the roof.

I explode onto the boulevard. The creeper meter is in the red. Skanks, vandals, and tattered souls are on patrol. A security gate covers the entrance to Fedele Costumes.

"No."

I wrap fingers around the bars and shake. They whack against the window frame as the odor of onion and cigarette wafts across my face.

"Need help?"

Whipping around, I face a trio of vandals. Black grease is smeared from cheekbone to the base of their necks. These filthy hands will not touch my investment. I wedge the parachute pack behind me and thrust both wrists through the crossed slats of the gate, locking fingers around gray metal. My cheap ass guitar slides to the ground.

"What's in the pack, kid," says a squat man in black, his voice gravel under a tire. Triplicate stares bore into me from beneath backward baseball caps.

I rattle the gate as loud as a thunder battle between Greek gods. Lights blast on inside the store, sending yellow shafts across vandal war paint.

I max my vocal cords and yell, "SANTINO!"

My assailants surge forward, sensing their chance to snag my gear leaks away. Fingernails dig into my upper arm. Using the gate for leverage, I drive high top heels into two different groins. Both dudes bend in half, knocking heads on their way to the ground.

The last vandal jumps over his groaning comrades. "Bad choice, jacklick." His punch lands in the same place Timmer nailed last night.

Fire pops across my face, igniting enough adrenaline to lift a minivan. I scissor kick. "Now who's the jacklick!"

He grabs my shin and wedges himself between my knees. When he yanks, my fingers lose their grip on the gate. He pulls me free of the pack and grabs it. I wrestle it from him and drop into the fetal position around my gear, wishing the helmet inside was on my head.

Vandals growl, a hunting pack closing in for the kill. One of them stomps my guitar. Pain flares across the back of my neck from a boot heel. Damn, these moves could paralyze me. I clench my pack tighter. Grimy paws slap and dig at me.

"Back it up, jacklicks!"

For once, it's not me who's being jacklicked. A menacing *click* breaks through vandal grunts. In the dusty beam of a streetlight, I see a badass pistol slide through the bars.

The vandals trip over one another, crab walking off the curb to get away from Santino's gun. They rise in a collective blur to dash across the boulevard, rats to Santino's cat. Me-fucking-ow.

He unlocks the gate, pulls it up a bit, and tugs my collar. "Get inside, you mad shitiot."

My gear and I roll into the store while Santino secures the perimeter. "Thanks, man."

He lifts my chin with a finger, assessing. "Ice."

"Thanks, man."

I follow him through a door camouflaged by a flock of feathered Mardi Gras masks. The storeroom smells of dust and packing tape. He gestures to a staircase behind a tower of cardboard boxes.

I grab the rail. "Thanks, man." My head reels.

"That's three 'thanks, mans.' Consider yourself paid up."

I make it up one step and then stumble.

"Whoa." He crooks his arm through mine.

"Thanks, man."

He chuckles, helping me to the top. "I see you're a man of two words." After tapping a code on the keypad, he pushes the door open. "Welcome to *La Mia Bella Casa* Fedele."

The apartment mimics the size of the shop below. Santino sweeps an arm toward a sunshine yellow sofa that sits between a pair of ass-ugly tangerine armchairs. A long shelf cluttered with books and knickknacks runs the length of the room, serving as the bottom frame for picture windows that overlook Hollywood Boulevard to the hills beyond.

Santino waves a hand at the windows. "Lucky my front row seat to the boulevard has terrible sound proofing."

My nod lights my head up with pain.

Around me, the huge room is half-kitchen, half-living room. I aim for a place to land on a checkerboard of black and white linoleum squares that hosts an aluminum dining set dropped out of a 1950s time warp. Aqua squiggles swim across its yellowing tabletop.

Santino pulls the handle crank of a white, single door, bubble-cornered fridge with plant-on silver letters that spell P-H-I-L-C-O. The freezer compartment is iced over like a glacier.

Dropping onto the aqua padded seat of the diner-style kitchen chair, I ask, "Should I order a malted?"

He laughs. "Then we'll do the twist."

"This place is totally vintage. Where's the ghost of Buddy Holly? We could jam." Santino tosses me a bag of frozen corn. "Not vintage. Original. Try the couch. Your ass will dance with every spring."

The veggies sting at first, but they douse the throbbing.

"This apartment originally belonged to my grandparents. My pops carried his bride over yon Fedele threshold, and a couple of years later my sis and me joined the party."

"You seriously grew up on Hollywood Boulevard?"

"Technically, above the boulevard."

"Are your parents gone?"

"All the way to Santa Barbara. They retired and passed *Casa Fedele* to me." He opens a door next to the kitchen and jerks his thumb into a dark hallway. "And my sis, Liliana. Her apartment is down that way. Actually..." He blushes. "Everything from the costume shop to the corner is Fedele land."

I wince as the bag of corn peels away from my skin. "You're a Hollywood robber baron."

A water bottle slides across the table followed by four aspirin tablets. "Thanks, man." We share a laugh at my two-word mantra. I toss back the pills.

Saint Santino grabs a chair opposite me, releasing an exhausted breath. I take it as a hint my freeloading pass expired.

"I'll split. Only came for a refund." When I stand, the room spins. I grab the edge of the table.

Santino jumps up, clamping a hand on my arm. "Fizz down. You're not going anywhere until your eyes stop rolling back in your head." He leads me to one of the tangerine armchairs.

"Dude, those vandals know I'm here. They'll come back and screw with you for helping me."

"Naw." Santino pulls the gun from the waistband of his jeans, waving it at the windows. "Vandals are no-ball wonders."

I gawk at the gun, and he laughs.

"I'll put this baby to bed." He opens a door in the wall across from the kitchen and flips the light on.

The room is Mission Control. I stumble to the doorway. A huge flatscreen surrounded by posters of indie bands takes up most of the back wall. Four laptops are lined up on an L-shaped desk that grips a corner of the room. Monitors play feeds of club stages or dance floors packed with humanity.

One stream is tuned to the reality show, *Kickin' It With Midas*. Midas Lear, president of Golden Pipes Records, and his trio of influencer daughters slink down a red carpet. Santino tucks the gun into a small safe in the corner.

I nod to the shrine of tech. "Are you actually a scientist-billionaire with a hero complex?"

Santino snorts. "You caught me. I'm a business mogul by day, closet superhero who may or may not wear a metal suit by night."

"What is all this?"

"Side biz. Web, graphic design, social media consultant for fellow boulevard dwellers."

"Boulevard dwellers! That's *Blitz*." I point at one of the screens recognizing the venue from TV. "The capital A of the A-list clubs in Hollywood."

He shrugs, face pinking. "Neighbors. The boulevard is a small town, Jumper."

Jumper. The title nips at my ribs. I lean on the doorjamb. Tonight was my last jump. "I'm retired. Need a refund on the rig you sold me to buy a used laptop and burner phone. Straps, toggles, helmet, and every inch of chute still mint condition. Can we deal?"

Santino gestures for me to sit. "You are a dude with a story, aren't you?"

I collapse onto an armchair. "I'm a dude with a steaming pile on my doorstep. If I had a doorstep." I drop my head onto the backrest.

He claims the tangerine twin of my chair, draping legs over one of its arms. "Tell me a bedtime story."

The warmth in Santino's eyes reminds me of Feisty B. I've barely met this guy, but I'm getting the vibe I can talk to him. Either exhaustion or the cumulative knocks to my head break the dam. Santino becomes the victim of my emotional TMI– the short version of Timmer dumping me after the Zeli mob shred, Gothel tossing my ass out of the tower, and the Summer Number One miracle.

His eyes wiggle back and forth absorbing it all, not completely focusing on me. My words compete with a silent dialogue in his head.

"Problem is, I'm an Internet zero. My phone took a swim in the Rampion moat. I have no tech. No way to connect with fans. Death sentence before I sing a note."

I almost leak the particulars of Zeli's tower sitch to illustrate the entirety of my pathetic quest to pluck her out of Gothel's grip. A surge of protectiveness for her shuts my mouth. My former feelings for Z have crumpled and transformed. Our duet in the dark drives me mad to save her. Me, alone. I'm not auditioning backup, the more the riskier.

Santino shakes his head. "You're screwed."

"Ya think?" I cover my cheek with the pack of frozen corn.

He stares as if he can see through my skin. Dude is intense. Too intense. Hairs on the back of my neck rise. What do I know about this guy anyway? He could be a psycho. I just told him nobody on the planet gives a crap where I am. This is the part of the story when he skins me to make a sicko skull mask to sell in his costume shop.

I stand and aim for the door. Santino blocks me.

Stammering, I put more distance between us. "I get it, man. All sales are final. Thanks for the corn." I toss him the bag. "Later days."

He holds up a hand. "Dude, you'll be vandal chow if you hit the boulevard. You're welcome to crash here."

Damn, I want to believe this guy is cool. My face must tip him off to my internal freak out.

"I get the invite is weird. I'm practically a stranger. Let me call my sister or my friend, Robbie, or a dozen club managers if you need character witnesses. I promise your eyeballs won't end up in my freezer."

Dude sounds totally genuine. Dude saved my carcass and gave me frozen corn. Dude and his family are freakin' Hollywood Boulevard royalty, not predators.

"And you're wrong about being a net zero." Santino flies into the tech room. I linger in the doorway while his fingers dance over a keyboard and the flatscreen explodes with the video of me zipping around the Slinging Seven. "You got hits with an exponent on this clip, man."

"Those hits are for Zeli."

"The hits are for a rad jumper. I've been to a couple of Singen Mot's jumps which were damn fine to watch, but what you pull off shatters my brain."

At least my professional jump finale hit the bigs. It's shit I can't cash in on it. "That jumper is dead. Justin MacKenzie has to be history. It's death by Gothel if he recognizes me."

Santino stares at my jump footage. "Justin, this is going to sounds nuts." He bounces the rubber tip of his high top on the pea green carpet. The logo of a speed freak superhero covers his right shoe and the ultimate do-gooder in a cape, the left. If you can't trust a guy with superhero footwear, there's no hope for the planet.

"What if I conjure you a legit web presence for The Summer Number One? Visibility with a capital V. Will you teach me how to B.A.S.E. jump?"

A bubble forms in my chest. I'm on disaster's doorstep, and Santino is offering me a life preserver. "How can you do that in one night?"

His lip quirks into a sly grin. "This is Hollywood Boulevard. Between my tech skills and various, ah, connections, we've got you covered."

"I can't deliver on the B.A.S.E. end of that deal. Singen Mot's a better bet. You gotta learn to jump out of a plane first. There are tests and certifications, guild licenses. I'm sure he could hook you up better than me."

"Singen's cool but not the mentor type. That's what I need. Walk me through the right steps. My first jump can be off the freaking couch as long as my end game is somewhere in Hollywood. No rush. The dream is to see my boulevard from the clouds."

Falling from the sky is a dream I relate to. It's easy to share the necessary steps to get him airborne. What he offers is not a deal, it's a gift. Trust is not my default, but Santino is two for two in being a good guy, first hooking me up with jump gear and then the vandal save. A guy's gotta take a stab at trust sooner or later. I stretch out my hand. "Santino, let's rock this."

His frown is not what I expect. "Before we pull the trigger, how good are you?"

My turn for a sly grin. I bust out the opening bars of *Just in Time*.

"Holy shit."

"Holy shit bad or holy shit good?"

He grips my hand. "Webmaster at your service." Tears gather in the corner of my eye. This is piss embarrassing. I didn't cry when vandals freaked me up, but Santino's kindness breaks me apart.

Acting as if he doesn't notice, Santino slides behind a keyboard. "Let's start with your name."

15

THE DAWN OF TIME

A CREATIVE TORNADO TOUCHES DOWN. CYBER WIZARD, SANTINO, casts spells to create a Justin Time website and social media accounts. He pauses to appraise my face. "I need profile pix. You look like you lost a cage fight." His finger circles the worst of my bruises. "I can doctor pixels to pretty up your profiles. You concentrate on ice to ditch that swelling before tomorrow."

I open the fridge for new frozen veggies. Footsteps approach from the shadowy hallway off the kitchen. I back away, prepared to yell for Santino and his gun. Instead of a grizzled boulevard maniac, the poster boy for the California Lifeguard Association steps into the light. The shirtless dude is over six feet tall with a cliché tan and sun-bleached hair. All he's missing is a surfboard.

"Ah, Tino's latest stray rat," says the God of Summer. "Let's see the damage."

Before I suck in a breath, the dude's got my chin in his hands. He whistles at my swollen cheek.

"Jesus, Snapper," says Santino, emerging from his tech cave. "Try introducing yourself prior to pawing. Justin, this is my sister's boyfriend, Snapper. Snapper, meet Justin, the soon-to-be winner of this year's Summer Number One, not a rat."

Two more figures pop out of the dark.

Santino jerks his chin at the newcomers. "This is Robo Robbie, master of creative I.D. and used tech of questionable ownership."

Robbie's face pings in my memory. "You're the street clown."

"He's a clown all right," says Snapper.

An eye-poppin' hot chick tucks under Snapper's arm. She steams from her painted-on jeans to the orange creamsicle hair on her head in a chaotic pile.

Santino clears his throat, catching my straight up ogle at the hottie. "Meet my sister, Liliana."

"Leeni," chirps the goddess. "Robbie said to come meet the next Summer Number One chart buster. You'd better be worth my little bro's faith. If you screw him over, I'll roast your balls."

"Snapper's an EMT," says Santino. "Let him check you over."

Leeni eyes me like prey. "When do I get my hands on your hair? You're in desperate need of rock star treatment."

"After I steal leftover eggplant parm from Tino's fridge," says Snapper.

"You made eggplant parm and didn't invite me?" says Robbie, clearly offended.

Santino claps his hands. "Justin first. Eggplant second."

Their banter shines with the energy of connection, of family. This quartet reminds me of Slinging Seven hang outs after a gig in a hotel room strewn with pizza boxes and Timmer's whisky stash. Once I had glue that attached me to other people. Those bonds dried up and flaked away.

A legit icepack and a heap of kickass eggplant parmesan later, I swivel back and forth on a chair in front of Santino's tech console. My Robbie-generated driver's license rocks. On paper, Justin Time is for reals.

Santino's hand flies over the keys like he's playing a concerto. "You cool with me listing myself as your manager? That way I can field any glitches with your reg."

"You're hired."

There's a pop as he hits *enter*. "Justin Time ammie number 200, done and doner."

My Summer Number One registration is uploaded and bulletproof.

Santino clicks his tongue as he tinkers with my profile picture. "You up to record a vocal snippet?"

I rub my throat. We laid down *Just in Time* instrumental tracks, but vocals are another matter. "My pipes need rest before I sing tomorrow." I glance at the clock. "Make that, tonight."

"Just a couple of bars." He taps his temple. "I've got an idea."

My chin thumps to my chest. I have no energy for singing. My body wants to crash and sleep until noon.

Santino pushes aside accordion doors, and a rush of energy zips me to my feet. It's no closet. Inside is a comfy padded sound booth with all the trimmings. This mini studio is totally what I envision in my own digs. Two guitars, a sweet Fender electric and an acoustic, lean against the wall. "Yours?"

"I dink around," he says. The tips of his ears turn raspberry. "Maybe later you could give me pointers."

"Pointers! I'll give you a kidney."

He points to the stool in the center of the mini studio and hands me the acoustic guitar. I'm barely acquainted with the instrument when he shuts off the lights in the room. A blue sheen from the strip of LED lights behind me spills over my shoulders to cast a shadow across the carpet.

"Mess your hair," Santino orders. "Make love to the guitar. Look badass."

The words "make love" flip me right back into the sky, singing with Zeli. An urge to continue our lessons beyond kissing tightens my balls. After I spring her from the tower, will we have a chance at something together, or will I be nothing more than the dude who opened her cage? I haven't earned it yet, but I want to be more.

With his phone, he snaps pics from different angles. "Nailed it," he says and flips the screen my way.

Santino is Picasso in his blue period. There's my wild-haired silhouette, making intense love to the guitar in brooding rock star pose.

"This, my friend, is how the world will meet Justin Time. We'll tease. No clear face yet, just your sound. Make the Summer Number One fans rabid to see through your veil of mystery. That'll keep them on the plaza for number two hundred. Now shut up and sing. Make it raw. Make them beg."

I bust out a cover from Da Da Da Deacon, one of Rampion's former stars, imitating his syrupy notes with ripped edges.

My personal tech magician fabricates clips of me singing live onstage at boulevard clubs like *Enigma* and *Rhythm,* nebulae where rock stars are born. My faceless, moody, blue form bleeds across social media.

While Santino finesses his creations, I amble to the living room picture windows.

Zeli's voice, the version made with delicate strands of moonbeam, drifts through my mind. Its softness spreads through bone, smoothing the sharp edges of my guilt for sticky fingering her tune. I must claim our song as mine in the Summer Number One. It's the only melody with enough power to bring my soul to the surface and win this thing. Even though it's my voice, Zeli's spirit will color the notes.

My whisper slides into the fading night. "Forgive me for stealing your song, Rapunzel. It's the key to spring you from Gothel's tower. I promise, we'll..."

Our song glides across my lips. "Banish loneliness, find love to stay."

A star clings to the failing night above the Hollywood Hills. I swear it shines pink.

After a day of cat naps and succumbing to Leeni Fedele's rock star hair treatment, I'm frog marched by Santino and Robbie to Rampion Plaza. It's full dark, and they refuse to leave me solo as vandal bait on the boulevard.

Robbie busts out a *whoop*. "J.T., you hit ten thousand plus followers across platforms. That ranks you fifty-sixth of the two hundred amateurs before they've even seen your face. Welcome to legitville."

"How?"

"Clubs, my friend. Tino has access to databases. Justin Time sent requests to everyone in Hollywood to follow Ammie Number Two Hundred. This town, hell the whole country, goes batshit crazy over the Summer Number One, and who doesn't dig a mysterious underdog." Robbie laughs.

Santino fist pumps hard enough to dislocate a shoulder.

"I'm still last to the stage. My audience will be owls and vandals."

"Kill the bad juju," says Robbie. "Let Tino worry about bodies on the plaza." With a salute, he zips back to Fedele Costumes.

"Robbie will handle your social," says Santino, flashing me his phone with towers of comments on my profiles. Justin Time answers them. "Trust him. Dude's got the gift of chat and turbo powered texting thumbs."

Kaydance will snap a copper nail when she beholds my cyber sizzle.

I stop to face Santino. "What you've done for me blows my freakin' mind. I've given you nothing. I'm totally at a loss here, man."

Santino lays a hand on my shoulder. "Get used to it, JT. You've been adopted by the boulevard."

"The boulevard?"

"Leeni, Snapper, Robbie, Singen Mot, me, the clubs." He waves an arm toward the Hollywood Hills, and then zeroes in on my face. "You're weirded out."

"It's all weird, Santino." Santino, *who the hell are you*, Fedele. A knot forms behind my breastbone. There has to be a catch. "This is surreal. I'm totally grateful, but be straight with me. Why the intense investment in a guy you know jack about?"

He scopes the distance for five beats. "Think of me as one formerly displaced dude helping another. Call it Karma."

"Displaced? You're a boulevard dynasty."

Santino shakes his head. "An honor I nearly pissed away. Before college, I rebelled. To me, the family biz equaled death by boredom. I turned boulevard rat, living in a pack with runaways and scaring the shit out of my folks. A month in, I got caught ripping off the tourist shop by the movie theatre with the footprints. Guy who owned the shop, Rand Diggs, didn't give me up to the cops."

Rand Diggs, there's a rock star name.

"Rand gave me a place to crash with no questions, no strings. Said he saw a good 'light' in my eyes. He introduced me to the real pulse of the boulevard with its deep connections. I learned how to have someone's back and let them have yours. Our corner of the city has a presence. It's a freaking gift to be part of this insane boulevard community, our tapestry."

I glance down the boulevard. Each storefront announces itself with a different voice. Some have chase lights. Others boast awnings that belong in a modern art museum. None succumb to any code of conformity. I feel Santino's tapestry.

"He convinced my folks to let me do online college instead of disappearing into a gorilla suit."

"Sounds like a movie."

"This *is* Hollywood." His lip crinkles. "Rand taught me not to flush my legacy. Now, I double dip. Keep the family biz healthy and do my P.R. thing. Not a bad gig for a dude between drinking age and thirty."

Memories rewind to Feisty B. and his Hollywood and Vine place, a wing that sheltered me for a time, another weave in the boulevard tapestry. I wonder if Santino knows him.

"J, I've never met anyone like you, a bro who jumps into the sky one sec, and then sings for the bigs the next. It's my turn to offer payback to the cosmos."

He's not asking for anything but trust. I survived the tough first steps in that direction with him, so why do I still have the urge to slap his hand away? It's Timmer's fault for burning my ass. It's Ma's fault for turning ghost.

"Trust always bites me in the ass."

"I'm passing the good on to you, Justin Time, for reals."

The confident way Santino says Justin Time makes this whole mad plan shine with possibility. I study his eyes and find the tangible glow of *good* in those cinnamon peepers that Rand defined.

I take a step closer to trust, something I've never been good at. How can I pass up the chance with this guy and his crew? They invented me.

"For reals." I stick my hand out. We shake.

Santino slows at the edge of the plaza. "Someday, you'll meet someone in trouble who needs you."

My mind jumps to Zeli locked in the Rampion Tower. Someday is now. What if I screw up? Maybe I don't have the chops to save another person. Can I be more than a song-stealing jacklick who dreams of living a life of music, and damn it, fame?

"I'll do what I can if that day comes." My promise swirls like a glow around my heart, a light filled with Zeli.

Santino hands me his guitar just as a groupie girl takes in my *look*.

"Are you in the Summer Number One?" She leans in for a closer look.

I offer a hand. "Justin Time. Nice to meet you."

"Justin Time! The Blue Shadow!"

Blue Shadow. Great name for my backup singers. *Justin Time and the Blue Shadow.*

Her friend whips out a phone. "Is a picture cool?"

Santino holds up a hand. "If you swear not to post until after his performance."

"Swear," says camera phone girl.

I squeeze into a selfie sandwich.

"Allow me," says Santino, grabbing her phone.

The girls cover my cheeks in kisses while Santino clicks away. They skip off, a pair of twittering cartoon birds.

"Buckle up, J. Roller coaster is heading for the loop," says Santino, grinning. Like the sun hidden by a cloud, his smile fades and a crease forms between his eyebrows. "It could happen for you, Justin. The bigs. You're that good. Keep your head on straight."

"I'm not going to piss this away, Santino. I'll be smart."

Smart.

Stealing Zeli's song isn't genius territory, but I'm past the point of no return on that one. Our sky duet stokes the boiler of my artistic engine. The need to sing *Just in Time* and what it could do for both Z and me consumes me at a cellular level.

I long to sing with Z again and see if a second kiss might blossom into something more. That's not going to happen as long as Gothel's got her locked in the tower. For a legit shot at freeing her, I've got to be invited into the Rampion Tower instead of sneaking in through the moat and praying I don't get busted for trespassing. The only road to accomplish that is by being the ass who sings a song written by hitmaker Zeli instead of my own untried tune. My gut tells me *Just in Time* will secure my place to sing with the pros and build the bridge I need to reach Zeli.

I make two wishes on the Hollywood sign. First, that Zeli hasn't played *Just in Time* for Gothel yet. Second, by some miracle, Z will forgive me for the dumbassery of stealing her song once she understands I'm singing it to save her.

Santino holds up two fingers, crimping each in turn. "Wristband? Thumb drive?"

I raise my wrist and pat the pocket of my costume. "Check, check."

"See you soon under the moon, JT." He slaps my shoulder and jets.

I stare at his retreating form. He twists back to throw me two thumbs up. Santino Fedele is the first person in my life to look back.

My sight drifts to Zeli's penthouse prison at the top of the tower. Does Santino's boulevard tapestry have room for one more? Another lonely soul with a voice to fill the sky with stars. God, I hope so.

16

THE BIGS

THE SPECTACLE ON THE PLAZA IS BIBLICAL. SUPPLICANTS WORSHIP AT the altar of Rampion Records. Across the panels that define the performance space, a digital thunderstorm rages around the current singer, a visual match to her lyrics about torrents and downpours. Off to either side, Jumbotrons flash the live feed to the audience.

I weave through the myriad of humanity swarming between stage and grandstands. Folks are tucked in for the Summer Number One long haul with camp chairs, beach umbrellas, and even a blow-up wading pool. Groupies wave signs with the names of their favorites.

MELISSY CHRISSY - PIPES OF GOLD

TAKE 'EM DOWNTOWN CAMA RAMA

The Cama Rama contingency claims an entire section of grandstand and a dozen patches around the lowlands. They're the biggest fan clique in the crowd. His posse flashes *Team Cama Rama* tees plastered with the ammie's face. Between singers, they chant for their boy.

"CAMA RAMA."

"Who is this guy?" I tap the Summer Number One link on my newly acquired phone.

Fifteen fucking thousand followers!

He's ranked in the top twenty of the whole competition, ammie and pro, before he sings a note. Dude's bio claims that he's a "Badass Purveyor of Rock." The bastard's headlined at every top club in Hollywood.

Cama Rama's profile picture boasts a mane of black hair as substantial as any lion's and long enough to tickle his ribcage. He leans on a tomato-red, electric guitar that matches both the six-inch, vinyl belt wrapped around his waist and a headband masking an ample forehead. Between knee-high boots trimmed in fringe and a black velvet sleeveless tee, Mr. Rama wears slate gray, cheetah print tights. The final touch is a swatch of red fabric tied around his thigh.

"What a shitiot." He's the picture on the front of a prepackaged Halloween costume labeled *Rocker*.

I feel a twinge of remorse for the *trying too hard* extensions Leeni pasted to my noggin'. I don't want to be the package. I want to be the contents.

A guy working the crowd shoves a coupon in my face. "Two for one at Vegan Delish." He nods to silver tents hawking food and Summer Number One logo merch.

I've only seen the Summer Number One on TV. Standing here, the real phenom pulls energy from the core of the planet.

I'm pumped. Get me on that stage.

Purple, blue, and green spotlights wash over Ammie Number 190 as she croons her depressing ballad. By mid-song, 190 loses the crowd.

My gaze drifts to Floor 33 $^{1/3}$. Is Zeli plugged in, watching the scene down here? In my dreams, she'll hear me sing *Just in Time* and concede the song is perfect for me, graciously handing it over. I pray the connection we shared in our sky duet will help her understand that I'm doing this for us. The tune is our beginning, not our end.

I catch sight of Kaydance barking at a Gothel goon in front of a black tent between the stage and Rampion Tower. Above their heads is a brushed metal VIP sign. Target acquired.

The former Ms. Foil Jacket rocks a silk poncho with a Navajo blanket print. The orange, brown, and white faux weave could be my old musty bedspread.

As I saunter toward Kaydance, a doofy smile tugs the sides of my lips. "Cue Mr. Time."

I've dreamed of being in the Summer Number One so often, I'd begun to believe it was forever relegated to the land of fantasy. But I'm here. Number two hundred. Before the moon sets, I'll be up on that cavern of a stage under rows of lights streaming fairy dust onto dreamers below.

"*Goodbyeeeeeeeee.*" Ammie 190's final screech surely made every hound in Hollywood slap paws over their ears. "I'm Jennilee Orbit," she shouts and waves. Lackluster hoots ripple across the plaza.

"Oh, darlin', you just dropped out of orbit," I say under my breath.

God, what if I unleash a clinker like that? We've got three measly minutes to sell our souls. That's not enough time to recover from any imperfection much less an eardrum splitter.

The Jumbotrons flash *Amateur 191.* The next ammie claims center ring of this mad circus.

They're on schedule according to the vertical window running up the edge of each Jumbotron. Every thirty seconds, names and headshots of the top 25 ranked amateurs replace the schedule. Cama Rama's name holds firm at the top of the ammie list. How did that guy shoot up so fast?

Voting is open to the whole planet until U.S.A. west coast midnight. That's when I'll know if I'm moving on or falling down the Summer Number One rabbit hole.

As I mosey up to the VIP entrance, lights from the stage reflect off the oversized orange glasses than swallow Kaydance's face.

"Good evening, Ms. Kaydance," I drawl.

Her fingernails echo the Navajo weave design of her poncho. This babe escalates matchy-matchy to an art form.

She waves me through an opening past the Gothel goon standing guard.

I set my expression to *bored rock star* and stroll past the ammies waiting to go on. In the corner of the pavilion, a pyramid of bottled water rises within a cascade of mist. Tables along the wall hold steel cylinders of a dozen different teas. To my disappointment, none of them are labeled Rampion Tea, Zeli's drink.

Goons guard openings that lead deeper into the complex. My shoulders go rock hard. If Gothel materializes from the inner sanctum, I'll have to duck out fast to insure he doesn't recognize the jumper who ignited Zeli's platinum shitshow.

T-shirt moment: B.A.S.E. Jumping Not Spoken Here.

Kaydance scans my jumpsuit. She covers the mouthpiece of a headset, the only part of the apparatus free from the coils of orange and brown braids on her head. "Thought I wasted a wristband on you, Justin Time."

"You thought wrong."

"Caught your website." She bites her lower lip and nods. "Never expected slick from you." After a tongue click, she holds out a hand. "Gimme. I'll load your tracks into the system."

I press the thumb drive across her lifeline. My heart skips when she tosses my treasure to a woman in a plastic yellow sundress.

I half expect Zeli to waltz through the curtain and hand out pink guitars to the ammies. I'll bet she's laying down backing tracks for pro night. I suck in a breath. They're the wrong tracks.

If only I could explain the big picture before she hears her song coming out of my mouth. She'd know my theft is justified because I believe *Just in Time* is the song to keep me in the competition. Once I'm mic to mic with the pros, I'll have enough access to Rampion

Records to figure out a way to knock down her tower walls. Zeli would totally get why I have to sing her song and appreciate my overall plan.

Who am I kidding? In a few hours, she'll hate me.

I snug into a corner to warm up my voice. The notes find a home in my chest where rock songs belong. Through the VIP entrance I see a buttercream moon watching the Summer Number One from its front row seat in the sky.

I slide down a beam to the light at your feet.

The lyric surprises me. A melody fills my head. I snatch the guitar to catch them both. Visions rush through my mind in a series of snapshots.

A glimpse of Zeli's real hair woven underneath her highway of extensions. "River of gold is banished beneath."

The song comes to life sliding gracefully from heart to lips to fingers.

Night breeze whispering through my chute. "Voices join in the mist of the night."

I whisper phrases over and over, keeping guitar strings hushed as minutes tick away at too rapid a pace.

A woman frozen in front of a window high above the ground. "Behind walls of glass, you'll linger no more."

This song finds me like a visitation. It's not for me. It will be my peace offering to Zeli. A trade. This new song for the one I stole. Harmonies deepen around the main melody line, clearer and clearer. I must commit this to my spirit and hold tight to what I've written for Rapunzel.

From outside the tent a rhythm begins, slow at first. Soon, it quickens to thunderous proportions as *Amateur 195* flashes on a monitor. A string bean with a familiar black mane sweeps up the stage steps.

"CAMA RAMA."

His throng goes nutzilla. The mix man has to restart C.R.'s backing track several times. When 195 finally sings, my heart splatters onto my high tops. Dude's got the goods with his perfect blend of growl, technique, and a bitchin' song.

I swig a water bottle and sing, "Fizzzzzzzzzzz down," to keep my throat from clenching. I'm not deluded enough to assume other singers won't give me a run for my money, but damn, this dude is one serious threat.

When Cama Rama bounces offstage, the scene at the top of the steps makes me gag. Kaydance slaps his leather-covered ass and matches him pelvis to pelvis. He returns her enthusiasm by gripping the crossbars above their head and grinding against her. Kaydance's bright orange lipstick disappears between his teeth as she wraps a leg around his thigh. They break apart with a juicy smack, leaving no doubt of her choice for the Summer Number One's top spot.

I slink away from their PDA. Cama Rama is so sure of himself he's grabbing tongue time with Kaydance in full view. Bastard probably already has a contract from Gothel.

I close my eyes and summon the energy I'll need to perform. I dig deep for focus and ignore the trappings of injustice that writhe through this contest.

After a clone of Mistress Mango—a previous Rampion diva—peddles her wares on stage, Kaydance hunts me down. "Mix man instructions?"

Hugging Santino's guitar, my attention drifts to the stage. "Don't be shy with the reverb."

The flatness of my voice doesn't escape her. She tilts her head. "Where's Justin 'cocky ass' Time?"

If only I could B.A.S.E. jump and sing. That's a performance that would knock Cama Rama off the ammie throne already draped in his colors. I scrape a toe against the ground. I'll never sound as good as I did, falling through the sky, singing with the woman trapped behind glass. Never. But for her, I'll come as close as I can.

I can't see the plaza from backstage. Judging from the lack of sound, they've gone into hibernation. On the monitor in the VIP area Cama Rama's rank sits at number one. I need serious online voting love just to reach the base of his mountain. My heart plummets. No matter what Santino drums up, how can it ever revive an audience burned out from hours of ammies?

Ammie 199 pulls off a series of gritty, half-singing shrieks. My confidence flickers back to life. I'll sound like freaking Sinatra after her, poor thing.

"One more and we're out of here," Kaydance calls to the people hanging in front of the last remaining row of water bottles. "Two hundred on deck." She jerks a thumb to the steps.

A weary stagehand plugs a cable into my guitar. "Thank God you're acoustic," he says, jerking his chin at the instrument. "I won't survive another screeching bass."

From here, I catch sight of a Jumbotron. It flashes my number across the plaza like lighting. The stage glows purple except for a single spotlight, awaiting the last ammie.

I step onstage. Beneath me the floor is a chessboard of LED squares. They pulse in a hundred different colors dazzling enough to light the bottom of the clouds. I stare straight up into the spotlight making the circle I'm supposed to hit as my mark. Rookie error. Bright bursts fill my vision. Beyond the curtain of fireflies, I make out swaths of blue and purple searchlights chasing one another through the dark plaza and into the sky. I can't judge the size of my audience.

If there is one.

From behind me, the guy sitting at the mix board calls out. "Hit it, Last But Not Least."

A gust of wind plasters my jumpsuit to my body. I prepare to sing to a graveyard.

My spot-burned vision settles. In the haze, I imagine Feisty B. in the crowd. Which ghost of Justin past will appear next? Ma? Timmer? The whole Slinging Seven?

Above me, moths flap through spotlights. I step up to the mic stand as follow spots from light towers target me. Their warmth cuts through the night's chill. Beneath my feet, the floor starts to shake.

Alarmed, I shoot a glance to the mix man who stares out at the plaza, eyes wide. A beat later the rumble rolls over me. I pull out the earpiece to confirm what I think I'm hearing.

"JUSSSSTIN."

Rumbles turn into a rhythmic boom.

"JUS-TIN."

The boom goes supersonic.

"JUSTIN."

Fan-freaking-tastic! Santino stands front and center twenty feet from the stage. A sea of people surround him, chanting my name ten times louder than Cama Rama's groupies.

Stagehands and Gothel goons peek around curtains. A mass of humanity streams onto the plaza from the main artery leading to Hollywood Boulevard. My music starts, and I stuff the earpiece back in.

Kaydance flags the mix man to cut. She flattens the headset against her ear, hollering into the mouthpiece.

The Jumbotrons flip from my onstage image to a grid of footage around Hollywood. Reporters stand in front of a dozen music venues while lines of club goers dash past them, under awnings, through double glass doors, and down steps, leaving the clubs. The trail brings them here. They're storming Rampion Plaza. A crawl across the bottom of the Jumbotron feed pulses:

SUMMER NUMBER ONE SHOCKER – JUSTIN TIME – AMMIE NUMBER 200 – CLEARS THE HOLLYWOOD MUSIC CLUB SCENE

Kaydance's voice blasts from the wings. "Call Gothel."

Santino and his boulevard family keep the chant alive. Sound ricochets off every building edging the plaza.

I'm so choked with emotion, I hum to keep my throat open. Beyond the Jumbotron, I hear a hubbub on the moat bridge. I barely make out a cluster of black suits pouring out of Rampion Records.

I settle the guitar strap around my neck and lean into the mic. "I'm Justin Time. Your number two hundred."

My Santino-created fan base goes nuclear. The mix man cranks up my music like I'm on my own platinum tour. He tweaks the sound, amping it, adding reverb and background rhythms.

I push lips against the mic as my mind cries to Zeli.

Hear me. Forgive me.

"Just in time, our stars crossed just in time..."

As I sing, the audience settles, wrapped inside each note. Suddenly, I'm back in the sky with Rapunzel.

My song flares as bright as a falling star. The tapestry of Hollywood Boulevard weaves me into its fabric.

I own the plaza. My heartbeat is the music. My soul, the words. I lay my offering on the altar, sustaining a note here, syncopating there. *Just in Time* reincarnates with more beauty, more hope than ever.

"We banished loneliness, found love to stay."

For you too, Zeli, I promise.

I hold the last note, longer, longer, and then settle into a natural fade.

The clubbers of Hollywood go ballistic. Spotlights blaze. I'm a ball of fire.

Santino jumps. He kicks heels to ass and fist pumps the moon. I throw him a salute for saving my ammie bacon and drop into a bow that sets the plaza off on another Justin chant.

This is for us, Z.

In the wings, a face appears. Uplight chisels Grant Gothel's features into a stone gargoyle. The Justin love on the plaza escalates.

"ENCORE."

I dip my head in deference to Gothel, the man poised to change my life. His expression leeches every drop of blood from my body. Reality hits. Gothel knows what I've done.

I'm toast. I deserve to be toast.

The shitiocy of my logic and overblown ego hits me full in the face. Risking the chance that Gothel hadn't heard Z's song yet or rejected it for the contest is insane, but I sang it anyway. After my sky duet with Zeli, my sense of self-preservation shorted out. I've become so obsessed with ripping Z out of that tower, I adopted the fantasy that song-stealing wouldn't kill my shot at the Summer Number One.

I'm burned toast.

Gothel's face says *eviscerate*.

T-shirt moment: Justin Time – King of all Jacklicks.

Gothel's snarl bursts through the rising chants on the plaza as he aims a finger at my heart. "That punk stole Zeli's song. Grab him."

17

GOTHEL'S FANGS

GG GOES OFF LIKE A GRENADE. "NAIL THE THIEVING RUNT."

Spotlights and LED squares go berserk. Every figure has ten shadows all closing in on me.

I spot the only possible exit point. Clutching Santino's guitar, I leap off the front of the stage and drop as soon as I hit concrete. Rolling under the weighted bottom of curtain that spans the front of the stage, I make it out of sight as the plaza lights up like midday.

A voice shouts, "He ditched onto the plaza."

Through the mesh curtain, I see a legion of black leather shoes push into the crowd: Gothel goons.

I force my breathing to quiet. Did I truly think I'd get away with this, that Gothel would toss this gorgeous song aside for not being on brand enough for Zeli?

Yeah, sure I did. I believed self-righteous intensions would be enough for me to pull this off. Joke's on me.

Crawling across scaffolding, I tuck deeper under the stage.

"Mange!" Gothel stands on the plaza near the stage. "Get me Justin Time!"

I tuck Santino's guitar against an upright piece of scaffolding so I can navigate more easily. It'll be safe here while I slip out from under the stage, use the mayhem for cover, and high tail it to Fedele Costumes.

A time machine would be handy to rewrite the lasts two days. I'd never check on Zeli after the mob scene, keep my lips to myself, and avoid trading notes with her in the sky. Top of the list would be to get my ass back up on stage and take my chances with my own original tune.

A bolt tears the sleeve of my jumpsuit as truth tears at my heart.

I'd rather die than erase one moment with Zeli. The woman twisted my brain from the second I first wandered into her twilight room.

"That little piss better be standing in front of me in two minutes." Gothel's rage threatens to crack every letter of the Hollywood Sign.

Above me, I hear Mange. "Mr. Gothel...the Jumbotron."

There's a two-foot square opening at the back of stage. A quick peek confirms no goons patrol this vector, so I slip through and scramble to my feet. I catch a glimpse of a Jumbotron. My face fills the screen next to a counter ticking up so fast, it's impossible to make out a single number.

The votes are mine.

Feet pound this way. There's no time to drop back under the stage. I attempt to dart into the crowd but smack a chest of stone.

Snapper's fingers clamp around my upper arm, yanking me into the middle of a cluster. Robo Robbie flanks me while Santino throws a hoodie over my head. As we move alongside the stage, Gothel still flames.

"Get Zeli on the phone."

Shit, not Zeli.

Santino buzzes at my ear. "Head down. This is all kinds of ugly." My human cocoon heads toward the back of the grandstands. Gothel's fury folds my guts into an accordion. Zeli can't take the fall for my epic blunder.

We stop in the same stretch of shadow where Timmer beat the crap out of me.

Santino punches my shoulder. "A Zeli dive into the crowd, seriously?"

I stare at the circle of faces. They don't know Gothel wants my head stuffed as a trophy.

"How did you find me?"

Robo Robbie nods toward the plaza. "We saw you ditch under the stage."

Santino is amped enough to buzz. "Show him." Two-dozen phone screens point my way, forming a ring of light. Snippets of *Just in Time* fill the air.

"You're the number one download on Tuneful," says Robbie.

"Number Two Hundred obliterates the other ammies," Leeni squeals. The moment should be sweet, but I've soured it with my thievery. I have to warn Zeli what happened before Gothel gets to her. Who knows what a guy who locked her in a tower and possibly shoved her to the floor last night is capable of when he's really pissed?

Santino waves his phone back and forth above his head. "I've got requests from a whole list of clubs begging you for pop-ins tonight." He jumps into the air completing an entire revolution. "Justin Time knocks the lid off Hollywood."

He hustles me in the direction of the boulevard. "Let's blow this pop stand."

A dude in a leather blazer with a clear plastic bow tie pulls on Santino's arm. "Rock Out is holding main stage mic time for your boy."

Santino whoops. "We'll get for reals club footage for the website."

I pull free incapable of moving off the plaza and farther away from Zeli. My new home team of Santino recruits waits for me to speak.

"Y'all rock." I strain to keep the waver from my voice. Now please move along so I can get to Zeli. They close in like I've granted them permission to approach the royal personage. Some hands slide over my bod while others thump me on the back. A babe in our entourage slinks in fast. Her lips grab mine in a wild kiss.

"Put it in reverse, you vandals," says Santino to our fan group. He laughs and slings an arm around my shoulders to shield me from any more benevolent mauling. "You want more Justin?" A cheer goes up. "Meet us at Rock Out." He waves his hands. "Keep the online love going. I want ten times the number of bodies on the plaza tomorrow night."

A guy flashes a tablet with my performance blasting across his screen. "We'll saturate the web, Tino. You'll have people falling from the sky to catch Justin live."

Santino launches the group away with fist bumps, and then turns to me. "First we hit the clubs. Leeni insists you crash at her place. I guarantee you'll wake up with longer extensions."

I feel hollow enough for the breeze to carry me over the hills. Santino thinks he rescued me from pandemonium, not Gothel.

"Can't go, man. I've got to do a thing."

"A thing?" Confusion crosses his face. "With Rampion? Already?" He shrugs. "Well, let's make it quick and get to the clubs. Don't want to kill the momentum. Where to?" He scans the crowded plaza. "Put your hood up."

This is torture. Santino blew me out of a cannon to light up the Hollywood sky. He gave me a real shot at the Summer Number One, and I'm about to smash it to bits. *I have to get to Zeli. I'm scared as piss Gothel might hurt her.*

I pull Santino to the corner of the closest building. "I've got serious shit to deal with."

"No kidding. Everyone on that plaza wants a piece of you."

"Not that," I say, pointing to the crowd writhing around the stage. "I screwed someone big time."

Creases form black lines across Santino's forehead. "Okay. Let's fix it, and then make the club rounds."

He's earned the truth. Santino saved my life from the vandals and made Justin Time a phoenix rising from a pile of ash. One night and he's more family than I've experienced since the days with Feisty B in the dinky apartment on Hollywood and Vine.

"You don't want to know."

His expression shifts into caution. "Tell me."

Old Justin would shut up or lie. I owe Santino more than that. Hell, if anyone can help me through this, it's him.

"I stole Zeli's Summer Number One song."

Santino's face relaxes, and he laughs. Of course, he does. This is ridiculous.

"You're hilarious. What did you do, crash her session and steal her tracks?"

"Close."

The corner of his smile goes south. His face blanches white enough to glow in the dark.

Taking a deep breath, I plunge. "I heard her singing the tune in the tower. I have a knack, like a photographic memory, but with music. The song, "Just in Time", it's hers. She wrote it for her Summer Number One performance."

"Don't shit me. Not only would that be totally vandal, it's stupid."

I dip my head. Extensions slide down my collar.

"You said you had your own song."

"I do."

"Then why steal hers?"

How can I explain when Zeli offered the song to the night, it soaked through my skin, wrapping fingers around my heart?

"Answer my question."

Words tumble over one another. "I went nuts from the crowd shredding Zeli's hair and Timmer ditching me. I heard her sing "Just in Time", and it sent me reeling. I for reals thought Gothel would nix it as not pop enough for Zeli and that she'd sing some other tune in the Summer Number One." I'm panting now. "My twisted mind made serious bad choices."

"Twisted mind, my ass. You have a twisted soul." My shitiocy snuffs the good light from Santino's eyes. His stare lingers a beat before he turns his back.

"Santino, I'm so sorry."

He whips around and looms over me, dark and dangerous. "I let you in, Justin. My boulevard family launched you viral." His snarl cuts the air. "You sucker-played me." His breath is as hot as a spot-light. "Took my help for a stinkin' lie."

"Not true." My knees wobble. Lies scorch my insides. "I need your help to fix this."

He snaps fingers half an inch from my nose. "I'm out." His knuckle thumps my breastbone. "If I could, I'd take it all back." Santino scuffs his heel against the concrete. "I'm the shitiot, buying your 'alone in the world' act."

"It wasn't an act. I didn't play you, Santino. Swear. You are my lifeline. I screwed up."

"Then unscrew it. Step out of frame and take a good look at yourself." Santino follows the same path Timmer took away from me. *Déjà*-freaking-*vu*.

It hurts to breathe. Timmer may have used me, but he gave me a place in the world. Santino helped me crack open the door to the future I've always dreamed of, and I'm screwing it up. I've driven them both away with my shitiocy. I pray there's still time to turn things around with Santino.

"I sang "Just in Time" to save Zeli."

Santino slows.

"Gothel has her locked up in the penthouse. I need to get her out."

He turns back but keeps his distance. If I tell him everything, at least he'll know I didn't steal her song for myself alone. It's for Z too.

"I need access to the Rampion Tower to get to her. I'll score a pass inside by going all the way to the finals. "Just in Time" is my chance to make that happen."

He scowls, digesting my words, and then shakes his head. "I'm not buying any more of your fantasies. I don't exist until you clean up your shitshow." Santino pivots toward the boulevard.

"I will fix it. I promise, bro."

Santino spins like a cyclone, blowing back in my face. "I am not your bro. You have no clue what that means."

The faraway lights from the plaza catch an angry tear in the corner of Santino's eye. "What kills me, Justin, is that your voice is as perfect as I've ever heard. You had a serious shot to win this competition without stealing Zeli's song."

Even though he clearly wants to smash me, he's still here.

"You're right." I want to grab his jacket and beg him to believe I can fix what I broke. He is good people, and my tune-grabbing stupidity is flushing our friendship down the crapper.

Santino steps backward, putting distance between us.

"Justin Time is off my list until you do right." He wipes his hands together, and then jabs his thumbs toward the ground. I watch the most decent person on my playlist become a shadow.

18

SOME PAPA

SANTINO DOES NOT TURN BACK. EMERGENCY LIGHTS THAT LIT THE plaza snap off. The hunt is over.

Smoke rising from scattered barbeques adds an eerie layer to the scene. Fans sing "Just in Time." A nasty taste fills my mouth. The price for my triumph is too high - Santino's rejection – Gothel somehow blaming Zeli for my actions.

I flip the hoodie over my head and set off on a suicide mission to breach a fortress filled with Gothel goons.

I've got to get inside the Rampion tower and face Zeli. I need her to know that I sang "Just in Time" for both of us. That's not all. I shudder. I've also got to explain how the jumper who stole a kiss became the man who stole her Summer Number One tune.

The moat pirouettes around the tower, its hiss louder than any other sound. There's no walking through the lobby this time, pretending I'm with Gigabyte. My face isn't random anymore.

I'm in for another swim.

I slip into the moat, up the tunnel, and onto the floor of the maintenance dock. My shoulder cramps from holding my cell above the water. I ditch my sodden hoodie and slip a hammer from the wall through a loop on my jumpsuit. I may need a weapon for a goon fight.

By the time I cat burglar up to Zeli's ready room, the hallway is deserted. I grasp the door handle.

Locked.

I ditch back into the service ring. I'll jimmie the vent open, squeeze through, climb the spiral stairway, knock on Zeli's double doors, and–

"I'm sorry, Zeli. I'm a shitiot, Zeli. Off with my head, Zeli. Forgive me, Zeli," I mutter to myself.

Kiss me, Zeli.

Desire to touch her hits me like a fist to the temple. I have lost my mind if I think she'll ever let me touch her again.

T-shirt moment: Zeli Lips Are Only for Singing.

I attempt to shove the claw side of the hammer under the edge of the vent. It doesn't budge. There aren't any screws on my side to strip out. My only option would be to bash the vent out of the wall and slip into Z's ready room, but a shaft of light coming from the open double doors kills that possibility. I'll be heard.

SMACK!

The sound rings out from Zeli's penthouse. That was skin on skin. I peer through the vent, heart galloping.

Zeli's silhouette clutches the doorjamb, eyeing the distance to the spiral stairs as if she plans to jump. Gothel looms behind her.

"How did this Justin Time sweet talk that song out of you?"

Blood thickens in my veins when a string of interjections pour out of Gothel. "I told you not to touch social media." Gothel punches the wall near the doorframe. "What did this online Romeo promise you? Love?"

Another odd barrage erupts from his lips. It sounds like a curse.

A broadcast blasts from the penthouse at high volume.

"Justin Time exploded from zero to phenom in an unprecedented takeover of the Summer Number One amateur round. Vegas odds place him ahead of pros who won't take the stage for another two days."

Gothel jabs a finger toward the sound. "Your song gave the punk propulsion."

"Papa, I had nothing to do with it." Zeli collapses in a heap on the floor, dropping her face into her hands as she weeps. Extensions clump around her in a multicolored pile of designs and patterns.

Gothel lifts her by the metal lace vest. The only color on her skin is a reflection of the diamond ceiling.

"You betrayed me over the promises of an online asshole? I should send you back to Rampion Ranch."

Gothel looks as if he's either going to sink his teeth into her or heave her across the room. All I can do is watch as his freaky fire fingers begin to glow. I've never felt so useless in all my life. I want to call out, run to her, shove Gothel out the open double doors, but his glowing digits stop me. What is his freaky power capable of? I could make things worse for Z by busting in. I press a fist to my lips to keep silent. If he hears me, I'm next to the grave.

"Papa." Dainty hands rest on his cheeks. "It's me, your Rapunzel." They stare at one another. "If you hurt me, you won't forgive yourself."

How can she be tender to this maniac?

As if Zeli cast a spell, Gothel gently sets her on her feet. He examines his dimming hands.

"You know not to make me angry."

"Justin Time made you angry."

Fantastic. She's aimed his death ray fingers between my eyes. Not that I don't deserve it.

"I think I know where he got the song."

She leaves the frame of the double doors, and I strain to keep her in view.

"I didn't write "Just in Time"."

I stuff my hand into my mouth at the same time Gothel shouts. "What!"

"It's from the family memory files you gave me at the ranch. I played it every night. My father sang it."

Gothel barks a laugh. "Sweet irony. The song you stole from dear old dad was taken from you." I shudder as his laugh grows in intensity. "You resurrected some trash lullaby for the Summer Number One?"

Zeli paces back to him. "It's a beautiful song with a happy ending. Maybe Justin Time's parents sang it to him."

It's more than a song I've taken from Zeli, I stole a memory, and still she's defending my ass. Santino was right to ditch me.

Gothel snaps his cell to his ear. "Kaydance, search Justin Time's song—copyrights, recording, any trace of it."

If this song is copyrighted, I'm going down in flames. Only original tunes qualify for the Summer Number One.

Gothel kicks a pile of Zeli's extensions out of his way. "1958!" he shouts into his cell. He narrows his eyes, tapping teeth with a fingernail. "I want a rule change – tonight. Copyrights over fifty years old with new orchestrations are now eligible." With no goodbye, Gothel slams the phone into his jacket pocket, ending the call.

My breath catches. Did Gothel resuscitate "Just in Time"?

Zeli's delicate profile is split between the light of her apartment and the murk of the twilight room; an angel with a demon's shadow stuck to it.

"Well, Rapunzel, maybe you didn't piss away a hit to some clown who–" He lays both hands over his chest. "Touched your heart."

Zeli's expression is toxic.

"The copyright of this tune belongs to Midas Lear and Golden Pipes Records." He snaps his fingers. "Did that old buzzard send in Justin Time as a mole to snatch the Summer Number One win out from under my people?" Gothel belly laughs, amused by his own notion. "Not a chance. Midas Lear would send in someone a thousand times more polished than that punk."

Screw you, Gothel.

"I've never spoken to Justin Time, Papa."

"News flash. Your lullaby is from an old school musical, *Star Crossed*."

She hangs her head. "I thought it was a family song."

Bile burns my throat when Gothel lifts her chin.

"I'm the only family you need, Angel." He waits until she nods. "Even so, bad things come to those who plagiarize."

He's got that right.

"If you want to keep the Zeli train on the tracks, you'll come up with an original tune to knock Justin Time out of the Summer Number One. If you don't, I will send you back to Rampion Ranch until you're nothing but a memory. I've got other talent ripe for harvest and new opuses to be sung."

"Don't send me back. I'll write you a platinum hit."

What the hell is Rampion Ranch? It's freakin' the hell out of Zeli. She practically genuflects to Gothel. "I'll make you proud."

Zeli is brainwashed, a prisoner deifying her captor. I've got to get her out of the tower and deprogram her insane loyalty to this slime-coated jerk. I've got a new song for her to make that happen. The one that came to me today before I stepped on stage. My peace offering to the woman who sings to falling stars.

"You will beat this Justin Time jacklick into the ground. Now, send me into the sky."

My heart skips. I try to dislodge the vent one last time and take a risk, swinging at it with the hammer. The freakin' thing must be welded to the wall.

My only way to get to Zeli's place is to score a return ticket on Gothel's zip line. To do that, I've got to hot foot it over to the roof of Singen's building where Gothel will land.

19

DANGLE

DROPPING LIKE A COW OUT OF A TWISTER IN THE SERVICE ELEVATOR, I reach plaza level. I crack the door to the main hallway. There's no one around. Dashing out the main lobby doors in front of the Rampion guard could end with a Gothel goon snagging me so I head in the opposite direction for a quick scan. I'll swim the moat if I have to. I come to a door marked *Scene Dock* and head inside to find the place deserted. I've still got a few notes of luck working for me.

A sprint across the space leads me to an outside door behind the stage complex. Nearby, a smaller version of the main bridge spans the moat. I fly over it and round the tower until I'm under Zeli's open window.

Above me, a foul Gothel bird soars. I've got to get to the roof of Singen Mot's building before that zip line rig returns to Zeli's penthouse. I hug every shadow and slip over to the building. I'm cooked if GG catches a glimmer of me.

The lobby doors to Singen Mot's building are locked. I sprint to the side of the building looking for a way in. A security guard on cig break yaks on his cell next to a door propped open with a chair.

Skittering silently like the rat I am, I ease through the door unnoticed. God willing, if I'm caught, Mot's put my name on the list. With a gut full of dancing worry worms, I ride the elevator to the top floor and find the door to the roof stairs.

I sweat enough to fill the Rampion moat. If we meet, Gothel will smash me into a million pieces.

I promised Santino I'd fix this. Even though she doesn't know it yet, I made a promise to Zeli—no, Rapunzel, with our song in the night.

Never have I felt a connection with anyone the way I felt wrapped in her voice. Destiny rarely gives one a choice when it comes knockin'. I won't abandon her the way everyone in my life walks away from me. I'll ride that zip line over to her and begin to make things right if she'll give me the chance. I swear I'll do whatever she asks to earn it.

I crack the door to the roof. Unless the stars and Hollywood Sign give me away, I've got a stab at this. I creep onto the rooftop. Backlit by the Rampion Tower, Gothel chats on his cell while he slides free of his tricked-out harness. I tiptoe closer.

"Hang on," says Gothel, tapping his screen. "Goodnight, my angel." He taps again without waiting for her answer. "Mange, Justin Time will not hit that stage tomorrow until we have a chat. Don't mess him up. I have plans for the dillweed."

Dillweed?

Plans?

The creep passes my hiding place. "He's going back on stage."

Gothel wants me back on stage? I'm dying for deets, but the empty rig slides closer to the edge of the roof.

"And get on the song copyright. I want to own every note of "Just in Time"."

I can't wrap my head around this. A squeal from the cable yanks my attention back to the zip line. Gothel isn't through the roof door. The harness under Z's platinum record extension is nearly out of reach. Praying GG is too preoccupied to look back, I dash to the harness and leap.

The force of my impact sends the rig over the edge of the building. Two handfuls of twisted guidelines are all that hold me airborne. If I don't wiggle into the harness before I lose my grip, I'll be plaza splat.

The harness sways back and forth in a wicked arc. Straining every muscle in my upper body, I manage to jam belly down far enough into the rig to stop mentally writing my obituary.

Zeli stands next to the window, back to me, leaning on the sword that controls the payout line of her extensions. I have less than fifty feet to figure out how to explain why the hell I'm riding her hair.

Inside her apartment, a huge flatscreen suspended from the ceiling broadcasts my performance. My image is real rock star material. The dude onscreen has "it," the thing, the sound that draws you in, a voice that makes an audience beg for another song. I'm for reals, not a fabrication of Santino's cyber handy work. Seeing myself on screen really brings it home. If I don't mess this up, I might have a real future. But I've got a boatload of damage control to rock first.

Far below a tip tap percussion interrupts my reverie: Gothel's shoes on cement. One skyward glance and I'm done for. He's not my only worry. If Zeli faces me now, she'll scream and be the death of me.

"Eyes on the screen, pop queen." I plead with the great gods of Hollywood.

The track grinds to a teeth-cracking halt, sending the rig into a mad spin. I lock arms around knees to keep from sliding out.

I slow to find Zeli's jaw dropped in the prelude to a scream. I flap the *SHUSH* sign and frantically point to Gothel. The motion sends me slipping through the harness down to my armpits.

"Don't yell," I whisper-hiss as Zeli's focus switches between Gothel and me. Her nub of a nose scrunches.

I slip farther. My chin pokes above the harness. Fingers still clutch the guidelines while the rest of my body droops below. I kick a high top toward her flatscreen. "That's me."

She leans out the window with her own hiss. "Justin Time?"

"Yeah." I shimmy and pant until my stomach once again presses into the harness. "Douse your lights so he can't see me."

Her place goes dark. Together we watch Gothel vanish around the curve of the tower. I blow out a metric ton of carbon dioxide.

She faces me dead on, hands clamped to hips. "You thieving bastard. Give me one good reason why I shouldn't push this sweet release button." She jerks her chin toward the window frame. "I push–you drop."

My voice hits a serious high note. "Paleeeeeese."

The faintest trace of a smile quivers at the edge of her lips. "Having a ball-squeezing moment, Justin Time?"

"Haul me in." A wobbly streak of neon reflects off the moat far below to define my height. I long for the reassuring pressure of a chute pack against my backbone.

Zeli leans against the window frame and blows on her finger-nails. "I'm enjoying your dingle-dangle." The woman takes charge when she wants to.

I feel like a shitiot, floundering in midair. "Bring me in. Swear I'm not a vandal."

She snorts. "I have, let me count..." She unfolds five fingers and then flicks her hand. "Zero reasons to believe you."

"I'm here to belly crawl and make amends."

She tosses her head. It doesn't go far before extensions pull it back into place.

"A little late, doncha think?" Her hand shoots to the lever. A grumble sounds along the track above me. I swing back toward Singen's building.

How deluded am I to believe she'd forgive me or even allow me to plead my case? In less than a foot, my direction reverses, closing in on the tower. The rig rocks in a gag-inducing rhythm. A second later, I'm moving away again. She messes with the lever, bouncing me back and forth under the track.

Zeli's laugh has sharp edges. "Got the pukes yet, thief?"

I nod my head furiously.

"Now you know how I felt, hearing *my* song coming out of *your* mouth."

"It's not your song." The zip line whips to a stop. She gapes at me. "I heard the truth from Gothel's lips back there on the rooftop."

Zeli crosses her arms, trying to look tough. It's freaking charming, but she can't sustain it. Her shoulders droop. "I believed it was inspired by a memory."

The to and fro torture of the rig has brought me close enough to the window to make out blue neon tears pooling in her eyes. "I wish you had written it. It's beautiful."

Her peepers flare.

"I kinda saved you by stealing it."

She waves her finger in the direction of the "drop Justin" button.

"Let me explain."

Zeli doesn't move.

"It would have been a disaster if you sang "Just in Time" first and been nailed for plagiary."

"Cut the knight in shining armor crap. You had nothing to sing so somehow you sticky-fingered my tune."

I shake my head and zero in on her eyes. "I first heard you dialing in the song after your concert, but when you sang it out the window last night, it pierced my bones."

She grabs the casement to steady herself.

I flip a finger between us. "Our duet."

"That was you? It was real?"

Shyness washes over me along with fear that she'll hate the fact I'm the other half of our night song.

"All me."

The breeze licks wisps of yellow hair around her face. Instead of a woman with millions glued to her head, I see a precious pink bird perched on a branch, searching for the moon.

"Zeli, I truly wish I could hit undo and change everything."

"None of us have an undo button, Justin Time."

I swear the second O on the Hollywood Sign winks at me to say, *you are super screwed, dude.* "But I have a fix."

Zeli's head clicks to the side. "Steal another song?"

"I wrote one...for you."

Sharp notes sprinkle from her lips. "Why should I believe you can write anything?"

"I've got the chops. Bring me in. I'll prove it. Please, give me a chance to make this up to you."

Zeli's hand wavers over the lever but doesn't make contact. Finally, she points at me. "Prove it from there. Sing me an unstolen song, punk ass."

"Singing with my gut clenched doesn't show me at my best."

"You should have thought of that before you hitched a ride."

This is my one chance. If I don't do what Z asks, she'll never trust me. *Trust me, hell, at this point, I'm hoping she doesn't kill me.*

"Turn off your flatscreen." I swallow hard and take seven lucky breaths. I have a promise to make to Zeli with this song, a tune that rose from my heart before Justin Time ever stepped on the Summer Number One stage. Through my music, I'll prove our duet last night transformed me. Without guitar or backing track, the melody flows from my heart to the woman in the tower.

"Falling to Earth brings such wonders to sight
Colors unfold like the flutter of kites
Sparkling seas roll topped with crests of white down
Highways and hills melt into this town of dreams

Falling, falling, down from the moon
I slide on a beam to the light at your feet
With hopes and ambition, I pray we will meet

So, my heart may fall open to you

One night when I fall, a vision appears
Tender blue eyes set afire with tears
A river of gold is banished beneath
Ribbons and patterns to feed this town of dreams

Falling, falling, down from the moon
Our voices will join in the mist of the night
I'll storm your dark tower and enter the fight
Then my heart will fall open to you

Believe in my quest. Blaze courage inside.
Your jailer I'll slay and crash through the door
Behind walls of glass, you'll linger no more
On wings, we shall soar above this town of dreams

And my heart is now open to you.
My heart is now open to you.
My heart is now open to you."

A graceful sob floats out the window.

Currents of warm air from inside touch my face. I imagine it's her breath on my cold lips. "I'm for reals, Zeli. I want to make things right for you."

A hand rests over her heart.

"Are we chill?" I don't dare blink until I see her nod. "Then bring me in."

Z balls her fists up under her chin. "I don't know you. I don't trust you."

"Close your eyes."

Eyelids stay open under knitted brows.

"Please." I hold her gaze for a beat before closing my own eyes. "Trust this, Zeli." My voice rides the mist rolling in from the ocean as I sing. "Just in time. Our stars crossed just in time." This isn't the growling rendition I delivered on stage. It's a love song. "To blaze a path across the moon drenched sky."

Through the darkness, she hums our song with me. My eyes pop open. Hers follow. Neon turns eyelashes into the blue bristles of a paintbrush. I see the thread of chance beginning to unwind. Slowly the rig moves toward her window.

"Lift your feet over the sill."

I pull knees to chest and cross the threshold into Zeliland.

She stands, arms stiff at her sides, clearly enjoying my ass plant as I slip free of the harness.

After freeing the last of her extensions, the platinum record, from a nasty-looking hook attached to the end of the zip line, Zeli hangs the harness on a peg next to the window. Free from the track, extensions slide across the floor as she moves. Without a word, Z waltzes toward me, not stopping until we're toe to toe.

"Thanks for letting me in."

A wicked slap pops every blood vessel in my cheek. I stagger backward. "What the..."

She's an icicle with thorns. "You know '*what the*', you song-stealing bastard." Zeli shakes her hand and whines. "That wasn't supposed to hurt."

"I'm your first?" She blushes as red as the handprint that surely stains my cheek. Even though every part of me says not to laugh, the right corner of my lip curls up. "First face smack? Well, Miz Z, you're dang good at it."

She stares at me. Not a blink. Not a sound.

"What?" I check to make sure my fly is zipped.

"Lift your extensions."

I lift an eyebrow.

She stamps a foot. "Do what I say, or I'll call Gothel."

"How will that turn out well for either one of us?"

She taps her phone. I hear the ding of voice command. "Call Pa-"

I'm ninety percent sure it's a bluff, but my role here is to grovel. I twist my extensions into a mangled lump between fingers.

Zeli flips the lights back on. Hands fly to her mouth, and her cell falls to the carpet. "You're him."

I drop my hair and dip into a bow. "Justin Time, song stealing bastard. Guilty as slapped." Before I have a chance to add, *and Justin MacKenzie former base jumper,* Zeli growls.

"No. *Him.* My lucky star."

T-shirt moment: Cause of Death – Shitiocy.

Of course, she immediately recognizes the fool who sent her diving into a mob. I should have respected her intelligence and led with who I really am. I'm already blowing my shot with her.

Zeli snatches her cell from the rug and zips around the counter of her stainless steel-everything kitchen. A span of hair stretches from the top of the couch to the counter, forming a barricade.

I spring off the cushions and leap over her extensions. As gently as I can, considering I'm diving on top of her, I grab for the phone. An elbow separates two of my ribs. She skitters toward the window. Extensions are everywhere.

"Don't touch me again, whoever you are." Z sets her jaw and pulls a chunk of her hair up as a shield.

In three strides, I'd be on top of her. I stop at two, close enough to snatch the phone from her hand. "Why are you running? I'm the same dude you kissed."

She rushes me and lassos my neck with a length of hair. The thin metalworks on the underside of her extensions press into my skin. This scene is not playing out the way I wrote it.

"Give me a chance to expla–"

She gives a wicked yank. I grab at the vise around my neck.

"Something crapped you out of the sky to ruin my life. I never should have kissed you. Look where it got me with Gothel."

The room bleeds into a pink haze. I push words past smashed vocal cords. "Swear I'm here to make up for that. Help you–" My knees go first. When I collapse, my neck slides out of the hair noose.

Zeli gathers her locks for another attack. "You're a liar, jumper."

She's right. That's all I am anymore, lies and impossible dreams. Screw ups thunder in my head; blowing the jump at Zeli's platinum gig, her hair shred, Timmer's fists, vandals on the boulevard, Santino's '*you're nothing to me*' face, stealing Z's song, making an enemy of Gothel. A steaming pile of disasters with the name Justin blinking on top.

Once, she cared enough about Justin the Jumper to charge across the plaza. To kiss me.

"The song I just sang, that was truth. Zeli, I'm not just here to help you. I'm here to save you."

20

A WORTHY KISS

ZELI'S LAUGH IS SOUR. "SAVE ME? DELUDED MUCH? YOU'RE THE ONE I need saving from. Everything you've done since you walked into my life screwed me." She waves an arm. "You ruined my show, stole my song, and–"

Softly, I sing to her. "Believe in my quest. Blaze courage inside. Your jailer I'll slay and crash through the door. Behind walls of glass, you'll linger no more. On wings, we shall soar, above this town of dreams."

Her bravado melts to a whisper. "Why?"

I take a step closer. "I know it sounds mad, but that first night we met, when I heard you sing–total blindside. I saw the real you, not the version Gothel shows the world. When we shared the song in the sky, I saw myself. I've led a careless and reckless life. Our voices together make me want to take another path. With you."

She doesn't back away. "There's no sense to this. I don't know who you are, a jumper or Justin Time."

I'm close enough to lightly touch her arm. "I'm Justin MacKenzie. A twenty-three year-old former B.A.S.E. jumper who plans to win the Summer Number One."

The beginning of a smile rides her lips. "That much I figured out."

"I want to make music with you, Zeli." A shiver runs down my back. Do I dare ask more? What if our night song was different for her? A one-off. A sweet duet on the surface with no substance. If I'm truly finished being all about me, I must ask. "What did you feel when we sang together?"

She is the essence of stillness. "Hope. The music, singing with you is different. Like nothing I've ever experienced. It's–"

My breath stills, waiting for the word I long to hear, the word that describes the connection, the beauty of what rose between us in the night.

Zeli slowly closes the distance between us until her lips brush my ear. She whispers, "Magic. I do want more magic with you."

I slide a hand down her arm and twine my fingers with hers. "I was so afraid it was only me." The tide of purpose pools around us. Together, we'll free this woman from Gothel. We will be music and magic.

Her cheek brushes mine as she pulls back. I lay a finger under her chin to tilt it up. "And what did you feel when I kissed you?"

A heavy breath slides from her mouth, warming my lips. I find an in road under her extensions and cup a hand around the back of her neck.

"Something you'd like to feel again?" Bringing her closer, I marvel anew at the perfect angle between her lips and mine. Before the kiss becomes real, she drops the top of her head to my chest.

I'm screwing up again. "You can say no."

She raises her gaze back to mine. Her voice tinkles like a bell as she lays a finger on my lips. "When you came to find me..." Bluebell eyes glitter. "Gothel's never given me enough space to kiss anyone."

I go full Zeli pink. My hand falls from her neck. This sweet soul did not deserve her first kiss to be a hot rocket mouth smash from a full-of-himself music wannabe looking for a favor. I do need magic now to reset that moment, spirit her unkissed. Santino is right to dub me the lowest life form in Hollywood.

"That was not a worthy kiss. An ego stole a lip lock from you."

A mischievous smile sneaks across her lips. "An ego, or a soggy jumper in a banana suit?"

I brush my pinkie across the curve of her lower lip. "I'm wiping it away."

Zeli's breathing quickens as the pad of my finger travels to each enticing peak of her top lip.

When I finish, I flick my fingers toward the window. "Gone."

"This..." I bring her in until our mouths touch. "Is a kiss."

My lips graze hers, oh, so lightly, a whisper. In moments, we shift into a roar. The woman sends electric twinkles across every bit of my skin.

Zeli slips her hands around to my ass and yanks, increasing the pressure of our bodies against each other. We twirl to the couch, refusing to break the kiss, swaying to silent music. I sink into the cushions and pull Z into my lap, caressing her soft little tongue with mine. Her hair winds around my legs. I'm trapped.

This is not just Zeli's first real kiss. I've never flown so high. She breathes fireflies into my blood stream.

She runs her hands up my chest to find the tab of my jumpsuit zipper. "There's something else you did to me." Slowly she pulls it down, exposing skin down past my navel. Her fingers trail though the fine sandy hair between my pecs and then dance across my nipples. "When you touched me like this."

The way she's perched on my lap leaves no mystery of what her touch does to me. She peers down to where our bodies connect. The circle she makes with her lips heightens my arousal.

"Do that to me again," she whispers.

My breathing doesn't come easy. "It would be my pleasure, as you can tell. Z, I'm going to have to lose this jumpsuit or permanently squash something I'm very fond of."

She practically leaps aside. "Am I hurting you?"

I slide out of my jumpsuit in an eye-blink and adjust Zeli back on top of the bulge in my shorts. "Far from it."

I pull her mouth back to mine and circle my tongue around hers until she moans. Working my hands along her sides, I find the hem of her flowered sundress and slowly pull it up until I can drop a kiss on her navel.

I stop cold. Next to her skin is the lacey metallic vest that supports her extensions. I trace a finger down the mesh from the hollow of her neck, stopping between her breasts.

"What do we do about this?"

With the flexibility of a contortionist, Zeli wriggles her arms and head through the contraption until the vest spills out the neck of her dress to dangle down her back, still attached to her extensions. "I'm sorry it doesn't come all the way off. This is as loose as I could trick Gothel into making it."

Trick Gothel? A surge of anger at Gothel infringes on our intimate moment. "Does it hurt? The vest?"

"It feels strange, but it does help support my extensions along with..." She cups the side of my face with her warm palm. "Please pretend it isn't there."

Was she about to come clean about Gothel's crazy ass deal with her tears? I pry a bit more. "How do you manage all that hair without snapping your neck?"

Zeli stares at nothing. The battle to tell me or not to tell me rages in her eyes. I walk up to the edge of spilling what I know but manage keep quiet. The tear collecting, Gothel's fire fingers, those are her stories to share not mine to steal. I've stolen enough.

We're only at a beginning, she and I. It's a fragile thing. If I push, we might fall apart.

I lay a hand on the vest. I want to rip the fucking thing off and burn it. "I promise we'll figure out a way to get rid of this soon."

Z moves in to drop kisses up my jaw until she reaches my earlobe for a hot nip. She guides my hands back to the hem of her dress.

For an amateur, Zeli knows how to get back into the game. She giggles as I continue to peel her wrapper. "Higher?"

"Yes, please."

I tug and her bra slips off with the dress. She gasps as cold air slides along her bare breasts.

"Tell me if it's too much, Zeli."

She shakes her head. "I want a repeat of that..." One finger traces her breast, down her stomach, and stops at the top of her panties as she searches for the right word. "Zing."

I can't hold back a laugh. "Zing?"

Z slaps both hands against my chest. "Don't laugh at me."

The movement sets her sculpture-perfect breasts swaying in the twinkle lights from above. She's sweet and inexperienced but also daring and willing. It's a mind and dick blowing combination. I pull in a singer's deep breath and attempt to keep my mounting desire at bay. This is Zeli's night, her first step. I'm not going to ruin it by ploughing into her because I lose control.

I take her hands and kiss her palms one at a time before setting them on my shoulders. "Hold on to me, close your eyes, and lean back."

Her hips rock forward as she obeys, bringing my own zing perilously close. I circle a finger around each of her plum-colored nipples. They grow into a pair of perfectly matched nubs as she groans. Next, I lightly scratch my nails across the rising bumps until I'm rewarded with a drawn out "Ohhhhh."

"I'm...it's—" Zeli tries to speak but only succeeds in dropping her head back.

This slow dance is as new to me as it is to her. My trail of lust with overeager groupies after jumps falls into the fast and rough category. I love this coaxing, the build, the appreciation of each moment of pleasure Zeli and I share.

I adjust her hands behind my neck so I can lean in for a taste of her. The slightest flick of my tongue over her nipples doubles their size, and I'm lost. I first take one in my mouth to suck and graze with my teeth and then the other. Oh, the taste of Zeli. She's new and tender and freaking fantastic.

"Justin."

Even with her panties and my shorts as barriers, I can tell she's deliciously wet as she glides against my cock. I grab her hips and guide her back and forth. Zeli revels in the friction, increasing speed with no coaching from me. Her adorable squeaks tell me she's close. On the brink of losing my mind and last shred of control, she arches her back. An ear-splitting note bursts from her lips as she reaches her peak.

It's going to take me a fucking month to lose this erection. Racing to the brink even without a payoff is worth it to see the thrill on Zeli's face as she experiences her first full zing.

She falls against me, breathing hard in my ear. I ease her down next to me and hold her, dropping kisses onto the soft golden hair above her ear. We linger in the embrace until her racing heart calms.

Zeli nuzzles the side of my neck. "I'm glad Justin Time is my jumper." She pulls back in a flash. "I'm still pissed at you."

"You should be." I smooth a strand behind her ear. I don't want to leave. My gut tells me if I stay longer, we'll trip up and get caught. She's too willing, and I'm too tempted. "It's late. Let me in tomorrow. We'll work on your new song."

"I can't sing your song. It's so beautiful, but too on the nose. Gothel will figure it out."

I kiss the corner of her lips. "Then I'll write you another." I wriggle back into my jumpsuit. It's still snug in a particular area. At least I'm most of the way down. She twists back into her dress and that damn metallic vest.

"Zeli, there's more we need to work out than a new song."

She raises her eyebrows.

"We need a plan to get you out of this tower. Gothel has no right to control every part of your life the way he does." I take her hand. "You're the expert on his routines and any opportunity for you to slip away. The Summer Number One is a perfect distraction to use since we're both part of it. We'll find the right moment, I promise."

There's raw fear in her eyes that makes me even more determined to get her the hell out of here.

"This is too big for me to digest right now. I need time," she says, clutching my hand tighter.

I lay a finger on her lips. "I understand, but time is something we don't have much of. Think on it, and we'll work on ideas tomorrow night."

Zeli nods, and I lead her to the window. Worry cuffs me on the back of the head. "Does it hurt when I ride your hair?"

Zeli crinkles pouty lips, shooting a frown to her locks. "My hair doesn't hold the weight. It leads the harness across and back."

I long to crack open the secrets between Gothel and Zeli. Even with the vest and Gothel's boost, I marvel a woman her size hauls those extensions around.

Her fingers play with mine. She's as reluctant for me to go as I am to leave. I climb into the zipline rig.

Zeli puts a hand on the jeweled lever. "Goodnight, Justin MacKenzie."

"'Night, Zeli." I ride beneath her shining platinum record extension. On the far rooftop, I escape the harness and look back at the window. Zeli stands with one hand outstretched in a frozen wave.

I flip my fingers her way and murmur, "Goodnight, my angel."

The difference between Gothel and me is that I believe Rapunzel has wings. I long to deserve the honor of helping her learn to fly.

21

NUMBER TWO WITH A BULLET

I SNAP AWAKE IN DARKNESS FROM A NIGHT OF FALLING DREAMS, broken chutes, and lost pop queens. "Zeli!"

In the road box, my sleep mind folds into my waking one as I wipe a layer of sweat from my forehead with a hunk of curtain. Zeli is safe above me in her penthouse, as safe as she can be with Gothel.

A new sense of wonder fills me. I've never awakened thinking of anyone except myself. Zeli's claimed that spot.

I swipe sound files on my phone and find the one labeled "Z" and listen. The new song I wrote in the wee hours is good, written for the elegant sound of Rapunzel's authentic voice. I press the phone to my heart. A heart that now holds the lovely pink presence of Zeli. Two days ago, I wanted to set her hair on fire. Now, Rapunzel is seared to my soul by the power of sharing a song that only the stars witnessed. I swam too deep in my own ego to realize it at the time, but this woman began to take up residence in my heart from the first moment I heard her singing in the twilight room the night we met.

My cell rings. I check the time. Shit, the next round of the

Summer Number One is well under way. After burning moonlight to write Zeli's new song, I've slept the day away.

Restricted Number.

Nausea harmonizes with my pounding heart. Was Santino pissed enough to whistle blow? Is this call kicking me out of the Summer Number One? My fingers shake as I cup the phone in my hand, and whisper, "Hello."

"Justin Time?"

"Yeah."

"Kaydance from the Summer Number One."

Here comes the Rampion portcullis to crush my skull.

"Well, Time." I squeeze my eyes shut to soften the sucker punch. "Remove the double zeroes from your number."

I forget to whisper. "What?"

"You're number two, buckaroo."

My brain sizzles. "For reals?"

A single *tsk* breaks the silence. "Try checking out Summer Number One media threads like every other good little ammie. You need to get your ass to the stage."

I'm not history. I'm freaking number two. I'd holler, but that would summon a swarm of Gothel goons.

"Enjoy *numero dos*. It's as high as you'll get."

A vision of Kaydance and Cama Rama in their sloppy lip lock blazes to mind. "Who's number one?"

"An artist destined to kick your ass, Cama Rama," she says as if she's announcing his set at the Grammys.

"That guy? You had me worried for a hot sec."

Her disdain oozes through the phone. "Meet Gothel at the V.I.P. tent in fifteen or you'll be Justin Time Out."

I replay his words from the rooftop last night. "*I have plans for the dillweed. We're putting him back on stage.*"

"Will do." I end the call and hold my breath. Fifteen freakin' minutes to metamorphosize Justin MacKenzie, resident of a road box, to Justin Time, viral rock hopeful. I rub my eyes. I've got to snag Santino's guitar from underneath the stage.

Why does Gothel want a meet up? To suck my blood, or give Justin Time a transfusion?

I could bail, ration the money I have left.

If I bail now, the walls of Zeli's tower may squeeze the life out of her. I'll be a stone in the pit of Santino's gut forever. My dreams of the Summer Number One flatline if I disappear into the Hollywood sunset.

Zeli alone is reason enough to face Gothel. I've made her a promise, and that promise defines who I want to be. I pray the high visibility of my Summer Number One ranking is a thick enough shield.

After grabbing my guitar, I dust off my jumpsuit and slink into the VIP area.

Kaydance, packaged in a neck to ankle rattlesnake patterned cat suit meets me at the bottom of the steps leading onstage. Her banging bod beneath a neckline that plunges all the way to her belly button nearly makes me drop the guitar. Knowing this she-snake belongs to Cama Rama gives me the sicks.

A voice bleeds around a black metallic curtain. "Mr. Time."

With deliberate strides and an intense glare, Gothel reaches me. Fingers twine through the strands Leeni glued to my head and tug. "This is a runt's tail. Are you the runt of the litter, Justin Time?"

My lips go dry. I haven't been this close to him since he ordered my moat-stained, ass out of the tower. If he makes the connection, I'll be at the bottom of the moat instead of onstage.

"Join me." He flicks a finger and the goon guarding one of the curtained mystery rooms steps aside. My mind fills with the sound of wind whipping through a rainstorm.

"Sure thing." I smile as if I expected this.

His eyes narrow, assessing. A goon with extensions flowing to the back of his knees holds the curtain aside for us to pass. We're in a room with flatscreens hanging from the metal skeleton of the stage complex. Across the bottom of the monitor, names of the top fifty ammies crawl from left to right.

I nod to the feed. "Do all ammies get a meet and greet with you, Mr. Gothel?"

He barks a nasty laugh. "Ammies come and go faster than I crap."

"I'm honored." It sickens me to kowtow to this jerk on a stick. Revenge bubbles against my spine, remembering his treatment of Zeli. He deserves a head butt instead of an ass kiss.

He sets my guitar on a chair and drapes an arm across my shoulders. "You and I have a problem."

My face tingles with the effort to stay neutral.

"Look, friend." His expression intensifies on the word *friend*. Was he about to say *Jumper*? Rivulets of sweat sneak down my neck. "There are consequences for the bruise you've dealt me."

I slide out from under his arm and roll my shoulders like I'm loosening up for the performance. Playing dumb feels like the correct note to hit. "Bruise?"

He grabs a handful of my jumpsuit and pulls me close enough to smell a hint of Zeli's heavenly tea on his breath. "Kill the innocent act. You stole Zeli's song, and we both know it." His eyes shine gemstone green, sorcerer beacons. Heat flows from his hand in a malicious wave. His face contorts. Is this the horror Zeli sees when he comes at her?

Grant Gothel is terrifying.

I fully expect his freaky fire fingers to scorch me. There's no way to fight this beast in a suit. He rules the kingdom.

"I'll walk away. No need to fry me."

He reveals teeth as white as a full moon. "You owe me restitution." He releases me. The front of my jumpsuit is still hot to the touch. "Talent such as yours, legal or illegal, is acknowledged at Rampion Records. I am a collector of phenom, and you have entered the zone."

"Zone?"

"The Zeli, Gigabyte, and Justin Time Zones. Zero to sixty phenom in an eye blink earns you a place in the Grant Gothel stable of stars."

My Hollywood dream rises, regaining its shape even in light of my ill deeds.

Gothel leans over me, a cat ready to pounce. Forty-eight hours ago, I thought Grant Gothel was the golden god of music. Today, I'm fully aware the dude dangling this carrot may be the devil's bestie.

I pause, acting as if there's a choice. A ring of Gothel goons forms around us. I don't even want to imagine what will happen if I say *no*.

My Summer Number One dream, as tainted as it is now by the truth about Gothel, is leverage I need to help Zeli. This is a win. I'm entering her world. I wanted this before I met her. Now, I need it for her.

"You're offering a deal if I win the Summer Number One?"

Gothel's hand clamps onto the base of my neck in a scorpion pinch. "You're not going to win. You'll stay in the contest for visibility."

I expect a rush of heat, but it doesn't come.

"The Summer Number One is my chess game. A game you'll no longer play if you reject my generous offer."

Message received. I take his deal, or I'll be a curb rat by nightfall.

"Well, Justin Time?"

"Of course I accept." I will join your stable to steal your prize pony.

He slaps me on the back. "Welcome to Rampion Records."

This moment should feel like Christmas colliding with my birthday. Instead, the edges of my soul begin to fray. A bargain with this man is tinged with darkness, not sparkles. I've seen how he treats the talent.

Gothel snaps his fingers. Mange slips a contract between them. GG fans me with the pages.

I nod at the flapping paper. "My manager has to check this out."

"Mr. Santino Fedele?"

How does he know about Santino? Shit, his name is on my registration.

"This is Rampion's boilerplate contract. You sing for me now. Give Mr. Fedele notice."

I pull the contract from his hand and pretend to read. Not a single word comes into focus, but numbers do. Five hundred thousand dollar signing bonus and plenty of zeroes to follow. That's security, a future.

The sticker shock melts. A Gothel contract may have given Zeli fame and a platinum record, but it also comes with abuse and a prison. "What's the term on this beauty?"

His head dips to one side. "How long do you plan to live?"

My gut bubbles. "Are we talking age or as defined by my number of Tuneful downloads?" What am I doing? Self-sabotage doesn't get Zeli out of the tower.

Gothel leans in until our eyeline hovers on the same plane. "My instinct for talent speaks for itself. That instinct points your way. I'm committed to this partnership. Are you?" An even stronger whiff of tea tickles my nostrils. With the aroma comes an eerie sense of calm.

Still, the creeps ripple through me as if Gothel reads my soul. I break eye contact. Gothel makes a figure eight in the air with a gold pen. I hold my hand flat. He smacks it across my palm.

This is a crossroads. Signing is my best chance at access to Zeli. If these papers hold my future, why does it feel as if they could burn off my fingerprints?

Memories of that freaky glow from Gothel's hands when he cinched Zeli into her lacy metal yoke play through my mind. The way he smeared her tears across the scratch on his arm. Am I entering the light or the dark?

I can't piss away this foot in the door. I may never get another shot. I sign the last page.

Gothel rips the paper from me, adding his curling signature next to mine. I expect a smoke demon to rise from the ground to consume me. My new manager swallows my hand in his, pumping twice before he lets go.

"Now go rack up a massive pile of votes with your opus." He sniffs the air. "Do I smell a number one ammie?" Mange holds Santino's guitar out to me and pulls the curtain to the main VIP area aside.

I hold my ground. "I don't need to sing Zeli's song. I've got another."

"It's far too late to change your tune." Gothel shows his teeth. ""Just in Time" belongs to you. My gift." Webby laugh lines flank his eyes. "Or should I say, belongs to us."

"If Zeli needs it–"

Gothel waves his hands, shooing a cloud of non-existent gnats. "Not your concern. Zeli's wave is overdue to flatten. It's your time, Justin."

Flat wave? The nasties I overheard him saying about Zeli on the rooftop jump into my head. I can't get up to Z's birdcage fast enough. I owe her more than a new tune. We have to hit the gas on a rescue from whatever darkness Gothel is brewing for her. Doubt joins panic for a dance. By signing this contract with Gothel, have I screwed her?

Again.

When I step out into the main VIP area, a sea of fingers tame my extensions and dab my face with make-up. Kaydance beckons me to the stage.

I'm now property of Rampion Records.

22

LOSE THE ZEROES

Cama Rama's voice caresses the crowd.

I scowl at Kaydance. "Why is your boyfriend on ahead of me?" She startles at the word *boyfriend*.

"Number One picks his time."

Ah, so the munch monkey chose to take the stage before me. Cama Rama must perceive me as a legit threat. Tonight, the freak's backing track is synthesized to robotic proportions. Cama Rama: half-man, half-techno. The fans buy whatever he's selling with ravenous applause. He milks the adoration by blowing kisses and rocking a series of pelvic thrusts.

He zeroes in on Kaydance. She subtly waves him off and mouths *later*.

"Two-hundred minus the zeroes, you're on," says Kaydance, giving my ass a pinch. If number two gets an ass pinch from the she-snake, Cama Rama definitely gets the whole shebang. Emphasis on *bang*.

At least I'm ass-pinch worthy in Kaydance world. She may be the only quasi-fan I have left. Santino made me. He's had the time and motivation to unmake me. Does it even matter anymore? I've signed Gothel's contract.

Cama Rama leaps with both feet onto the step in front of me. "Top my fan love, jacklick."

The dude is freaky tall and skinny. *Eat a hamburger, will you?* This close, his metallic eyelashes gleam. Both eye and lip liner are tattoos of multi-colored, jewel chips. His new and improved extensions dust the floor behind him like the train of a red, black, and silver wedding dress.

Cama Rama's black eyes narrow. "Justin Time. Douchey name." He bumps his bony hipbone into my ribs.

"Cama Ram-it-up-your-ama." I shoot him a salute that ends with my middle finger in front of his chin. He raises an arm to backhand me, but Kaydance leaps between us.

Cama Rama reaches around her to grab a chunk of my jumpsuit. "Look, tiny balls, you've got one more go before you're history in a bag."

Kaydance lays a palm against his chest to ease him away. "We're all artists here."

I point to my throat. "Some of us paint with the real thing." My chin jerks toward the mix board. "And some of us need tech to scratch out a decent sound."

"Bastard." He tries to push past Kaydance.

"We'll see who's history in a bag," I say, hopping around him and up the stairs out of range. Fantastic, an enemy with a backstage pass.

My gut flutters with iron butterflies. Tonight, there will be no boulevard posse or Santino waiting for me.

There's an emcee on day two. His chainmail tux jacket, gunmetal grey skinny jeans, and plastic, lime green high tops make a statement. When he turns, I recognize X.T., host of the *Making Mad Music* show on the Tuneful Channel. The ante is higher on day two.

"You rocked the vote for him," says X.T. My butterflies graduate to eagles. Talons rake my stomach lining. "This cat is literally an overnight sensation, last night to be exact. Everyone give it up for Justin Time."

X.T. gestures to me. Before I plant a foot onstage, I watch the emcee's face go slack. He dives behind the upstage platform that holds the mix console.

A lethal hum rises from the crowd. Something clangs that shouldn't be clanging. The floor beneath me vibrates. I grab a handful of curtains to keep from losing my balance. An ape parade of Gothel goons streams past me onto the stage. Gothel's perfect fingernails clamp around my upper arm. "Hang tight, Justin."

"What's going on?"

X.T. hovers behind the mix man. Their eyes stretch so wide I see mostly white. Above me, stage lights rock back and forth on trusses. The hum buzzes louder and my ears ring from the sound of metal hitting concrete.

SLAM

"BARRICADES DOWN," yells Gothel. He hustles me down the steps to the VIP area.

Vibrations shaking the complex become a word.

JUSTIN!

Gothel bellows into a headset. "Get the barricades back up, pronto. I want Time's face out there a-sap."

Gothel flags the camera crew, seeking asylum in the VIP area. "Get us on the Jumbotrons."

The plaza uproar flashes across backstage monitors. A mob rushes the stage. Two lines of uniformed Rampion security guards join goons to push them back.

JUSTIN!

The viral tsunami Santino launched grows teeth.

Kaydance passes Gothel a hand-held mic. He faces the camera lens. "In three, two, one." A red light pops on at the top of the camera. We're on every screen. Grant Gothel's voice booms over the cacophony.

"Heya, heya." He slings an arm around my shoulders. "Your boy, Justin, can't take the stage until you fizz down."

The *JUSTIN* chant shatters into smaller sound bites.

Gothel shoves the mic under my nose and hisses at me. "Calm them down."

I grin straight into the camera. "Let's get this party started." Pandemonium erupts. Gothel growls. Oops, his Justin puppet isn't doing the right dance. Point–Time. "How am I going to get to number one waiting back here?"

The chant changes.

NUM-BER ONE!

"Barricades back up," Kaydance calls.

I wave into the camera as the red light dies.

Gothel yells in my ear. "If they rush again, go straight upstage through the panels and jump off the back. We'll be there. Go."

I take the steps two at a time and then mosey onto the stage, the coolest character who ever grabbed a mic. The crowd blows their vocal cords screaming. The sight in front of me sends a sizzle through my synapses. Every square inch of the plaza and grandstands are maxed with fans.

My ego has always driven me to act bigger than I am. Right now, facing this crowd, I'm an ant under the shadow of an elephant's foot. The possibility of getting stomped is for reals. How did Zeli have the guts to charge into such a crush of humanity for me?

I need the *no fear* page from her playbook.

My music kicks on. The audience explodes. A flock of chicks with my name plastered across their chests perch on the shoulders of beefy boyfriends. A thousand feet stomp bleachers. Hands clap. Arms wave. I raise my hands for quiet.

They calm as if I cast a spell. I nod to the mix man. He restarts my music.

"Just in time. Our stars crossed just in time…"

My brain clouds. The sheer density of the audience shoots me into an alternate universe. The last note at the end of my phrase goes slightly sharp. *Fight the fear. Fear can kill a jumper. Sharps can kill a song.*

"To blaze a path across a moon drenched sky."

Zeli. Picture Zeli. Sing to Zeli.

A thousand bobbing heads disappear. In the center of the plaza, I conjure my sweet dream in pink, floating atop her mountain of extensions. A golden corona surrounds the wings rising behind her.

My angel – not Gothel's.

I sing to her and no one else. She sings back. Inside my head we harmonize and rock the tune that brought us together.

"We banished loneliness."

I refocus on the audience. It isn't Zeli singing with me. It's them, the whole plaza. They're pitch perfect. The Summer Number One crowd is my backing track.

Girls weep and stretch their arms to me. Dudes embrace and thump each other on the back. A flash mob, rocking a sweet waltz erupts off to the right.

"Found love to stay."

NUM-BER ONE!

Thank you, Santino. I swipe a tear. He should be here to see how he ignited Justin Time into a blaze. I spread arms wide and drop my head in a bow. The crowd comes on fast, rolling toward me as my music plays off. Barricades clang as they again topple onto cement.

Visions of Zeli's extensions being torn to bits fly through my mind. I hug my guitar to protect vital organs. The first line of bodies climbs the front of the stage. A foot crashes through a floor panel sending a shower of plastic shards into the air. The mob covers the stage like ants on a lollipop.

"I love you, Justin."

"Kiss me, Justin."

Magenta fingernails, each painted with a single gold letter to spell out

J-U-S-T-I-N-T-I-M-E, lunge for me.

This is the roller coaster Santino warned me about, but he's not my safety bar. A meaty arm snakes around me. My feet leave the floor. I'm swallowed into a tunnel of black suits.

23

FALLING STAR

AN HOUR IN THIS SALON CHAIR HITS MY LIMIT. GOTHEL'S GLAM SQUAD took a cue from Leeni's work, adding extensions in dozens of shades between dark blond and my own tawny color. An undercoat of silver and gold tinsel set the whole works to shimmer. The Rampion touch is a crimson streak starting dead center at the top of my head that runs all the way to the bottom of my longest strand. The red line pops like a trail of blood dripping from my scalp.

Gothel strides into the salon. "There's a Rampion star."

I scratch the nape of my neck. "How about derailing a few cars of this extension train?"

"Long locks bring a smile to my face." His smile curls dangerously close to a snarl.

If Grant Gothel is so freakishly enamored with extensions, why doesn't he rock any?

"I strain my neck, I strain my pipes."

In response, he moves in slowly, tilting his face down and exhales. The sweet aroma of Gothel's breath seeps into my senses. I salivate, overwhelmed by an instant craving for the flavor I recognize. It's Rampion tea. That elixir Zeli drank the first night I met her. As the fragrance wafts across my face, muscles unclench. I even hum Zeli's song, "Stars and Fireflies".

Gothel chuckles. I open my eyes. When did I close them? How long have I drifted on this cloud of tea?

"Will your tears be worth anything to me, Justin?"

I swipe at my eyes on the hunt for moisture. What tears?

"If you need anything, Mr. Time, name it." Tea fragrance kisses my skin.

What a generous guy. I misread bad blood between Gothel and Zeli. My boy, Grant, isn't on the naughty list. I'm a shitiot. Spying through vents and under door cracks doesn't show a whole truth. He whips Zeli's sorry ass into shape to protect her career. Mr. G. put her in a Rampion Tower time-out until she gets her head on straight and rocks her responsibilities as a sparkling bubble gum diva.

"Jussssstin?" The next wave of Gothel's tea breath covers my face, chasing every pocket of tension from my soul. This man cares. GG is my papa too. I rock new vision for Gothel, my fast-track music manager. He's not breathing fire or eating babies. If I want to play in the bigs, he's my ticket.

He snaps fingers in my face, breaking my trance. "Time to go, J.T."

"Where are we off to, Boss Man?" I dig the slick way his suit catches the light. I could rock a suit like that.

"To lay decent tracks and a Tuneful version of your song for fans to download. I can't stomach your syntho-babble backup one more day."

"I posted a Tuneful cut of "Just in Time"." Santino's version.

"I took that mess down."

We ride the elevator to a floor filled with recording studios. The doorframe of Studio A pulses with light and a monitor announces Zeli's recording session is live.

She's beyond that door. Suddenly the haze in my mind pops

like a soap bubble. Gothel comes back into focus. Gothel, the vandal. Gothel, the fiend.

Instead of moving past Studio A, Gothel opens the door to interrupt a song mid-riff. He shouts above the music, "We're finished here," and kills Zeli's session.

My throat drops to my knees. A wave of dizzy passes through me. I fight the intense yearning for Gothel's tea breath.

Zeli stamps a foot. "I'm not done."

Gothel pulls me inside. "Your song is rubbish. Write a better one."

The harshness of his tone clears the last of the kaleidoscope jewels inside my head. Five minutes ago, I nearly wrote the dude a love song. Now I want to knee his groin.

Z signals the booth. "Listen to me rock it with the full mix."

Her backup band fixates on their shoes. I peek past Gothel and nearly swallow my tongue. Zeli's band isn't a mix of random musicians. Behind her, frozen in concert formation, is Gigabyte.

The universe has pulled its head through its own blowhole if I'm booting Zeli out of a joint session with Gigabyte.

Gothel whistles into the hallway as if calling a pet. "Let's go, ladies." A gaggle of girls zips into the room. Her hair dancers spread out and take their positions under Zeli's locks. Gothel propels me farther into the studio.

Zeli's flesh-melting expression sends Gothel into bursts of laughter.

Unlike him, I fear incineration from those pop queen eyes. "Mr. Gothel, I'd prefer to wait until she's finished."

Zeli is right in front of us. She shoots a divalicious glower up at Gothel. Her stubborn streak cranks to full. "Well, Papa?"

Gothel's sneer flashes like headlights across Z's face as he calls to the booth. "Dump Zeli's entire session." He stares at her without a freakin' blink. "She's finished."

Z's eyes twitch at the dark edge to his tone, a crack in her boldness. I want to slap myself for the bizarre thoughts I've had in the past ten minutes sugar-coating Gothel's nasty.

He spins Zeli to face me. "Meet Justin Time, America's newest phenom. You remember what that's like, don't you?"

"Start the phenom timer," Zeli says with a huff. She hip checks me as she passes. "It runs out fast." The hair maidens rest extensions on their shoulders and file out the door behind her.

"Ding," says Gothel, slamming the door. "Someone's timer just ran out, and it isn't yours, Justin."

A roiling sizzle of fear twists through me. What if Z refuses to send her hair and the zip line harness over to me tonight because of this?

A ripping sound draws my attention. Gothel stands in front of Gigabyte's lead singer and tosses two halves of sheet music into the air.

I gesture to the studio door. "This isn't right. Shoving Zeli out after I–"

"Stole her song?"

The surface temperature of my cheekbones rises a hundred degrees as I'm shamed in front of my favorite band.

"Mr. Time, someone's always rising while someone else falls." Gothel points off in the distance. "Imagine, just over the horizon, a fruitful crop of talent each with an unsung opus poised to claim Zeli's place."

"No way is Zeli, THE Zeli, falling. That night at her gig, I saw the crowd." My words screech to a stop before I spill anymore. I can't drop a single breadcrumb that leads him to Justin the Jumper.

Gothel claps me on the shoulder. "There are stars, fixed points in the sky that eventually burn out. Then there are legends. Legends..." He takes in a long stream of air. "Legends swirl between the stars forever."

"Right. Zeli's a legend."

Gothel's stare bores into me like a drill. "Zeli is a star."

His words ring in my head hours later as I jog across the dim plaza still pumped from my session with Gigabyte, my stolen session.

Gothel's control tightens. He set me up with my own dressing room that looks more like an apartment complete with a closet stuffed with clothes. Everything I tried on fit perfectly. Too perfectly. It's freaky.

Gothel warned me to stay put in my new digs to stay safe from over-zealous fans. I agreed like a good dog until I dug free under his fence. If I'm caught, I'll say I'm meeting Santino, my recently relieved of duty manager.

I'd give anything to be welcome at Fedele Costumes right now. Did Santino catch my song tonight? I hope the trail of ghosts I'm starting to leave behind will not include Zeli.

My finger hovers over Santino's contact. Until Zeli accepts the new song I wrote for her, I can't face him.

A group of fans with matching scarlet swatches tied around their thighs pass me. They sing Cama Rama's Summer Number One song. I duck my head and speed to Singen Mot's building.

The doors are unlocked. I saunter to the desk. "Justin Time. Name's on the list."

The security guard flicks his wrist, and I'm in. Thank you, Singen Mot. Next to the elevator is an arrangement of silk flowers. I tuck a fuchsia-colored poppy in my pocket for Zeli.

Outside the roof access door, lines of crimson and ginger scratch the sky above the Hollywood Sign. I settle into a sheltered nook to wait for dark and Gothel's exit before I call for Zeli's hair.

Anxiety nudges me. I hope Z's bluffing about the harness release button. After stealing her session, she may be motivated to give it a push.

I kill time by polishing her new song. Last night, I proved to her I can write music. Tonight's tune is another peace offering, one I hope gets me inside.

When the night sky is a plum-colored bruise, the squealing of the zip line snaps me out of composer mode.

Gothel sways in his rig above the plaza. "Enough incompetence!" GG's bellow sends me deeper into shadow. "I told you to raise our offer for the copyright of "Just in Time" until Midas Lear agrees." He rails at the poor sap on the other end of the call until he makes roof fall.

Gothel taps his cell. "Goodnight, my angel." His words reek with insincerity.

Zeli's hair heads west, back to the tower. "Two things better go down before midnight, Mange. First, get me exclusive rights to "Just in Time". Second, tell P.R. to plan Zeli the longest overseas tour in history." His boots tap like gunfire across the rooftop. "If she screws up the Summer Number One, she fades to background noise. I have a tastier fish on the hook without tapping into any Rampion Ranch talent."

I slide along metal ducting to stay close to Gothel. He pushes the door to the stairs open. "Of course I mean Justin Time."

My name skitters across the rooftop like a moth heading into a bug zapper. Gothel is setting me up to replace Zeli. I would have danced naked under a full moon to ruin Zeli before I knew her. Now, I want to help the woman tear Gothel's heart out.

Where's the justice in all this? If we manage to spring Zeli from the tower, the future Gothel's orchestrating for Justin Time bursts into tiny pieces of flaming rock.

Plans change. Gothel isn't who I thought he was. I chew my bottom lip. Am I? Is viral Justin subsuming Justin MacKenzie? The original Justin built the instrument and the dream that got me here. Santino would tell me to honor the music ahead of the fame.

Santino is the kind of man I want to be, that blend of integrity and kindness. There's only one road that leads me to that end. Zeli will be holding my hand as we walk it together.

The decibels rise in Gothel's voice. "Green light the Zeli exhibit in Vegas. I'll personally rip the extensions from her head and stick them in a glass case if it sells tickets." His malevolent stare slithers through the night to Zeli's window.

24

WINDOW PAIN

ZELI HASN'T MOVED FROM THE LEVER BY HER WINDOW. I LEAN OVER the edge of the roof to watch Gothel cross the plaza. Halfway to the tower he stops, staring at the figure slumped against the side of her window, watching the stars. The bodies of both singer and man deflate.

I know that pose. I've rocked it twice this week. After Timmer knocked the crap out of me and when Santino walked away without looking back.

Gothel begins to surge forward but spins back toward Zeli. He holds two fingers to his lips and extends them in her direction.

Is the gesture a kiss goodnight or a kiss off?

I tap her contact and send up a prayer to the Hollywood Sign that she answers. My lips tremble with memories of kisses, and her invitation to kindle a passion wholly new to her. Damn, that's a brand of trust I haven't earned. I want to. Behind closed eyes, I'm falling through the sky again, singing with her.

I push send.

Nothing.

My fingers shake. Again, I hit send.

A siren from the boulevard plays in stereo, live and through Zeli's cell.

"Zeli?"

"Screw yourself."

Call ended.

Send.

"Do you need a picture?" she says. Across the plaza the middle soldier on her right hand stands at attention.

Call ended.

Abuse is better than flat line.

Send.

"How long before your battery dies?"

This time, Zeli doesn't end the call.

"Just charged it."

She grunts a stream of mean into the phone.

"Z, I screwed up." I'm not cut off. "A decent person would never take your studio time, but Gothel didn't give me a choice."

A sigh like bubbles under water floats through the phone.

"We've established Justin Time is not a decent fellow. I'm trying to change that."

"Maybe that's a waste of time."

"That's a better name for me, Justin Waste of Time." A snort sneaks past her armor. If I don't go for it now, I may never have another chance. "Rapunzel, Rapunzel, send me your hair."

Her gasp rides the night breeze. "How do you know my name?"

"Bring me across. I'll spill everything. If you can't deal with what I have to say, you never have to speak to me again." I'm afraid she's going to end the call. I nearly drop my phone over the edge of the rooftop. "I have the new song I promised."

Her silence guts me. This isn't about a fantasy or a fling. Zeli redefines me. Without her, the essence of the better man I want to become withers.

She ends the call. Time morphs as I stare at her window. Nothing moves. A thousand heartbeats later, her platinum record extension sails out the window with the zip line harness. Anticipation of Zeli's ultimate rejection cuts my breaths shorter and shorter as I approach her open window.

When I touch down in the penthouse, her face is a mask of stone, no warmth, no invitation for me to plead my case.

It's the expression of an ending. The same one Timmer and Santino wore before they turned to vapor. Seeing it on Zeli's face flips my overload switch. Brain waves combust. Body systems go haywire. The room spins. My knees wobble as my vision dims.

So I do what any totally cool dude would do in front of the woman who's squeezing his heart into a pulpy mass between her fingers. I drop to my knees, head to the floor, ass pointing to the ceiling. Checking my balls at the door, I harmonize blubbers with whimpers.

"What is your freakin' problem?" Zeli growls.

"Can't...breathe. Heart attack."

I roll onto my side and clutch my chest.

Zeli leans over me and clicks her tongue. "You're no 911."

Panting, I untangle the extensions plastered to my face. I use the arm of Zeli's couch to pull up and then collapse onto its cushions.

"Your ticker is still ticking, Justin Time Clock," she says, hands locked on hips.

Scorn is better than ice. "How do you know? Ever had a heart attack?" I lay a hand over my chest. "Code blue." I try to gulp deep pulls of oxygen.

"Ribs popping?" she asks.

"Horrid pinch."

"Lungs closed for business?"

I wheeze to make my point.

"Burning goo in your throat?" She taps her temple. "Blurry vision?"

I loll onto my back, opening my mouth wider for increased air intake. The next sound makes me snap it shut.

Zeli laughs. Not the high frequency, bubblegum rock queen giggle that floods every interview. Her snickers are an octave lower. The sound is rich and delicious, a return to the quality I first heard in the twilight room and again in our midnight duet.

"You're having a panic attack."

I manage to sit up but have to drop my head between my knees. "It's worse. I'm unhinged."

She plops into the armchair. Extensions climb up over the back. "Tough luck, you're not dying tonight."

The whirlwind spinning through my body subsides to clear space for embarrassment.

"You better grow a stronger pair if you plan on staying in the music biz." When I raise my head, Zeli grins. "Thanks for the show." Her smile fades. "You're poison to me, Justin Time."

This is my opening. The single chance to keep her in my life. "If I'm poison, answer one question."

She stares me down.

"Is that a regular thing with you, duets with jumpers falling outside your window?"

Zeli's gaze slides to the moon. Its lower curve touches the top of a building across the plaza. "Just the one." Her ice begins to melt. "When you complicate someone's life, you go all the way don't you?"

"I might ask you the same question."

"What have I ever done to you?" she squeaks.

"I got booted from my B.A.S.E. jump troupe and made Gothel's hit list because you ran into that mob. I blamed you and like a shitiot, stole your song for the revenge I thought I was due."

"You stole my song because I gave a damn you didn't die?"

"At first." Nerves radiate up my legs, then my spine, warning me to shut it, but if I don't come clean with everything now, I'll always be poison to her. White twinkle lights and crystal swags draped from the ceiling turn the room into fairyland. Pointing to the double doors, I continue.

"I watched them weave that vandal frame under your extensions. I lost my shit when Gothel stole your tears and zapped you into that vest."

Zeli's hands fly to her mouth.

"I know your real name because Gothel used it when I saw him mess you up and lock you in this tower."

Blue irises sizzle. "That's where all the details in the song you sang to me last night came from. You spied on me. You know too much."

"Yes. Full disclosure, I snatched more than a song and studio time from you. I stole that first kiss because I wanted you to introduce me to Gothel."

Her face turns ashen.

"That guy was a walking overbloated ego." I kneel at her side. "If I could go back and kick his ass, I would." I brush my thumb across her cheek. "I wasn't supposed to feel anything when I kissed you. I never intended to care about you, but I heard your voice, your real voice that first night. It wiped away everything I thought I knew about you." I rest a hand on hers. "That first kiss felt like a golden thread, tying me to you. And last night, when I was lucky enough to kiss you again, and you trusted me to bring your body to a place you've never gone–"

Hands fly up to hide her face. "Stop."

Gently, I ease her hands away and force her to look at me. "Don't turn away from me now. That's everything. I swear, there are no more revelations about what I've done. I'm ashamed, and I'm sorry." I drop my forehead onto her hand to regroup before I lift my head. "When we sang under the stars, that song lit my soul. I knew there was nothing else besides "Just in Time" I could sing in the Summer Number One and have a chance. Because it was ours."

Zeli's eyes glisten.

"Rapunzel, you are the light in my soul. Will you give me the chance to be the light in yours?" I never want to leave the shining blue of those eyes. Retrieving the silk flower from my pocket, I tuck it behind her ear. "My heart is in the new song I wrote for you. Will you listen for it?"

Her hand rests feather light on my arm. "Do you swear there are no more surprises?"

"One more. Before my performance today, Gothel gave me an ultimatum. Join his stable or watch my career burn to the ground for stealing your song."

She shakes her head. "I was afraid of that. Tell me you haven't signed his contract."

"It's cool. He said it's standard, boilerplate. I'm sure I can bail if I want."

She runs a finger along the red streak in my extensions, and then examines my newly manicured fingernails. "You're Gothel glammed." Her fingers dig into my arm. "He's trapped you, Justin. His contracts are a never-ending story."

I ease her fingers out of the death grip. "Everything ends."

"Not when you sign your life to Gothel." She takes fistfuls of my extensions and shakes them. "Never ever trust him." She pushes my shoulders. "Get away, before your soul bleeds."

"If I bail on him now, I lose any leverage to get you out of here."

Her hands rest on top of mine. "Wanting to spring me is the craziest, maddest, most–" A single gilded tear falls. "Wonderful thing anyone has ever tried to do for me."

I catch her tear on my fingertip. It's heavy and warm as if there are sparkles inside.

"Oh, Justin. I felt drawn to you, too, the night of my concert. It confused me, scared me. It made no sense." Her fingers close over my finger and the tear. "The night we sang together, I felt that same pull again even though I didn't know it was you. It broke me apart."

"Z, I'm sorry for all the wrongs I've done you."

"Don't." She lays a finger on my lip. "These feelings, our duet, the song you sang me last night, you've brought me to life."

I brush a kiss across her knuckles. She clutches my shoulders and squeezes. "It's too late. If you don't run from Gothel, you'll lose more than the Summer Number One. You'll lose everything. His contracts are unbreakable."

I run my hands along her arms to her shoulders. "Then we'll have to break him."

Zeli startles at my words, but then her eyes go dewy. She leans toward me, lips parted. I accept the invitation. We fall into a hungry kiss. Her fingers dig into my back as I pull her body to mine. We are the sparkles inside her tears. This is what together feels like. I'm hers on this crazy ride. I'll be hers long after we're free from Gothel. We'll make music and love. I've found my light, and I will never let the darkness take her from me.

We separate, both smiling, both teary, both sinking into the happiness that a song and the stars had been waiting for us to find. She doth teach the torches to burn bright.

"Rapunzel, did my heart love 'till now?"

She grabs my hand and places her palm against mine. "Oh Justin, how I've longed to love. It wasn't until you that I understood the depth of that longing."

I twine my fingers through hers. "I think we're writing a new song." My lips smile against hers as I part them for another kiss. The kiss of a man in love with a woman who loves him back.

The crackle of her flatscreen steals our moment. With a frightened gasp, she shoves me to the floor.

25

TRUSTING TIME

ZELI PILES A MOUND OF EXTENSIONS OVER MY BODY. I GRAB A DEEP breath and prepare to be smothered by the weight. To my surprise, Z's extensions are lighter than I expect.

I'm plastered against the couch, Zeli's bare feet underneath me. Through the loop of extensions that start with an Egyptian hieroglyph and end in a section woven with botanical sketches of flowers, I make out a sliver of flatscreen.

Gothel's face lords over the room. "Answer your phone, Rapunzel."

As cool as they come, she laughs. "Forgot to charge it."

"You're in studio in sixty."

Her cool disappears. "Tonight?"

"Time to dazzle me with your chart-busting, Summer Number One tune."

I want to drive a fist through the face behind the sarcasm. Z's leg shudders against my side. Still on full charge from her kisses, I'm dying to run a finger along the soft skin of her leg.

"It's too late tonight. My voice, the song...it isn't ready."

My anger blossoms blood red at this calculated Gothel sabotage. I gently squeeze Zeli's leg above the knee to calm her. Her skin is as smooth as I imagined. She tenses at my touch. I squeeze again with less pressure, willing her to read the signal as *don't fight.*

"Drink your tea and warm up those platinum pipes. End of discussion."

Zeli presses a leg against me. I've got to convince her this is more than Gothel flexing his pissy muscles. He's digging her a tiger trap with a stake at the bottom.

"Do you enjoy freaking me out, Papa?"

"That's when you do your best work." A sneer bleeds through his voice. "Be ready when I slide the stairs back in place."

As soon as his smug face pops off the flatscreen, Zeli flips her hair off me. I grab the remote to kill the flatscreen's power and any possibility of Gothel reappearing without an invite.

Zeli takes it from my hand. "He can control the monitor from his end."

The fireball of fear in my gut must show on my face.

She lets out a joyless huff. "Don't freak, there's always a crackle pop when he's about to bust in. You know where to dive." Zeli grabs her extensions and shakes.

I take in the double doors leading to the ready room. "I don't get it. If Gothel can tippy tap up and down the stairs, what's with the circus act out your window?"

Her lips form a straight line. "Haven't figured him out yet? If there's an over-the-top way to go, Gothel takes it. Ever caught the videos of him riding my extensions out over the plaza so the people can enjoy–" She busts out a Gothel imitation, opening her arms as if bestowing gifts on the masses. "The artistry and magnificence of Zeli's marvelous muse. Her glorious hair."

She flips a few extensions up into the air and watches them fall to the carpet. "This is his circus. Every move is a reminder of who the ringmaster is."

Acid burns my throat, imagining Gothel's thrill that Zeli is stuck at the window while he exploits her extensions over the plaza. The burn goes molten, remembering how Gothel described putting

Zeli's extensions on display in Vegas. Bastard has no regard for the woman who gave the mad hair traction in the first place with her talent.

I lunge at Zeli. "We've got to get you away from Gothel now. He's making his move to kill your career."

She twists out of my grasp. "Has B.A.S.E. jumping deprived you of oxygen one too many times?"

I pace back and forth in front of the table, pounding fists to my thighs. "I overheard his plans for you. Long term overseas tour, and–"

I don't have the heart to repeat the grim statements Gothel made about Z after he kicked her out of the session.

A dissonant undertone runs through her voice. "I'm due for a tour. Dude's not the ogre under my bed. You misunderstood. I hit platinum."

"You've got to believe me. He's setting you up to fail."

I should man up and spill the specifics that her "Papa" is poised to trade in Zeli for Justin Time. Words stay glued to my tongue. I'm a damn coward, but I can't risk her calling him out on things she shouldn't know. He might go full psycho. Spider legs crawl inside my bones imagining what he'll do to her.

"Zeli, I know Gothel's pointing a spear at your heart." I kick the chair. "Why do you need more proof after the way he abuses you?" We lock into a staring contest. She's first to look away.

Zeli pops her lips, attempting to cue attitude. Instead, she wilts in a heartbeat as she avoids the question. "I've got an hour to shine a platinum hit."

I clutch her hips. "Hits. Are they what's really important to you?" My hand sweeps the room. "Is this?"

Zeli reaches behind the couch to retrieve a guitar made of bleached cherry wood so shiny and pink, her reflection is as intense as the real thing. "This is what's important to me."

I fall even harder for her. Damn me for ever assuming glitter and fame were her motivation.

"Trust me." I take her face in my hands. "And I promise you'll never lose your music. Just your cage."

Her shoulders sag. "And how does a B.A.S.E. jumper who's on minute seven of his fifteen minutes of fame plan to pull that off?"

"It starts with a song." Nerves vanish as purpose replaces the last tatters of doubt. The woman before me holds my heart, and I hers. I'm a legit contender for the Summer Number One. I will take Rapunzel's hand and lead us both from this tower.

I hold a hand out for her guitar. "The song you'll nail and break hearts."

The intensity in her eyes makes me light-headed. "Justin, why do this? If I win the Summer Number One, you don't."

"I only need to stay in the contest until we get you the hell out of here." Her expression says I'm gaining ground. "I have friends." The tapestry of Hollywood Boulevard gives me courage. Santino. Leeni. Robo Robbie. "With serious I.Q.s who will help us free you from Grant Gothel."

"So we can all spend the rest of our lives hiding from him?" She closes her eyes for a long second. "You have no idea how powerful, how lethal he is."

I lay a finger on her lips. "Every monster has a weak spot."

She shakes off my touch. "Don't call him a monster." We square off over her guitar.

His mental grip on her is tighter than I imagined. I break eye contact first and slip a finger under the shoulder of her lacy metal prison. "Only a monster would do this." I press on. "Ten minutes ago, you told me to run from him."

Tears fill her eyes. She hesitates. "I feel like I'm being ripped in half, Justin. I'll tell you something that Gothel will freak over if he ever finds out you know. I don't know how else to make you understand why I hear what you're saying, but all this screws with my head." Z composes herself. "If you knew what he's been through."

"You mean the story he's fed you."

She shakes her head. "He grew up in a violent neighborhood

and lost his only brother in a street fight. Not long after, both parents died." Zeli's voice breaks. "Anyone's heart would harden."

Anyone telling the truth. Gothel plays her like a pink guitar. I know it in my bones. Gothel was my idol. I've read a bazillion articles about him, and not one let out a peep about this convenient mega-tragic past that has her drowning in sympathy. This is the obstacle that terrifies me, her insane connection to *Papa*.

"He's really done a number on you."

"We're both alone in the world. That bonds us." She shakes her head. "After everything he's done for my music, it kills me to cause him more pain and betray him."

The bridge I'm building to Zeli could snap any time. She's trusted Gothel forever and bought into his urban legend. Carefully, I slide my hand around the side of her neck and lift the first extension woven into her golden strands. "He betrayed you the second he hid your beautiful hair under these."

Zeli grips the top edge of her metal vest tight until her fingers turn white. She lets go and pulls the guitar toward her chest, bringing me with it. This close, I make out the last echo of the bruise left by Gothel's smack across her right cheekbone.

Trailing a fingertip across the reminder of Gothel's rage, I whisper, "No more."

"I want believe in you, Justin. I'm scared."

"You will never hurt him the way he's hurt you." I give her a beat to let my words sink in. "If you trust nothing else about me, trust the bond we found when we sang for the moon." If she can't tear herself away from Gothel, I'll turn to dust.

She searches my face. A thin band of blue gray, ten shades darker than the rest of her eyes, swirls around her pupils. The stream of tears falling down her cheek shines. Gradually, the skin underneath lightens, erasing the bruise that was there moments before. I blink to clear my vision and touch a fingertip to her unmarred skin in wonder. Zeli's tears did this. Tears Gothel steals to fuel whatever brand of ugly he's using on her.

"I swear. It's his control you're leaving behind. He'll survive. Will you trust me?"

She touches her forehead to mine. "I'll try."

I wish there was time to kiss her. "Let's get to work." When I twist to search the room for a place free of Gothel's notice, my own extensions whip me in the face. I spit out a rogue strand of hair.

Zeli giggles. "Bringing sexy back. Definitely rock that move on stage."

Urgency tugs at my groin. I yearn to push her down on the sofa, kiss her senseless, and give her another taste of the pleasure she's newly discovered with me. Our bond deserves the chance to grow, but the tickety-tock of Gothel's deadline kills that plan.

I tickle the strings of her guitar to quench my mounting desire. "We need to polish any rough spots in the new song. Where are we safe from a Gothel pop in?"

"In here." She tugs my arm.

I nearly trip over a width of hair, following as she beelines in the direction of the walled-off space behind the kitchen. Lights fade up when we walk through the doorway of Zeli's bedroom, the place where no one is watching.

26

ONE YOU

THE ROOM IS ALL Z. OUR REFLECTIONS STAND SIDE BY SIDE IN THE whitewashed wood frame of a full-length mirror. One of her shelves holds a line of Zeli dolls with waxy dead faces, freaky reproductions of the real thing.

She catches my disgust and stows the dolls under the bed. "Creepy, huh?"

Pink treble clef-shaped magnets hold sheets of music to a white board that covers most of one wall. A stack of empty staff paper sits on a desk of whitewashed wood matching the mirror's frame.

Z sits on the edge of her round bed and crooks a finger. I blush as pink as her bedspread at the thoughts of what I'd like to teach her on that bed. I focus on the guitar. This is no time to dissolve into a pile of lustful goo. A packed plaza didn't unnerve me as much as the urge to share a bed with Zeli.

"Tick tock, Time," Zeli says, thumping her foot on the rug. She's so jittery, I expect her to start spinning. Pop queen feet kick against the bed while I find the beginning of the song. Losing patience with me, she jumps up and shoots her arms straight to her sides. "I'll make my Rampion tea." She zips out the door leaving a pile of extensions behind.

I need brain space and oxygen to recover from the effect of my fantasies. My voice is rough. After singing scales, it's still strained, hitting flats instead of pure notes. Zeli returns with a steamy cup and snugs in next to me.

Tea fumes tickle my nose, and I relax.

"Major to minor key?" she asks.

"Right here. Make your audience lose hope and then–" I jump into the major key. "Pull them back in." When our eyes meet, my fingers falter on the strings.

"Will it help if I don't look at you?" she says.

"Sit over there." I point to a rocking chair in the corner.

Time to focus and make Zeli the vessel for my creation. The underlying truth to making art with the word, the song, the brush-stroke, is that it's a solitary act of the soul. Dedication adds dimension and harmony but expanding the oneness of creativity by sharing it with another is love. Does Rapunzel offer me that?

She carries the teacup to the rocker. The Rampion tea aroma rising over its edge nearly makes me follow. I recognize this feeling. It's the same bizarre brain haze I experienced when Gothel breathed tea fumes in my face. Something is not right with a tea that gives you a contact high.

I pluck a note and will this woman to stop short-circuiting my body long enough to make it through the song. "Ready?" I drop the guitar pick on the carpet.

The corner of Zeli's lip rises as she retrieves the pick. "Are you?"

In answer, I grab the front of her ruffly blouse and pull her lips to mine, fuel for my creative passion. I pat her ass, nod toward the rocker, and sing as Romeo to my Juliet.

"My untried heart hides from passion's call
Where hope speaks only in whispers
Frightened to flee its shadowed dream
Of love blessed by an angel's beam
Fearing love. Fearing joy. Fearing you.

Kisses come and kisses go
Tempests roil and stars burn out
My love lies deep inside a shell
Protecting me from fear and doubt

Cupid teases with such sweet visions
Of dear lips brushing close to mine,
That disappear at dawn's first call
His heartless tricks on my heart fall
Bring love. Bring joy. Bring you.

Kisses come and kisses go
Blizzards blind and oceans swell
The key descends from clouds above
To free my heart that yearns to love

Your soul's fire reveals the love I seek
In promises pledged under stars
Throw Juliet's dagger to fate
No longer in tears do I wait
Found love. Found joy. Found you.

Kisses come and kisses go
Lips now freed do join in song
Sweet rhythms hidden soon will soar
As winged hearts fly evermore

One love. One joy. One you."

The rasp of my last note fades. The glint of blue eyes blur through mist rising off the tea. Their beauty is another song.

Her voice swirls through steam. "This one is about me too, isn't it?"

"Every note I write from now on will have a piece of you inside it."

She doesn't speak. Numb fingers rest on the strings. I've disappointed her. The song isn't good enough.

"Tell me what to change." Is she breathing? "Or I'll help you with the song you're working on." I pluck random notes on the strings to fight silence. Eyes downcast, I track the advance of sparkly pink toes until her leg leans into mine.

Did I bring her sand when she needs sugar?

Slender fingers cover the hand I press into frets. "You make me crazy," says Zeli.

"They say the blade between creation and madness must be trod carefully, or the knife's edge will cut your feet."

Zeli tilts her head. "Who says that?"

I shrug my shoulders. "Me." I squirm under her gaze. "It's cool. I get it. The song doesn't track for you. A minor key is too dark for the "Stars and Fireflies" woman."

"Fuck fireflies." She shoves a hunk of extension over her shoulder. "This song – it's longing, fear, love." Zeli moves her lips against mine until we're both oxygen deprived. "And hope. That's worth singing about."

"Milady, dare you trade pop for the bite of alternative rock?" I snap my teeth together.

She traces my lips with her pinkie. "Sometimes when you wish upon a star, your soul comes out to dance, doesn't it?"

She's spun the planet backwards.

"Teach me every note."

The surface of the glass nightstand fogs under the teacup. A similar haze fills my brain. Rapunzel accepts my gift and gives back something more valuable: my redemption.

When I tell Santino I've written her Summer Number One song, the one that I swear on Zeli's twinkling tears will take first place, he's got to forgive me. The real payoff is what we will be able to do for her. With Santino back on my side, Zeli can kiss this tower prison goodbye.

Truth rattles my core as I listen to Zeli. This song is as much about Santino and about me as it is Zeli. I'm afraid to trust and believe in people because of the hurt and abandonment that always seems to follow. It's all I know. Deep inside, there's a part of Justin MacKenzie that longs to trust, to believe, and to give himself to others. A part that's been awakened by the kindness of a soul who reached out to a dude he'd never met, and a love song shared under starshine and moonlight.

Zeli charges into the new song. She picks up a tune as fast as the speed of sound, as fast as I stole "Just in Time" from her. Her tinny warble is gone. This woman is a solid musician.

Why does rock star Zeli sing with a ninety-nine-cent voice when Rapunzel makes clouds stop moving and a guy's breath pool in the air outside his lips?

"Here," I say, handing her the guitar we've been passing back and forth. Our hands meet again. Electricity rises between them. Neither of us pulls away. Her breath sends a flyaway strand of golden hair across my cheek and shreds my self-control.

There's an echo of my longing on her face. "Believe me, Justin. I'd like to do more than sing right now." With a saucy smile, Zeli retreats to the rocking chair. She feels the tune with her fingers and flies across the notes giving them wings.

I forget how to blink. "God, you're amazing."

The corner of her lip rises for a beat. Rapunzel claims the tune. Every time she sings it, adding a swoop here or a sustain there, the depth and grace of her true voice sends my melody soaring. The song that started as a jumble of notes on the edge of sleep finds its rightful home in Zeli, the legend, not the star. The Summer Number One crown is hers.

If Gothel ever lays a filthy hand on her again, I'll kill him.

My body thrums as Zeli wraps herself more deeply into the song. Sliding the phone from my pocket, I surreptitiously record her. I can't think of a more perfect ringtone to hear when she calls me.

Her head pops up, a crease drawing a line between eyebrows.

"What's wrong, Z?"

"Title?"

I shake my head. "Are you feeling one? Please not "Kisses Come and Kisses Go"."

She laughs. "Too poptastic?" Her smile turns soft and shy. "What about, "One You"?"

Her suggestion nails the essence of my song. This is the language of your perfect match, the one that lights your soul.

"You don't like it?" Zeli's lips pucker into a pout that flashes *kiss kiss kiss* in pink neon across my vision.

I make it to my feet despite a skeleton the consistency of pudding. "It's perfect."

Like you, Zeli. Like you, Rapunzel.

I kiss her once slow and deep, and then back away. I won't rob her of any more precious seconds to hone the song she's about to present to Gothel.

"My tea's gone cold." The fuzzy skirt of condensation has disappeared from the table. She pulls her phone from a pocket in her jeans' shorts. "I've got fifteen minutes to run through the piece and drink my tea."

"Keep practicing. I'll pop the tea in the microwave." I swoop the teacup off the table and dart to the kitchen. Out here, I'm free to go weak kneed, wrapped in the perfection of Zeli's singing without her as a witness to my swoon. She's got to be on her A-plus game to wow Grant Gothel into rewriting his vicious plan to dethrone the pop queen until I can fly away with her.

The tea's aroma massages the knots in my shoulders. I press my nose against the glass door of the microwave, soaking in the smell. My head begins to swim in the tea fumes.

Carrying the cup as if it were as fragile as a hummingbird egg, I pause in the doorway. "Cool if I taste this?"

She waves me off and adds grit to another bar. I hover within the steam curl and sniff.

Rampion Tea is water to a man dying of thirst. Bringing the rim to my lips, I sip, letting warmth coat the inside of my mouth. The brew flows down my throat. Steel fingers smash my windpipe.

The cup crashes to the carpet, spraying my pant legs with tea. I grab my neck as vocal cords scorch and burn.

27

TEA TIME

ZELI RUSHES TO ME, WAVES OF HAIR SNAKING BEHIND. "YOU'VE NEVER had Rampion tea. I should have warned you."

My vocal cords shrink, pulling into a tighter and tighter coil.

Staggering to the kitchen, I guzzle cold water. Zeli clutches me while I gulp and sputter. When the squeeze subsides, I still hang over the sink.

"That tea is ten shades of nasty."

"It's only weird the first time." She grasps her own throat. "The Rampion tea pinch actually relaxes you and makes it easier to hit high notes." Zeli rubs circles on my back. "You'll get used to it. Papa Gothel has all his singers drink it."

"It's poison." I chase the cold water with handfuls of warm. "I've got to gargle. Do you have salt?"

Zeli frowns. "Don't fight it. Papa doesn't tolerate variation from the Rampion tea gospel according to Grant Gothel."

Her face turns pearl white as the flatscreen hums to life. Zeli forces me to the floor behind the counter.

Gothel's voice is greased with a layer of smug. "Go time in five, Angel." He harrumphs. "If you've got anything to work on."

"Another platinum coming your way." She tickles me gently with her toes, and I nip her ankle.

Gothel doesn't temper his grunt of disbelief. *Bastard.* The flatscreen buzz goes silent.

Zeli fills a new mug with tea. I put a hand over the top. "Don't."

She lifts my hand. "I'm recording in the middle of the night. I need my tea." Before I stop her, she throws back the whole cup.

I rub my throat as she slurps. "Zeli, please, no more tea."

"Shush. We've gotta stash you."

My gut drops to my high tops. It's back, her popcorn voice with the screechy edges, Zeli's trademark warble. The rich beauty that's been dancing from her lips is stretched as thin as gum you poke your tongue through to blow a bubble.

"Can't you hear what it does to your voice? You're Zeli-fied."

"Stop freaking out. This is my sound. Not that dull pre-tea drone."

"Dull!" I sputter. "You're nuts. What you were doing five minutes ago was singing." I grab her arms. "You know how a song feels when it's right. A note trembles, floating in inner space. It glides inside you, an ethereal mist next to your heart before it flies through the resonating chambers of your instrument." I take her face in my hands. "You either coax a gentle note, or push out a quiet roar, gritty or harsh as it travels from inside to outside." I slide my hands to her shoulders. "Songs are a complete relationship with your spirit, deserving of devotion." Our bodies barely touch. "Zeli, the way you sang before that tea touched your voice is the reason music exists."

She pushes me hard. "Stop messing with my head. I exist because of this tea." Her eyes narrow. Z raises a section of hair above her head and slams it to the carpet. I leap aside to avoid the chain reaction of extension ripples snapping toward me. "You still don't get it. We can dream of escapes, but Gothel owns us. His word is the ONLY word."

Her complete one-eighty staggers me. It's that damn tea. I

circumvent the extension current and seize both her hands in mine. "Not for long."

Zeli jerks away. When she opens her mouth to blast me again, the clacking sound of the rolling spiral stairs rises from the twilight room.

"Hide." Zeli flails an arm toward the bedroom. "Wait half an hour, then take the stairs. No one will be there."

I crush her body to mine. Lips claim hers in a fury that leaves her breathless. "Sing your ass off."

Heavy footsteps followed by a chorus of lighter pit pats ring on metal stairs. I bolt to the bedroom, kill the lights and pull the door closed a second before I hear Mange's voice.

"Grab her hair ladies." Gothel didn't even bother to come himself.

Hair dancer giggles fade, and my Rapunzel is gone.

I drop onto the bed. Furious tears sting my eyes as I picture that demon tea ruining her voice.

On my phone, I bring up a Gigabyte tune. "Holy, shit." There it is the same plastic snap in their voices that kidnapped Zeli's natural sound. It's harder to hear across multiple singers, but it's there, the same stripe of Rampion rot. I fly through snippets of Da Da Da Deacon and Mistress Mango tunes. Tea squeal bleeds through their sound. Gothel has infected everyone in his stable with throat-clenching poison.

That vile crap will never touch my vocal cords again.

It's more than just the assault on the vocal cords. My head swam breathing in those tea fumes. My perception fractured. Gothel tunes his singers and tames their resistance with his brew. Zeli's flip flop between Gothel as the big bad and then a poor lonely man makes sense now. She's been on that tea too long and become an addict.

I must convince Zeli that tea may be doing irrevocable damage to her gorgeous authentic voice. It'll take more stretching of the cord between Gothel and her before it snaps completely. I will break it.

Exhaustion grabs me hard. My body appreciates a real bed. I'll power down so I can think clearly about my next moves to separate Zeli from Gothel. A quick catnap can't hurt. I'll slink out of here long before her session ends. I set my alarm to vibrate at two o'clock.

As soon as dawn opens an eyelid, I'll call Santino to tell him I've mopped up my mess with Zeli. His brainpower is key to help me plan a way to free my darling.

Sleep almost pulls me under when inspiration hits. I know the perfect time for a rescue, the first night the pros and amateurs take the stage together. We'll both be there. Short of dropping dead, there's no way I won't finish in one of the top ammie spots. Since "Stars and Fireflies" is the latest platinum for Rampion, Zeli's performance as capstone of the pro pyramid will happen back-to-back with mine.

Less than forty-eight hours. That's all I've got to cook up a plan, earn Santino's forgiveness, and break what's left of the link between Zeli and Gothel. An unwelcome thought coupled with the lingering pinch of tea makes it hard to swallow. What if Santino doesn't believe I'm good with Zeli?

"Shit." I should have asked her to call him.

My head meets pillow, and I give into pink dreams.

Warm breeze tickles my skin.

"Justin."

The sound doesn't pull me through the veil of lingering sleep. It's not the lark, announcing dawn with its out of tune discord and a beak full of sharps. A nightingale tempts me back into slumber.

Fingers shake my shoulders hard enough to rattle teeth. "WAKE UP!"

I raise one lid.

Sparkly blue eyes in full panic mode hover inches from mine. "You're still here?" Zeli is on the bed next to me, up on her knees. Light outside the picture window is deep violet, the last shade of night before lavender dawn.

I sit up fast enough to make my head swim. "What time is it?"

"Four-thirty."

I fish out my cell and groan. Shitiot me set the alarm for PM not AM. "We've got at least an hour before it's light." I grab her wrists. "Did "One You" fly with Gothel?"

Zeli's smile is my lark. She stretches arms wide and drops her head back. "On silver wings."

I wrap her in my arms and pull her down on top of me. Our hearts hit a Salsa beat. Pressing my lips into the honey strands that frame her face, I whisper, "Platinum wings."

It takes my entire reserve of willpower not to flip her onto her back and roll on top. Instead, I settle her against my collarbone, sliding an arm to circle her waist as I make a silent vow not to steal anything else from Rapunzel. If we make love now, and I end up failing her, one sweet memory turns to lifelong regret. Whatever happens between us from here on out will be a slow and mutual burn.

"Did the tune convince Gothel to spring you from house arrest? Do you get to go home?"

The soft side of an extension brushes my chest. "He pulled the stairs."

Which not only is a big no, it also means her hair is my only exit strategy. One I'll have to take at the first sign of dawn. I'm not ready to leave her.

I rub my nose against her cheek and kiss the tender skin in front of her ear. "Zeli, where is home?"

Home. The thing I mean to make with my music money. Do I dare to dream a home with Zeli?

"Are your parents at that ranch Gothel talks about?" I curse the ask when tears swim in her eyes. *Shitiot.* I heard Gothel tell her parents to rest in peace the first night I met her.

"They're gone. Papa Gothel promised my mother before she died that he'd take care of me. All I have of my mom and dad are memory files with a few pictures and music."

"You grew up with Gothel?"

She shrugs. "In a way. I grew up on his ranch."

I nip her ear lobe. "You and cows? I don't see it."

The prelude to a giggle bubbles from her lips. "Rampion Ranch raises musicians, not cows. All the kids there are trained for a life in music."

"Like Olympic gymnast kids?"

She nods and nestles her head back into the hollow of my shoulder. "Something like that. I miss it, the community."

I trace her jaw with my fingertip. "You deserve a real home." As if I know what that is. Words catch in my throat. I do know what a home can be - an apartment over a costume shop with people who care about you, or a Hollywood loft with a DJ who tries to offer you a decent life even as your Ma chases her next unicorn.

Zeli's sigh ends in a quiet mew. "I told you, there's no breaking away from Gothel."

"Rapunzel, follow me to a different life, a better life. One that adores your authentic voice. No more tea."

She's trembling. "Fans won't recognize the sound. They won't accept me."

"They will as soon as they meet the real you." I brush my nose against her temple, desperate not to break this spell of our stolen moment. "I need to be certain that no matter how insane the escape plan, you're all in. Are you strong enough to trust me and leave Gothel's world behind?"

Her body crumples against mine. My heart swells at the way we fit together, pieces predetermined by cosmic design. Has Zeli always been my fate? Has she turned me Romeo, full of plans to be with my Juliet and write a different end to the story?

A whisper warms my ear, one filled with a tangle of fear and hope. "Okay, Justin MacKenzie. I'm in."

My insides fizz. *I'm in.* Sweeter words were never spoken.

"When you gave me your song, you reminded me of truths, and the joy of making music the way it should be—without conditions." She lays a hand on my throat. "Pure. I choose that."

I lay a hand over hers.

"I'm terrified, Justin."

"If you weren't then this wouldn't be for reals." A mantle of responsibility like I've never felt lands on my shoulders. It's as warm and light as stardust. There's no doubt this is the path I'm supposed to take with Zeli, no matter the consequences.

"I will make it happen, Z. I swear, but there's something I don't get."

Her expression turns wary.

"What's up with Gothel collecting your tears?"

Her eyes widen.

"I know about his vandal tea. I've felt the way it screws with your mind. Tell me the rest." The strain lines creasing her face gut me. "I won't tell anyone, but I need to know anything that could screw up springing you from this tower."

Z takes a slow, deep breath. "My tears give him a power. They create heat in his hands that strengthen my bones and muscles to make it possible to live with the extensions. I don't understand it, but I need it. He takes, but he gives too."

If I hadn't seen their bizarre exchange with my own eyes, I'd think she was off her nut.

She hides her face in her hands. "If you need to go—go."

I'm dying to ply her with more questions, ask about the words Gothel whispers when he lights her up. Not yet. She'll tell me more when she's ready.

I pull her hands away and dot her knuckles with tender kisses. "I've spent years falling through the sky, rocking moves that should end me. You learn to believe things not because they make sense, but because you feel the truth in them. I believe you, Zeli."

She gazes up at me. "And I believe you're the one who is supposed to know my truth."

I lean until my lips touch hers, and we move together. Every kiss is new. She suckles my tongue slowly sliding her lips along its length. I take her bottom lip in my teeth and tug until she moans. Our next kiss is slow-motion, lips grasping, then lingering.

I grow harder with every swipe of her tongue. She's electric with the performance high I know well after a brilliant jump. "I should go, Z."

Her hand snakes down my hip until she slides it between us, lightly rubbing the length of me above my jeans. "Because of this?" she asks.

The slow and mutual burn I hoped for blossoms like a sweet summer rose between us.

I drop my head back, reveling in her touch. "Oh, God." I can't lose myself with her, not yet. She's so untried. Reluctantly, I guide her hand away. "I have zero control with you."

"Good," she says, sneaking her blouse over her head.

The sight of that cursed lacy metal vest is like a bucket of ice to my groin. "We'll have our time, I promise." I thread my fingers under the bottom edge of her shackle. "After I destroy this fucking thing."

Rising to her knees, Zeli shimmies and twists out of her vest until it hangs off the extensions behind her.

I need to leave.

"When I said I'm in. I'm in for it all." She pushes me flat onto the bed and kisses me savagely, singing into my mouth. "Kisses come, and kisses go." She reaches for the buttons of my fly. "Let's make the most of our hour. I want more than your kisses tonight, more than a song."

I arch up and let her pull off my jeans. Her gaze falls to the bulge in my shorts and slowly she lowers her face toward it. Before she gets any further, I cup her cheeks in my hands. "There's only one first time, my love. I don't want to be the dude to take that from you."

Zeli turns her head to kiss both my palms, and then she slides a hand under my shirt until it rests over my heart. "Justin, I want you for my first and my last and everything in between. Teach me."

With those words, I'm undone. "I promise to go slow. Stop me if it is too much."

She nods. We kneel facing each other on the bed, and she pulls off my t-shirt. I slide fingers up the curve of her waist and under the lavender satin of her bra. I tease her nipples with my fingers until they rise beneath my touch. She rips her bra off and flings it off the bed, arching her back until we're skin to skin.

"Do what you did last night," she gasps.

I take each nipple in my mouth and let my tongue bring her to a state where she can no longer stay balanced on her knees. Gently, I lay her down, kissing my way to the top of her lacy panties. I run one finger around the inside of the waistband, easing it down inch by inch, kissing my way after.

Zeli arches, raising herself to my lips.

"More?" I ask, blowing soft breath beneath her navel.

"And more." She sighs.

I slide her panties off, savoring the smooth skin of her legs. The sight of Zeli naked, glowing in the warm yellow light of the bedroom, makes my heart pound in my chest. She's perfection. Those beautiful full breasts and the curve of her waist that flares to the shapely hips of a woman have been hidden beneath deceptive clothing.

My groin throbs, tightening to the point of pain, but I will be loving and slow to this woman who gives me reasons to dream. I pull her to the edge of the bed and kneel before her, sliding my hands up her legs to the inside of silky thighs. With the lightest touch I draw circles higher and higher until I reach softer, wetter places waiting for me.

"And?" I ask again and blow a teasing breath across the golden puff of hair between her legs.

Her fingers thread through my hair, pulling me toward her glistening folds. I begin with kisses that make her sigh and then probe deeper with my tongue, circling, teasing. I moan against her, overcome with the sweet sensation of her taste.

I've never been someone's first. I need this to be for her what it is for me. I slide a finger over her slippery nub and then gently circle one then two fingers inside her.

"And," she cries out.

I press in farther, feeling her stretch and slicken, ready and wanting me.

Fuck. I don't have a condom. I never dreamed we'd get this far.

I will make my sweetheart zing, but I'll have to wait. Again. Tonight may kill me.

"*And*, Justin. More *and*."

I slide up her body. "Sweetheart, there's only so far I can go. I don't have-"

"Oh," she says, flicking a hand toward her bedside table. "In there."

Shock, and a spike of jealousy take my ardor down a couple notches when I open the drawer to find condoms in Zeli's nightstand drawer. "Why do you have these?"

"I asked my hair dancers to get them." She raises up on her elbows. "I've asked them about a lot of things." Zeli gives a sly smile at my arousal, straining to escape its cotton prison. "May I show you?"

I'm so ready a single touch might set me off.

Zeli lays on her side and reaches inside my shorts. Her hand grasps me and begins to stroke. With a quick swipe, she yanks my shorts down and stares. Her breasts quaver as her breathing speeds up.

"You're so...not short there."

I press her into the velvety coverlet and cover her body with mine, rubbing my not so short against her to bring her back to the edge. I reach between us to discover all the places that make her squirm and moan.

Her hand finds its way to my tip. She swirls a finger around and over it several times before her fingers circle me, moving up and down my length. "I want to taste you."

Mother of God, just hearing the words makes me harder.

Zeli flips us, claiming the top. Extensions bunch and pile around us as she lowers herself to me. The flick of her tongue brings me to the brink. When she closes her lips around me, it's all I can take. I gently pull her back and grab a condom.

Zeli sneaks her knees apart, inviting me in. The adoring look on her face fills me with a joy completely foreign and new. This is a new level of trust, a trust I vow never to break.

I open her with eager fingers. She's as ready as I am. I enter her ever so slightly and pull back, tuning what's left of my senses to stay out if it's too much for her. I venture further, and her hips rise to meet me. Again, I retreat.

This time she screams, "And," in my ear, wrapping her legs around me. I travel the rest of the way until I'm completely buried in this woman who has become my life.

She tenses around me as I thrust. We move together in a rhythm as perfect as the notes we share together in song. Skin sets fire to skin as we rock and slide until one long sustained cry from Zeli's lips breaks the pre-dawn stillness. I follow her swiftly into perfection before her cry drifts to silence.

Deep, lazy kisses coax heartbeats and breath back to steady levels. We lay face to face. I can't ignore Zeli's vest resting on the arm I wrap around her. The symbol of her captivity.

Faint light sneaks between buildings, through the picture windows, and into the bedroom. Any longer, and I'll be stuck here for the day. Instead of performing, I'll have to hide under her bed with those freaky dolls.

I slide off the bed, navigating my way through her hair. The disappointment on her face sends a rush of heat up my chest as I dress.

"Promise you won't bring any creepy Zeli dolls with you when we blow this place?"

"Promise."

I scratch fingers through my hair, surprised all over again that it goes beyond the nape of my neck. She stares at me with wanting eyes and adorable round lips. I'd better leave before my rpms rise from 33 $^{1/3}$ back to 78.

The bloom of dawn opens wider. Soon, the plaza will wake, and I'll be spotted.

"Rapunzel, Rapunzel lend me your hair." I stand, reaching for her. She takes my hands. Together we fit her back into the vest and wrap her in a pink chenille robe. Circling an arm behind her back, I lead the way to the window. When she slips her hand into the back pocket of my jeans and squeezes my ass, I almost combust.

Cotton candy light plays across the sky, waiting for the sun to catch up. Even the sun wakes up Zeli pink.

I pull the harness from its peg and climb in. She attaches the metalworks of her hair onto the zip line. A quick glance reveals an empty plaza. Throwing thumbs up, I say, "All clear."

"Come back tonight." With a smirk on her face and a tease in her tone, she says, "I'll set the alarm." Zeli raises the golden sword handle, and I fly.

My gaze never leaves the delicate beauty at the window. Even after I land on the far rooftop, we keep our sight locked on each other until her extensions travel back into the tower.

She lifts a hand to her lips. Through the brightening sky, Zeli blows me promises tucked inside a kiss.

If I'm going to stay true to my vow to make a life with her free of Gothel, I can't do it alone. I pull the phone from my pocket to call Santino.

28

DAWN PATROL

I SHOVE THE PHONE INTO MY POCKET. THIS IS A FACE-TO-FACE moment.

Thoughts race as I make a beeline to the boulevard. I've got to make sure the signing bonus is in my bank account so Gothel can't snatch it once Zeli and I make our getaway. I hope she's got some way to access to her funds as well. That money is our nest egg to a new beginning.

Fragments of a shiny future fill my thoughts, Zeli free from Gothel and leaving Rampion Records behind to offer ourselves to Midas Lear at Golden Pipes Records. We'll reinvent ourselves as a duet. Only it'll be Zeli's real voice dancing with mine, not tea infested tripe. Gothel will be the one who's yesterday's news, not Zeli.

By the time I hit Hollywood Boulevard, I'm winded. Dropping hands to knees, I catch my breath. A trio of shadows elongate around me on the sidewalk.

"Dude," calls a gritty voice from behind. "We know you."

Being the only dude in the vicinity, I turn and paste a lazy morning smile on my face. Grit Voice wears a suit jacket with an iridescent green shine, lizard skin. His black hair has green high-lights. I wish there was more action on this stretch of the boulevard.

Next to Grit Voice, a guy with bleached blond hair and the build of a Gothel Goon chimes in. "Justin Time. You suck." They all laugh. "Look at you, all glammed up with extensions."

The tallest dude in their group, a human carrot in skinny orange jeans and a black button-down shirt, pipes up. "Is it true every ammie in the Summer Number One gets to nail Zeli?"

There's no possible way these shitbirds know about Z and me. The sound of her name coming out of that bastard's mouth makes me want to score a roundhouse kick to his nose. Taking the high road, I walk away. Justin Time in the news for assault won't win votes.

"You didn't sing us a goodbye song," says Grit Voice. The hair on the back of my neck turns to spikes. They're tailing me.

I shift into a faster gear and croon, "Goodbye."

Locked metal gates guard storefronts. The boulevard isn't awake yet. There's no one to receive an SOS.

"Not good enough, Justin Time," says Blondie.

I break into a full run before he finishes my name. Fedele Costumes is four blocks away. God, I hope Santino is up for saving me a second time from boulevard scum. The memory of him turning his back on me burns red.

I gain half a block on them when a gunmetal gray Aston Martin squeals up onto the sidewalk to block me. I skid to a stop, lucky to have all my toes. The door flies open, and Cama Rama slithers out.

The car is a right-hand drive. Who does this asshat think he is, James Bond? Cama Rama cranks an arm around my neck. I nearly gag on his tree bark cologne. A cold knife pricks hard enough to make my jugular throb.

"Good morning, Time."

"Let me go, pissweed."

He makes a buzzer sound. "Time's up on your Summer Number One cheat. Tell your hackers to pull the plug."

Timmer taught me one useful thing aside from B.A.S.E. jumping. When you're in the middle of a shitstorm, balls of steel are the best way out. "Drop the vandal act, loser, and I won't throw you under Gothel's bus."

Cama Rama squeezes tighter. My balls are anything but steel.

Dude enunciates his words. "A nobody from nowhere doesn't go viral without serious cyber backup. Call-off-your-hackers." The point of his blade cuts a dot into the skin at the base of my neck. "You get one warning. If I don't fly back into the number one ammie spot by tonight, I'll personally give you a tracheotomy."

My teeth clack together when he shoves me. He shoots a death curse look my way as he climbs back into his car. Before he slams the door, I catch a glimpse of a curvy torso and legs that go on for days in the passenger seat. I can't see her face, but the black lace cat suit is trademark Kaydance.

Something's rotten in Hollywood.

Cama Rama cracks the window. "Collect your finder's fee, boys." His car turns into a gray blur as it screeches onto the boulevard.

Blondie kicks my legs out from under me, and my back slams onto the sidewalk. Carrot Boy stuffs a sock into my mouth and rolls me onto my stomach. My hands are yanked behind my back. Plastic zip ties cut into skin.

"Watch the extensions," says Grit Voice. "I don't buy shreds."

Blondie drags me half a block to a chain link gate in the boarded walls of a construction site. I twist and kick. It gets me nowhere. Carrot Boy kicks the gate open, and we disappear from boulevard view. Inside, a narrow dirt shelf surrounds a massive pit.

"How much for his mane?" says Blondie, raking fat fingers through my extensions.

Grit Voice's bony fingers replace Blondie's. "Five hundred."

The human carrot grunts. "These are prime quality extensions. Real silver and gold strands. You'll sell them by lunchtime to another ammie who has a hard on to be Justin Time. A thousand or we keep the goods."

Zeli accused me that first night of trying to steal her extensions. I'm living the for reals version of her nightmare.

"One time offer, seven, or I walk," says Grit Voice.

Carrot shoves me. A boot presses into my back, pinning me while extensions are cut from my head.

The more I squirm the harder the heel of the boot grinds into my spine. I curse myself for not calling Santino. These vandals are going to kill me. Cama Rama will keep the top ammie slot.

No one will save Zeli.

I stop struggling. I have to make it through this. I can't leave Rapunzel impaled on Gothel's fangs.

I have a clear view of Grit Voice holding my extensions into the light and petting them. The red streak shines bloody in the sun.

"Pleasure doing business with you, gents." He lets himself out the gate.

Carrot shoves my side with the toe of his boot. A sickening realization hits as my body rolls over the lip of the pit. With my hands tied, I can't control the tumble. My cries are snuffed by the sock that does nothing to stop grit from collecting between my molars.

I splash into a shallow puddle of mud at the bottom of the pit. The sock flies from my mouth. Tears and dirt blur my vision. I'm left with nothing but distant car horns for company.

Despite glop-soaked jeans, I manage to get to my feet. The spot from Cama Rama's morning kiss stings. This is what fame buys you, the bottom of a ditch and competition ready to poke holes in your windpipe. Gothel and Cama Rama are both fiends, fame-seeking bastards. Is that what I've become by entering the Summer Number One? The answer stings as bad as the prick in my neck. I sold my soul to the lure of celebrity the second I stole Zeli's song and signed Gothel's contract. Shame heats my face.

To Santino, I am just one more Hollywood fame-seeking bastard.

Screw contracts. Screw the Summer Number One. Right now, there are two great loves in my life, Zeli and our shared musical passion. I must do them both justice. If that ends with Rapunzel and I singing for coins behind an open guitar case on the boulevard, then I will be a lucky man.

The gate clinks above and a sunburned face beneath a hardhat peers over the edge of the pit. "What the hell!"

"Dude in a ditch here. A little help."

A few autographs later, and I'm on my merry way. Dripping a trail of mud onto the sidewalk, I hoof it to Fedele Costumes.

The metal security gate is still down when I get there. I rattle it. No one comes. With shaky fingers, I text Santino.

On your doorstep. Talk?

I press my nose through the gate, hoping to see him head my way. Nothing moves inside the store. I send another text.

Everything is cool with Zeli. Want to spill the deets to U face to face.

I stare down at the phone. Superhero high tops appear on the other side of the glass. When I face Santino, my words go on lockdown. His face is marble.

Pushing through a wall of nerves, I gush. "I fixed my screw up and wrote Zeli a new song."

The Santino statue doesn't flinch.

"She's singing it in the Summer Number One."

Nothing I say pierces his armor.

This is not going the way I need. In Santino's view, I'm a vandal, a lying thief who took advantage of Zeli, him, and his whole boulevard family. Why should he believe me? I've given him no proof.

Zeli's my one chance to win him back, and I need to do that for her sake. I don't just want to be the guy who frees Rapunzel from the tower. I want to be the kind of man she wants to leave the tower with.

My finger twitches, but I stop before hitting her contact. I don't know if she's alone. If I call and the wrong people are near, I blow the works. We can't tip anyone off.

I hold my breath, waiting for Santino to speak or curse or flip me off. His expression is hard.

"I wish I could go back and erase my screw-ups. Your respect means more than anything." I clasp hands in prayer.

He lifts his cell and types. The message ping ties a knot in my gut.

Come back after Zeli sings your song.

Santino disappears behind his racks of make-believe.

I slide down the gate until my ass hits sidewalk and bury my head in my hands.

Forgiveness is a bitch.

The price to patch betrayal is steeper than I imagined. In the face of his rejection, I grasp the miracle of Zeli's generosity in allowing me into her life.

A flash catches my eye. Across the street, a work crew pulls the wrapping off a giant digital billboard rising on metal legs atop a building. Its brightness swallows the last early morning shadows.

The Rampion Logo chases in a dozen colors across the screen then fades into Summer Number One footage. I stare at my own face. My performance from yesterday blasts onto Hollywood Boulevard. Letters made of tiny platinum records scroll along the bottom of the screen as the notes of "Just in Time" wake the dead.

THE AMATEUR RACE FOR THE RAMPION RECORD'S SUMMER NUMBER ONE EXPLODES AS JUSTIN TIME CLAIMS THE TOP SPOT. CAMA RAMA DROPS TO NUMBER TWO.

I am freaking number one. I may be ripped apart and rejected, but I'm number one. That explains why Cama Rama picked this morning to go dark on my ass.

For one glorious moment, everything is perfect. My music dream and what it will bring to my life sparkles. I want to whoop it up and throw my arms around someone to celebrate. A shadow crosses my heart.

That someone is locked in the Rampion Records Tower.

29

WINGS CLIPPED

THE SECURITY GUARD'S FACE MORPHS INTO *THE SCREAM* WHEN I STEP inside the lobby. I've been wandering the boulevard for hours, straining my brain to craft a viable escape plan for Z on my own.

"Justin Time?" he says, and checks the flatscreen on the wall behind him that features my pre-vandalized self on stage. He snatches the phone. "Kaydance, I've got a hobo version of Justin Time down here."

I catch my reflection in the smoky glass wall. It's bad news.

My throat goes dry. If Kaydance was in on my boulevard attack, I'm not safe with her. At least the guard is a witness. Justin Time - last seen dragged away by a witch in a cat suit. The *ding* of the elevator causes sweat to break out under the grime on my forehead.

Kaydance wears cheetah print scrubs with a belt reworked from Dorothy's ruby slippers. The clickity-clack from nosebleed-high heels stops when she catches sight of me.

"What in holy hell chewed you up?"

I glare and bite my lip to keep from screaming an accusation that guarantees a return engagement of Cama Rama's knife.

"Vandals. Ripped me off, literally." I flick fingers under the ragged stub where extensions used to be.

Kaydance taps an earpiece. "Page Gothel to the salon." The future ex - Mrs. Cama Rama shoves me into the elevator. She acts totally freaked out. Either she's Academy Award material or clueless to Cama Rama's post-dawn activity and leggy seatmate.

Gothel fills the frame when the elevator doors open. His claw reaches in and plucks me out. Heat from his grip radiates through my sleeve. Overlarge black pupils bleed into his emerald irises.

"What in the name of grief?"

I salivate at the thought of outing Cama Rama to Gothel. The memory of his knife to my throat dissuades me.

"Vandals on the boulevard."

"What were you doing on the boulevard?"

Excuses snick through my brain like pages of a flipbook. "I left my friend's place too early before vandals slunk back into their holes."

A storm rises in his eyes. "Our agreement was for you not to leave your dressing room unaccompanied until the Summer Number One is over."

I toss him a bone. "Excellent plan. I should have stuck to it."

"You'll go to the beach compound with me at night from now on."

Zeli begged Gothel to take her to the beach the first time I spied on them. If Gothel spirits me away, I lose contact with her.

My palms go damp, and the place where Gothel's fire fingers touched aches. I can't go with him and miss my meeting with Zeli tonight. The thought of being away from her chills me. We've got escape plans to hatch.

"That's an amazing offer."

Gothel's thick brows meet at the wrinkle above his nose. "Not an offer, Mr. Time, a directive." He hustles me through the door of the salon.

I can't abandon Zeli. I will stay within sight of the Hollywood sign. I turn to face him. There's only one card left in my deck with enough power to shake this up. It might be a joker, but I have to play it.

"Mr. Gothel, I haven't been entirely straight with you." I direct my next words to the travertine floor, feigning remorse. "I'm not twenty-three. In fact, I'm not eighteen yet. If I don't show up at home tonight, my bro, Santino, will hit 911 before the moon sets."

For once, my baby boy looks better pay off. I pray Gothel won't stick my contract in a shredder and kill my access to Zeli.

His eyes narrow to snake slits. "I wasn't aware Mr. Fedele is your brother."

"Stepbrother and, ah, guardian. We jacked up my registration a smidge." My fingernail breaks the skin of my hand. *Buy into this, Gothel, please.*

He shoots virtual daggers at Kaydance. "Our Mr. Time was never eligible for the Summer Number One?"

Her skin turns snow white. "His I.D. checked out."

Gothel steps toe to toe with me. "I assume your ersatz brother will be here for your performance today."

"Of course." I'm a hundred percent cool on the outside, but my insides creep toward meltdown.

"Bring him in to chat. You will stay in the Summer Number One." Gothel shows teeth that don't pass for a smile. "I'll clarify how we will finesse your little charade."

My attempt at a smile is as weak as his. "One more thing, sir."

Gothel purses his lips. "Are you going to tell me you're the estranged son of Midas Lear, and heir apparent to Golden Pipes Records?"

A laugh never sounded as fake as the one I try to pull off. "No more secrets, boss." If he knew the enormity of that lie, I'd spent the rest of my days in whatever version of a dungeon he has under the tower. "I truly feel it's bad juju singing the song I took from Zeli."

My request is met with a bored expression.

"How about a greenlight to switch tunes?"

He reaches to rest a hand on my shoulder. The caked mud puts him off.

"I will say two things. You will say nothing." He jabs a finger in my face. "One, you ARE twenty-three years old. Two, Justin Time will ONLY sing "Just in Time" in the Summer Number One. Got it?"

I squeeze my hands into fists to hide the shaking.

Gothel's voice booms across the salon. "Kaydance, I'm heading backstage. Mr. Time does not leave your sight until you deposit him into my keeping."

The second he learns Santino is MIA from my life, GG will fit me with a shock collar.

Gothel wrinkles his nose at my mud-covered reality. "Fix this."

Kaydance shoves me in the direction of the salon's bathroom.

I shut the door behind me and turn on the shower for cover. Santino showing up today is vital. I tap his contact.

"Come on, man. Take one last leap of faith with me."

My heart squeezes as thin as a red vine. I wait for him to answer. It goes to voice mail.

"Santino. It's Justin. 911. Can't wait until tomorrow. Sitch is life or death, man. Life or death."

A text ping quickly swims through my despair.

AFTER Zeli sings

The 911 didn't diminish my jacklick status with him. *What the fuck am I gonna do?* When my "stepbrother" doesn't show, nothing will stand between my wrists and Gothel's manacles. How can I convince Santino to hit the plaza and buy me the freedom of one more night to plan with Zeli?

I jump when Kaydance pounds on the door. Chick's giving me no space.

"Quit diddling yourself and get out here."

I need time. *Time. Justin Time. Just in Time. Buy time. Time to see Zeli.* I dive under the shower spray, straining to jumpstart any idea.

Zeli is the answer.

Gothel is on the plaza, not with Zeli. There's no better time for her to call Santino. If she can't bring him back onboard, I'm going under. I emerge from a cloud of steam and slap on the robe hanging on a hook next to the shower.

I can't risk Kaydance overhearing a convo. I text my plea and stare at the screen, waiting for confirmation.

"Come on, Z."

I've got to bury my freak out deep so I can perform today. Staying relevant in the Summer Number One is the only legit power I have left to stay connected to Zeli.

Kaydance swings the door open. Still nothing from Zeli.

30

SEALING THE DEAL

AFTER HOURS OF BEING RE-GOTHELIZED, KAYDANCE DITCHES ME TO Mange. My new extensions, perfect replicas of the ones removed courtesy of Cama Rama's vandals, swish back and forth. I want to wrap fingers around every strand and tear them from my head.

Mange muscles me up the steps to the stage, elbowing Cama Rama out of the way.

"It's a fine day to crawl out of a hole, eh Cramit up your Ramit?" I raise my middle finger, making sure my nail scratches the underside of his rodent chin. He pulls an arm back to deck me.

Mange has him in a headlock before my flipped bird has a chance to return to the nest.

"Get on stage, Time," barks Kaydance. "Curtain rises at Gothel's go." She gives my upper arm a wicked pinch through my jumpsuit.

"Gothel?"

"The Boss emcees the last day of ammies."

Below in the VIP space, Cama Rama catches my eye and slashes a finger across his throat. I jerk a thumb at Mange, and then twitch my index finger back and forth.

T-shirt moment: Say Hello to My Not So Little Friend.

Kaydance drapes my guitar strap over my head. Gothel's voice streams from backstage monitors.

"Two days ago, this lad hadn't landed on our planet." Hands flit around my face to glue a hairline mic under my bangs and slide an earpiece in place.

"Today, you've crowned him your amateur king."

JUSTIN!

The reverb from the crowd's chant raises ear-splitting harmonics. Vibrations from the stage floor hum under my feet as light squares go mad. I walk center stage behind the closed black curtains and hug my guitar into place.

"Please be here, Santino," I pray to the Hollywood Sign.

"From two hundred to number one, Knights and Ladies of the Rampion Realm, I give you, his majesty–"

On the monitor, I watch Grant Gothel sweep into a courtly bow and gesture to center stage. My intro starts. The middle of the curtain scallops up for me to stroll through. The crowd has the density of a neutron star as the ground rumbles beneath their chants.

A nip of fear grabs me until I spy the triple barrier and a line of Rampion Security paired with Hollywood's finest police between the stage and audience.

I push pause to soak this in. This may be my last time on stage once Zeli and I flee Gothelland. I'm going to launch this plaza into orbit.

Gothel bends at the waist, waiting for me to release him. I return his royal bow with grace and majesty. For the next few minutes, I own him. I own the crowd. I own time.

Gothel's voice overpowers everything. "JUSTIN TIME."

Chants of my name continue to rise. My breath catches. I understand why Zeli felt safe flinging herself into the mob the night of "Stars and Fireflies". This is big time love. Fans are the core of energy and strength. My body turns from flesh to iron. No one can vanquish me.

I scan the crowd for the single face I wish for. Did Santino think Zeli's message was one more lie in the Justin string of deceit? Maybe Z wasn't alone and never got the chance to talk to him. I can't wait to be bailed out. It's brave time. Team Z 'n J will escape Gothel's fortress on their own.

I shut my eyes and imagine golden strands of Zeli's real hair brushing my cheek, the taste of her, the feel of her flesh burning into mine as we make love, her perfect voice.

I sing.

They sing.

My army on the plaza is my courage. Together, we raise a swell of invincibility.

I soak in and bottle the rush. I don't blame Santino for ditching me. Any honorable person would. He'll always be the spark that set Justin Time ablaze. I will owe him forever.

"To search beyond the clouds for lover's eyes. Destiny..."

And that's when "Just in Time" works its magic again.

Santino Fedele stands near the front of the crowd off to my left. I almost falter in my note when we connect.

Zeli did it.

Santino gives a single nod. His lips form a tight line until his mask cracks and light shines in those good eyes.

I sing through a smile, crooning the song better than ever. New variations flow. Shadings of gratitude and hope lift the notes. With my Gigabyte backing tracks, "Just in Time" is reborn. The crowd's voices leap on the back of the new riffs and ride them into the clouds with me.

Gothel's smile sizzles offstage. I have pleased the master. My position in the game strengthens.

In your face, Cama Rama. The top ammie ranking is mine to keep.

An hour later, Santino presses heels of his hands to his temples.

"Tomorrow! You want to yank Zeli from the tower, tomorrow?"

He's still got crazy eyes as we step onto the roof of Singen's building.

"I can't wrap my head around Gothel. I've admired the dude for years, and now you tell me he's totally dark."

The stars compete with the lights of Hollywood for bragging rights in an indigo sky. "You played him like a fiddle in that meeting."

"Who played who? I almost pledged my firstborn to buy you one last night at–" His fingers crimp into air quotes. "Home." He shoots a look around the roof and back to the stairs as if he expects Gothel to appear. "I shouldn't have settled for one night."

I grab his sleeve. "It won't matter. After we rock my plan tomorrow, Zeli will be free."

"Tomorrow." His groan carries on the wind. "You don't give a dude a whole lot of time to pull a miracle out of his ass."

Fanning hands in front of my body, I smile. "You pulled this miracle off in one night. Freeing Zeli will be a piece of cake compared to that."

Santino bends over like he's been gut punched. He springs up just as fast. "You're talking less than twenty-four hours to figure out how to snag you both from the plaza, during a live show."

"We don't have more time. If Gothel zaps me off to his beach complex, there won't be a way for us to talk without ears on every word." I chew my thumb callous. "My leash will be short and lethal." I take a stuttering breath. "Like hers."

Santino is jumpier than a frog crossing the boulevard when I step to the edge of the roof. He grips my t-shirt and pulls me back. "Not so close."

I laugh and flick my wrist at the drop. "Rooftops are nothing to a big bad B.A.S.E. jumper."

When our eyes meet, my lip starts to quiver. It's our first chance to be alone. Gothel bum rushed us to his office. He made Santino follow through on his guardianship claim by co-signing an NDA and updated contract listing my age as eighteen. Between fittings for my new wardrobe, I fed Santino details of Cama Rama's vandal attack, Gothel banishing Zeli to the tower, and the bastard's plan to ruin her career.

It's a pinch me moment that he's here at all. "I swear to keep my part of our deal. Santino Fedele, you will B.A.S.E. jump over Hollywood."

"It was vandal to ditch you, J." He rakes a hand through curls. "You seriously pissed me off. We spun you viral, and then I fed you to the wolves. It's my fault you were Cama Rama bait."

"Stop." I grab him in a quick bro hug. "The shit is all on me."

When he tries to speak, I hold a hand up to silence him.

"You did everything I ever asked of you. I dishonored that. Stealing and lying brought me down. You were justified to cross me off your playlist."

Santino searches the dark outline of the Hollywood Hills. With painstaking slowness, he looks at me. "All you ever asked me for was a refund." He kicks at the rail surrounding the roof. "I took the media ball and ran with it."

"I didn't stop you."

He studies my face. "Don't go to the tower. Come home. I'll gather the boulevard together. We'll nail down a solid plan to free Zeli."

Home.

The word crumbles the edge my resolve. He says it like I belong.

"I have to see her. I promised. Keeping my word is my new jam."

"The rescue scenario brewing in your brain has serious holes." He nods to the window. "Shit, J. What if Gothel shows up while you're over there with her?"

"Boss man bragged he's booked 'til dawn recording interviews and promos for the Summer Number One. Dude loves his moments in the spotlight." I'm already touching Z's contact on my phone. "I'm finished breaking promises."

He punches me in the arm. "I'm not leaving here without you."

In half a ring, her beautiful voice answers. "Hi." My love stands at her window.

"Rapunzel, Rapunzel send me your hair."

Santino's forehead scrunches. "Rapunz-who?"

I nudge his supersonic hero high top. "I'll be back faster than that lightning bolt and fill you in."

Santino holds the rig as I wiggle in. He darts another look over the edge. "This is crazy with a K."

"It's crazy being away from her."

His head tilts. "Wait." He points between Zeli and me. "You and her? For reals?"

"For reals," I confirm. The zip line swings me over the plaza.

He breaks into a grin. "Vandal."

As the distance between us grows, a ball of anxiety bounces inside my ribcage. "Santino, why'd you show up?"

He stares across the plaza to Zeli's penthouse. "She sang it for me. The song you wrote. It said what I needed to hear, who you really are."

I'm too choked up to answer. Santino, Zeli, I'll dedicate the rest of my life working to deserve them.

Zeli shifts from a two-d shadow to a three-d angel as I close in on the tower. My insides boil. I'm dying to touch the tender skin of her face and twirl a strand of golden hair around my finger. My burning ices over when I see a phone against her ear.

Is it Gothel? Is he going to tuck her in after all? If we can't predict his moves in the next twenty-four hours, any escape plan is screwed.

I'm shaking when I reach the window. What if Zeli chickens out? How can I keep her on board to go up against Gothel when we don't have solid specifics the night before her world cracks in two?

Zeli throws her phone onto the pink sofa and reaches up to guide me in the window. She kicks the lever with her foot as I roll out of the harness. When my feet touch solid ground, Zeli rockets into my arms. Tears glisten on peachy-pink skin and dribble inside my collar. Tiny bursts of heat tickle my chest.

"What's wrong, Z?" Has Gothel done something? I'll rip his throat out with my teeth.

Zeli tilts her head back but keeps her body molded to mine. "Nothing, fool." She runs her hands over my shoulders and clasps them behind my neck. "Justin Time, I freaking love you."

Her truth terrifies me, but not because I don't yearn to hear it. Everyone I dare to love disappears. *Please, not Zeli.* It kills me to imagine life without this woman.

Gently, I press my forehead to hers. "What you did for me, calling Santino...that was–"

"Not even close to what you've done for me, the songs, the way you're trying to change my life."

I bring her hands to my lips and kiss them. "Not trying. After tomorrow you'll never answer to Gothel again."

"That was Santino on the phone. Oh, Justin, I really like him. He said to send you right back over so you two can get to work."

I'm caught by the fire in her eyes, the beckoning curve of her cheekbones, that tempting nub of a nose ripe for a kiss. I can only think in small words, none worthy for what I feel for her.

She squeezes my hands, her expression full of worry. "How can I ask you to do this? Gothel will destroy you."

Gothel's name snaps me out of angel worship. "He can't." I keep one arm around her and grab the flatscreen remote with the other. When it snaps to life, my face fills picture.

The final votes are in. Justin Time claims the top amateur spot in the Summer Number One.

A flurry of close-ups flash across the screen. Fans scream their Justin love. I've conquered Gothel's kingdom.

"He can, Justin."

I kill the flatscreen and clutch her to me. A whiff of Rampion tea lingers on her breath. If I had any doubts, that flushes them. "Listen to me. You can't stop us. Not me. Not Santino. Not a kickass group of people from the boulevard you'll meet soon. We're all taking the risk, buckle up."

She backs off, hands on hips. "I get a say in this too. Wait until the Summer Number One is over. Papa will ease up and let me out of here."

Muscles tighten in my neck. When the contest ends, Gothel will relegate Zeli to pop history.

I steal her hands to pull them around my back. I press my lips to her in a slow-burning kiss. My hands roam her hips, her breasts. I'm consumed with the desire to fit our naked bodies together and once again share that burst of oblivion that trades thought for pure sensation.

Zeli's hand slips inside my jeans, evidently sharing the same thought. Her fingers dance up and down my cock. "Justin, I want you so much it makes me crazy."

I rock my hips into hers. It takes monumental restraint not to make love to her right here in front of the window. Running my own fingers down to her wrist, I lift her hand free. She tries to dive back in, but I hold her off.

"Oh, Z, I want you too. There isn't time." I nod toward the window. "And we have an audience."

She giggles. "We could hide under my hair."

"Even that would give Santino an eyeful." I dot a kiss on her nose. "Soon, my darling. I promise."

She nestles against my chest.

"Tomorrow is our best shot at getting you out of here–a perfect storm. We'll both be backstage. Gothel will be occupied with day one of the pros. It's our last chance before he whisks me off to his beach compound."

"His prison with a view of the Pacific." She shudders in my arms.

I glare over her shoulder to the pot of tea on her kitchen counter. "And I am done with Gothel's tea poisoning your voice."

Zeli drops her chin. I kiss the fine golden strands on the top of her head.

"You'll lose everything for me," she whispers.

"No. I'll give you everything. You and me together, Zeli. We're nuclear. Our combined energy will summon starlight." She tips her face up, my Helen of Troy. I'll start a war for her.

Electricity arcs between our bodies. Zeli grabs my ass. "I want you fast and rough, and then you can go." I'm on the brink of giving in when her fucking phone rings.

She flashes a glance at the screen. "Santino."

I grab the phone. "What!"

"Look, Making Time, get off the girl and bring your ass back here." His laugh flows through the phone. "Robbie's fanning the flames of your idea back at the war room."

This is war.

Zeli grabs the phone. "Don't lock anything in until you consult me. I have perspective you clowns don't." My gaze digs into Zeli's. If I reach in far enough, nothing will ever break our connection.

Zeli ends the call and flings her arms around my neck. "Whatever happens tomorrow, I do freaking love you, Justin Time."

"Me too you."

She raises a single eyebrow. "And by that you mean...? Care to elaborate?"

I laugh and steal another kiss. "I love you, Rapunzel."

31

DUET

WHISPERING INTO HER PHONE FROM UNDER COVERS UNTIL THE WEE hours last night, Zeli helped us sketch out our plan. With tonight's Summer Number One performances in full swing, it's time to set it into action. Nerves send me pacing laps around the fruit and cheese platter on the coffee table in my dressing room. On the brushed steel wall, a monitor jump cuts to past performances, interviews, and A-list Summer Number One parties around Hollywood.

My very own silver kettle of steaming Rampion tea lurks on the counter. Curls of vapor waft through the room. I stumble to the kettle, hand to my throat. Steam coats my face as I inhale deeply.

"You deceptive bastard."

What grand irony. The brew with a godlike aroma cinches vocal cords and sets brainwaves to Gothelvision.

My mind hazes the longer tea mist tickles my pores. How bad can one cup hurt? I tip the kettle over a mug with the Rampion logo etched on its side.

"That last note punctured my eardrum," says a commentator on screen.

His words snap me back to reality. I stare at the half-filled cup in my hand.

"What the hell are you doing, MacKenzie?" I demand of myself.

I drop the cup onto the counter and open the mini fridge to stuff the kettle inside, locking the demon in its cage. I can't drink a single drop of that poison. According to plan, Zeli can't either. If it was easy to almost fall prey to a smell I've never depended on, can she resist?

The feed switches live to the plaza. The grandstands from the amateur round have doubled in height. Rampion Plaza looks more baseball stadium than concert venue. The rows of black and silver theatre seats added up front fill with celebs.

Above it all hang the electric blue spokes of a wheel: zip lines. One of them is our lifeline. As the capper of Zeli's performance, a legion of flag bearers will zip line down to the stage. Each flag is embroidered with cover art designs from Rampion's top hundred albums.

Grandstands block the setting sun. Spotlights chase over the crowd, harbingers of the mega Rampion talent taking the stage tonight. The feed cuts to the red carpet choked with Gothel's parade of VIPs.

I'll be last to walk the carpet while Zeli sings. Thanks to her newest platinum, Z is the pro's big finish. Other chart-topping Rampion stars have been alternating performances with the top amateurs still standing. Gothel's benevolent showmanship is to grant the number one ammie the final slot tonight.

His face flashes on the screen. I imitate his slimy tone. "Even the little people in this world have a shot at the Summer Number One dream." *Liar*.

It would have been the ultimate out of body experience to take the stage tonight and just perform. I mourn the loss of such simplicity for half a beat. Zeli's smile steals my thoughts. She is the ultimate out of body experience.

The crawl along the bottom of the flatscreen shows four acts before Zeli is on. I'd love to witness the freak out on Mange's face when he discovers this Justin bird has flown the coop.

I jump when my cell pings. Santino sends me a picture of my target, the same square opening under the back of the stage where I escaped Gothel the first night of the Summer Number One.

Me: *Zip line good to go?*

Santino: *Check.*

Me: *Mix man onboard?*

Santino texts a thumbs up emoji.

Me: *Escape route clear?*

Santino: *Stop freaking out and GO!*

There's a special place in Heaven for Robo Robbie and his hack-tastic skills. He not only downloaded cues and the schematics of the zip lines but enlisted a friend to add a sweet little motorized rig on a dummy zip line to pluck us from the plaza. Zeli and I will be phantoms disappearing into the Hollywood night.

I grab the cup of Rampion tea and knock on the door. Mange cracks it a few inches.

"How much longer 'til go time?"

He checks his watch. "Ten minutes. Gothel says to finish your tea."

I'll bet he does. He wants me screeching out the signature Rampion sound.

"Half a cup left. You want some?"

His hungry stare locks on the tea. "It's for the talent."

I've rocked that desire on his face. Mange clicks the door shut.

That's my cue.

I tuck extensions inside the back of my jumpsuit. After cranking up the volume on the flatscreen, I stack a chair on the coffee table over the tower of cheese and pull down the vent. I hoist my body into the lungs of the Rampion beast, then kick the chair away. It takes a wedge of Brie down with it. Once inside the shaft, I pull the vent cover back in place.

It's a quick trip through the air duct and into this floor's maintenance ring. I take the stairs fast enough down to the first floor to win an Olympic trial. It's lucky everyone's attention is on the Summer Number One instead of the empty corridors of Rampion Records. Still, flecks of panic simmer in my bloodstream.

I find the door labeled *Scene Dock* and slip through. From there it's a short sprint to the outside, and I'm on the moat bridge behind the performance complex.

My heart splatters against my ribcage when I spot a matching pair of goons hovering next to the target hatch at the back of the stage. Santino's peeps have been caught.

They see me at the same time I see them. The goons flash wicked smiles and gesture me across the bridge. The wolves in sheep's clothing are on our team.

I fly into the shadows next to them. "Thanks."

They shush me. The tallest fake goon points to the double harness dangling from the zip line that masquerades as one of the flag bearers' routes. It stretches to the top of the nearest building. He mimes Zeli's long hair and stabs a finger at the line that will *zip* Z and me to freedom.

Shorter goon reveals a deadly looking pair of shears, steel jaws destined to cut through the thin metal skeleton of Zeli's hair. I shudder, visualizing the vulnerable place dangerously close to her noggin that he needs to chop to separate Z from her locks.

This is a one-shot deal.

I dip through the hatch and squeeze under the stage. The goon twins follow, their bulk barely navigating the metal bones of this maze. Bass resonates all around us as we crawl. I'm inside a beating heart. An orange cone marks the location of a trap in the floor behind the mix console.

Cama Rama's caterwaul provides all the sound cover I need to remove the square access plug to the stage. The weasel is the last ammie to perform before Zeli.

I slither out to tuck in between the mix man's knees and the black curtain draping the front of the console table. I'm invisible to every eye on the plaza and stage complex. My goons stuff in behind me. The mix man is a member of Santino's boulevard family, another link in this selfless chain helping Zeli and me. I clamp a hand around his ankle, the stand-by signal.

Mix Man uses one hand to work Cama Rama's levels on the console and passes me a mic with the other. The stage unleashes a light show when Cama Rama takes his bow. Through an opening, I watch him jump down the offstage stairs and slobber all over Kaydance. The ruckus fades. I picture Gothel waiting for his moment.

Sure enough, the snake's voice booms across the plaza. "The moon is up. It's magic time."

Mirror ball dots of cherry blossom-colored light speckle the stage. On the offstage monitor, I watch pink glitter rain over the crowd. Magenta and silver Mylar curtains travel in as a backdrop for the diva's performance. Metallic strands wave back and forth, playing with the light. Digital ribbons from powder pink to deep watermelon undulate across LED panels. I know without looking the Hollywood Sign pulses Zeli pink.

The slippers of Z's hair dancers pitter-patter by, winding her extensions into a spiral. I can't see Zeli.

"Lads and lasses, I give you Rampion's Summer Number One Platinum Pro, ZZZ..."

"ZZZZZZZZZZZZZZZZZZZZZZZZZZZ..." The crowd buzzes along with Gothel.

"ZELI!"

I use the hair dancers as cover to dart behind an amp before the lights come up. The adoration bubbling on the other side of the main curtain could fuel a rocket. Gothel lost his mind, believing Zeli is on a downslide.

Mix Man hits the intro to "One You." The song I wrote for my Zeli blasts through a hundred speakers.

My gut clenches when I hear the Rampion pinch in her voice. I pray she's faking the tea sound and is not a victim of its grip.

I close my eyes to gather one last dose of courage. The echo of stomping feet against concrete and grandstands supply rhythm to my anticipation. As the front curtain sneaks up, a pair of follow spots snap onto Zeli. Her double shadow waves against the dazzling streamers of the backdrop.

I falter as her presence fills the plaza, the hills, the sky. I'm taking all this from her. And then I remember Gothel's smack against her skin. Doubt escapes like raindrops down a pane of glass as the notes of "One You" fade out.

Slowly Zeli lifts her gaze to the plaza. She begins without music, singing with the rich voice that made me fall in love with her. "Just in time. Our stars crossed just in time." For the first time, the world hears her perfect voice, free of Rampion tea.

I flick my mic on and spring out of my hiding place. "You called?"

Pandemonium detonates across the plaza. Spotlights follow each of us until Zeli and I share twin circles of light. The Jumbotrons flash a close up as I take her hands in mine and kiss her cheek to a collective roar of approval.

Zeli opens up her voice like never before. Its beauty rends the sky. She plays to the crowd, while staying completely connected to the song.

I'm awed by her gift. The Gigabyte backup meant for me pumps through speakers.

"To blaze a path across the moon drenched sky."

I join. "My heart wept."

We trade phrases.

"Reaching deep for hope."

"To search beyond the clouds."

"For lover's eyes."

We cast our spell. Our lips nearly touch as we harmonize. "Destiny drew your kiss to touch my waiting lips. Magic chased the dark–"

It's all I can do to keep from bawling as the ecstasy of singing under the moon with my Rapunzel returns.

It's seconds to go time. Our song flies toward its end. I scan the barricades. Taking down those barriers is essential. Notes swirl around one another. At its zenith, our duet lifts the crowd high enough to glimpse Heaven.

Offstage, Gothel crushes a handful of curtains in one hand, thrusting his other at us like a dagger. A battalion of goons clogs the steps behind him. His mouth contorts, unleashing curse after curse. Teeth gleam in the stage lights, ready to tear chunks from our flesh when we step offstage.

We're not going offstage.

As the audience leaps to their feet on our final note, I holler, "NOW."

My personal goons jump from behind the mix board. I spin Zeli and yank the extensions away from her head. Blades slice into the color block and metal frame closest to her neck. The instant shears hit my angel's hair, a shower of mega-heated sparks rain across the stage. Every lamp above us explodes and LED panels die in an end of days conflagration.

Zeli screams my name.

I grab for her as the stars go black. An afterimage burns in my retinas of light flashing from Gothel's fingers like the blaze he used to close her metal vest that night in the twilight room. The burst races down the metal highway under Z's extensions, heading for her neck. It's the only light in the darkness as Gothel fries every electric cable and lighting instrument in the stage complex.

"ZELI!"

A cluster of sparks flare in a corona around her head. I lunge for her. My hands close around empty space.

She's out of reach.

An arm cuts into my gut and wrenches me backward. When I try again to call for Zeli, a hand clamps over my mouth. She should be with me, redeemed from Gothel's hell.

My captor and I blast through the metallic curtain onto concrete ground behind the performance complex. Overhead a hundred bodies with cover art flags ride gravity's pull to the dark stage late for their cue.

There's a jerk at my groin. I soar in one half of a motorized double harness on a zip line toward the moon away from the Summer Number One.

Alone.

32

MUSTER

MY FINGERS CRAMP FROM TEXTING ZELI WHILE SANTINO AND I switch from one zip line to the next in the series Robbie installed on buildings between the plaza and the boulevard for our escape.

"Last one," says Santino, leading me onto the roof of a ramshackle hotel.

Robbie who's been disconnecting the lines behind us so we're not followed, touches down a minute later. "Go. I'll ditch this last line and catch up."

There's a screech from the power tool he uses to remove the bolts connecting zip line hardware to buildings.

Santino and I climb to the bottom platform of a fire escape and jump to the sidewalk. We're east of the plaza in the heart of vandal territory.

I hit Zeli's contact again. Straight to message. Did our people whisk her along a different route to the boulevard? We turn down an alley. The silence from her end pounds my heart like a flaming battering ram. I pray she beat us to Fedele Costumes.

Santino rips the phone from my hand and throws it onto the pavement. He grinds the heel of his boot into the center of the screen.

"Gothel might be able to trace you."

He pushes toward a roof access ladder. "We're regrouping at Liliana's in case they come looking for you at Fedele Costumes."

We scramble up the nearest building and skitter across half a block of rooftops. Santino knocks a pattern on the metal square of a trap door.

A fury of gray hair atop a reddish-brown face covered in lines of deep wrinkles appears through the hatch. From behind a pewter-colored, handlebar mustache, a voice grates the air.

"Where's Robbie?"

"On the way," says Santino, looking over his shoulder.

We jump through the hatch onto the kitchen counter in Leeni's upstairs apartment.

Our gatekeeper pulls Santino into a back-thumping hug. "I'm getting too old to play cowboy." The older man's silver caterpillar eyebrows press together.

"Justin, meet Rand Diggs."

I know that name but can't fit his shoe leather face into the puzzle.

"Rand is the reason I didn't piss away my future."

Rand Diggs is the guy who pulled Santino off the streets.

"Welcome to the Boulevard, Justin Time," says Rand.

I should shake his hand, but the tumult in my brain releases one word. "Zeli?"

Santino leads the way down the stairway to Leeni's salon. "No word yet."

The doorway at the bottom step frames chaos. A posse of faux Gothel goons spread throughout the room, speaking in agitated whispers. Leeni attempts to comfort a figure lying on the floor who screams like he's been dipped in acid. Snapper pokes an IV into the guy's arm.

I move closer. It's the goon with massive cable cutters. Leeni and another gal are working the fabric of his sleeve out of hideous burns. This is my fault.

"Leave it for the E.R.," says Snapper, reaching into the red EMT case on the floor next to them.

My knees give out. Santino grabs me. My body shakes so violently I can't draw a breath. If our cable cutter is this bad off... *Oh God, Zeli.*

Santino shoves me into one of Leeni's salon chairs. "Justin, look at me."

I'm panting, tears gush, extensions knot around my face.

Snapper darts a look at me. "Shit, is Justin going into shock?"

I swallow hard before shaking my head, no.

Leeni pushes Santino aside and gets in my face. "Get it together, jacklick." And then she's back at Snapper's side.

T-shirt moment: Candy Asses Don't Save Pop Queens.

I grab a wad of long, snaky cotton from Leeni's salon station to wipe my face.

Robbie flies into the room and skids over to a table in the corner where a guy wearing a Summer Number One t-shirt pours over a laptop. Images of Zeli in pain fill my head. I launch off the chair and grab Robbie's shirt. "Where is Zeli?"

"All hell is breaking loose in Rampion land," says Robbie. He pulls out of my grip to take over the laptop, clicking keys with the speed of a bullet train.

I punch the back of Leeni's salon chair hard enough to spin it. "Get me back to the tower."

Santino hollers at me. "Not yet. Every Gothel goon in Hollywood is hunting you."

I kick the wall of the salon. The glint of metal from scissors on a workstation catches my eye. Grabbing them, I hack and curse until my extensions lay in a heap at my feet.

A knock sends Snapper charging to the door. Red lights flash across the salon.

I move close as they hoist our fallen warrior onto a gurney and head for the ambulance. "I'm sorry, man. I'm so sorry." Add another name to the list of collateral damage burned onto my scorecard.

Snapper folds Leeni in his arms. He kisses her like he's going off to battle, and then follows the gurney.

Santino locks the door and kills the lights. Steps pound on the ceiling above the apartment. A colorful collection of the boulevard tribe streams down the stairs.

Santino punches shoulders and throws hugs. "Great job getting the goons to follow you." He scans the group packed into the salon. "Everyone back?"

Two women, one with a saffron weave that flares like sunshine around dark mahogany skin, and another with a flock of red and orange birds inked on her bald head, swoop over to us.

Saffron hikes a thumb toward the boulevard. "We lost them."

"Meet Flo and Edie," says Santino, kissing each on the cheek. "Proprietresses of the vintage clothing store on the corner and excellent runners."

I'm buried under hugs and handshakes from various boulevard folk. These are the peeps who conjured my viral wave, the sculptures who molded Justin Time out of spit and nylon.

A decoy goon approaches Santino and me. The apology in his eyes turns my blood to ice.

"I'm sorry, J. We busted the barricade and tried to catch Gothel."

My vision turns gray around the edges.

"He got your woman."

The salon spins.

"Talk to me, Justin." Santino grips my shoulders.

"What have we done to her?"

Robbie bangs the table. His laptop covered in Gigabyte stickers skitters to the edge. "Gothel's fucking hardcore to hack. His diamond coating won't scratch."

Santino points to a throbbing icon on the screen. "Open his texts, Rob."

"They're locked tight." Robbie growls. "I need a password." He taps his phone. "The code generator is going to start smoking if it works any harder. Ideas, Justin?"

I've known Gothel fewer days that my hand has fingers. How will I crack his password? "Gigabyte? Zeli? Rapunzel?"

Robbie groans. "Tried 'em and everything else with a Rampion stamp on its ass."

My head pounds. Through Leeni's blinds, shafts of light from the boulevard leak across her glossy wood floor and flare into a pattern of multi-colored wings.

"It's *My Angel*."

A beat later, Robbie yelps. The screen goes ballistic with Gothel grime. Overlapping windows of emails, files, and texts pop up.

I want Justin Time roasting on a spit.

No one sleeps until every inch of her extensions are back in place.

Zeli's alive.

A mixture of panic and gall propel me to the front of the shop. "They deal with her extensions in the tower on floor thirty-three. Plan B. Let's go." I throw the door open.

Santino jerks me inside, pulling the door shut. "Get your shit together." He jabs a finger toward Leeni's apartment where the boulevard tribe congregates. "You're not the only one who fries if Gothel finds you."

He's right. I am not a solo act. The safety of all these people is on me. I sit my ass down.

Two hours after the world opened up and swallowed me, Robbie waves me over. "Look at this." He points to a window with Gothel text threads.

Goodnight, my angel.

I growl at Gothel's sick sign off to Zeli. "She's back in the penthouse."

Once again Zeli has been shackled to her extensions. Were we even close to setting her free?

Santino sticks his head next to Robbie's. "Get a GPS lock on Gothel's cell?"

Robbie dives back into the laptop, calling, "Here Gothel, Gothel."

I hold my breath.

"Bingo! I've got a signal. Gothel's on Sunset Boulevard slithering into the west."

I bellow and tear at my hair. "Get me back to the tower." My face is hot enough to melt glass.

Santino grabs the front of my jumpsuit. "Fizz the fuck down. I'd rather lock you in a closet than take you back to the Rampion Tower, but you have the best odds to lead Zeli out." He shakes me. "Are you capable of keeping your head on straight?"

"Straight as a freaking arrow," I assure him. The muddled pieces of my brain snap back together.

Robbie kicks a bulging backpack out from under the table. "Go for Phase Two."

We race back upstairs, and Rand boosts us out the hatch. I follow Santino and his lieutenants on a snaggle-tooth path across rooftops back toward the plaza.

Up here, the shine of Hollywood fragments. Ripped pieces of tarpaper roofing flap in the breeze while metal pipes covered in aprons of tarnish point fingers at the moon.

We pass a group huddled around fire in a rusty barbeque. In this landscape of despair, graffiti blooms like enchanted gardens, a mutiny of color against grime. Spray-painted portraits, geometric masterpieces, and quotes with drop shadows in a dozen hues line our tattered highway. Above it all, the Hollywood Sign stands guard over vandal and angel alike in this land of dreamers and dream smashers.

Which one am I now? I've mutilated my dream and in the strands of my self-destruction, smashed Zeli's future as well.

Rising unscathed, the blue neon rings of the Rampion Tower leer through a layer of fog. A newly rigged zip line yawns between the building beneath us and Singen Mot's rooftop. Santino and I take turns flying across the space.

Once we're on solid footing, I grab his arm. "Remember, in the moat, under the bridge to the main entrance are the handholds to the maintenance dock. From there, take the stairs to floor thirty-three. Her ready room is the last door before you hit the windows on the north side." I point to Santino's backpack. "Break the lock and any goon standing guard. Zeli will lead us out." I grab his sleeve. "If anything goes sour, I'll find a place to hide with Z. You ditch into the road box until we cook Plan C."

"We've got surprise on our side, J. Gothel won't expect us to come at him again this soon." He passes me handheld sheers more suited to prune roses than cut Z free from her locks. Through the mist, blue neon catches a slender figure leaning on the window casement of Z's darkened penthouse.

Ever cautious, Santino holds the phone to his ear. "Robbie, confirming Gothel's twenty?" He nods and hands me the phone. "Malibu."

We stand at the make or break moment in our plan. If Gothel has taken Zeli's phone away, we've got no way to connect. Plan B crashes and burns along with the last of my sanity.

I touch Zeli's contact on Santino's phone, fearing a repeat of the silence that's haunted me all night.

One ring and then an answer. I don't speak.

Her tentative whisper breaks the silence. "Santino?" At the sound of her voice, my bones turn runny like watercolors in the rain.

I breathe into the phone. "Rapunzel, Rapunzel, send me your hair."

Zeli recognizes my voice and gasps.

"Hang up, Z. Gothel could be listening."

"Justin, no." Her voice is atonal, hopeless. I can't stand the sound of it.

"Bring me over now, or I'll stand here until Gothel finds me. I will not leave you again."

It breaks my heart to hit *end*. I squint through gloom and wait for the familiar squeal of her extensions moving along the track.

Santino lays a hand on my shoulder. "What did she say?"

I can't bear to admit the loss of faith in Zeli's voice. She isn't sending her hair. All that's left is to dissolve.

Creak.

Beautiful music fills the night as Zeli's extensions unspool around the zip line. I come back to life.

The rig arrives, and Santino helps me in. He doesn't let go. "Let me call Robbie again to make sure."

I gently peel fingers off my sleeve. "We're good to go. This is what Gothel does. He messes Zeli up and leaves her alone."

I'm terrified of what I'll find across the plaza. How badly broken is she? Should she be in a hospital?

I wave Santino toward the stairs. "See you on the inside."

This time, it's me who turns my back on him as I settle into the harness. Reflections send wonky blue stripes across the glass of Zeli's place, distorting her silhouette. I want to sing to her. Instead, I wave my arms, praying she sees the signal to bring me over.

My answer is a tug. As I storm her dark castle, I reach above my head and grasp a strand of her sunshine hair from under a purple zebra stripe extension and press it to my lips.

"I'm coming, Rapunzel."

Under the shadow of a licorice disk, I swing to create a rhythm and launch my feet over the casement. The instant my high tops hit floor, every light in the penthouse snaps on.

"Welcome back, Justin Time's Up."

Standing next to the pink jewel encrusted pommel, with his paw slapped over Zeli's mouth, is Gothel.

I lunge. Mange grabs me in a headlock and pricks a needle into my neck. Immediately, my field of vision begins to iris down.

Draped over Gothel's arm, the sliced and fried end of Zeli's extensions dangles free. Z's real honey-colored hair sways just beneath her jaw. Her metal vest is gone. A white gauze bandage wraps around her throat. Below her right ear the bandage droops to reveal an angry scarlet welt. She tries to twist free.

"ZELI!"

Gothel tosses her aside and drives knuckles into my cheekbone.

She pulls herself up with the sword handle; leaning over it for a beat before spinning to face Mange, ready to fight. He plucks her off her feet and heaves her over a shoulder.

I'm screaming. She's screaming.

Gothel looms over me, a hand around my throat, tea breath flowing up my nostrils.

"It's over...Jumper."

The word scrapes my last hope away.

He knows who I am.

"Bravo. You kept me blinded by the dazzle of Justin Time's magnificent potential, but when I pulled the curtain aside, a rather different face appeared." He squeezes tighter. "Justin MacKenzie, B.A.S.E. jumping fool." Black dots splatter across my fading vision. "When I threw you out of my tower, you should have run."

PLAN J

THE ITCH ON THE SIDE OF MY NECK HAS A PULSE OF ITS OWN. IT echoes the hammer knocking inside my temples. I wrench my eyes open to face pewter-colored leather.

"ZELI!" I jolt up.

There's a tiger *chuff* in the vicinity of a huge flatscreen on the wall identical to the one in Zeli's penthouse.

Gothel's image laughs at me. "Don't expect a wake-up kiss from your lover." He waves the condom box I recognize from Zeli's night-stand drawer.

My insides hollow. I rise on wobbly legs and shake a fist. "Where is she?" If Gothel were in the room, I'd tear him into strips.

"The rat who comes to steal the cheese better get used to the trap." He flips a dismissive hand. "Listen carefully. You sing tonight."

My fingernails dig into the arm of the sofa. "I won't sing for you."

Gothel dismisses my threat. "Mange will drag your ass to the Summer Number One stage in an hour."

My voice is steel. "I will never sing for you again."

There's only one reason the fiend wants me back. Justin Time must be blasting his ratings to the stratosphere. I'll screw him by keeping my mouth shut.

Gothel's grin is the essence of vandal. "I suspected you might say that."

I swear his image darkens on the screen.

"You sing, Zeli smiles. You zip your lips, Zeli hurts."

My heart misses its next beat.

"What happens to her is wholly up to you." With a crackle, the connection cuts off.

I collapse against sofa cushions. "Zeli, what have I done?"

Above me, a tin ceiling stamped with a thousand stars stares down. With growing trepidation, I take in the layout of the space, stainless steel everything kitchen, furniture layout, bedroom placement. Out the window and across the plaza, a familiar chrome-topped skyscraper stands guard, Singen Mot's building.

This is Zeli's penthouse. That's how the bastard found the condoms.

The absent crystals in the ceiling are not the only change. Everything is silver, black, and white from the brushed steel wainscoting to the array of pillows on the sofa. Not a drop of pink.

I stumble into Zeli's kitchen. Splashing cold water on my face chases the lingering haze from whatever they stuck in my neck. A long strand of hair falls into the sink next to me.

My extensions are back.

If Mange is getting me in an hour, then the second night of the amateur vs. pro round of the Summer Number One is in full swing. I've been out the better part of a day.

A flurry of questions start blood flowing faster to my brain. How can I still be a contender after last night's disaster? What happened to Santino when he tried to blow the twilight room lock?

I rush to the double doors, now painted dove gray, and throw them open. As if anticipating my rebellion, the spiral stairs have been rolled across the room. I'm trapped in this penthouse, utterly useless.

I shout at the flatscreen and press every button on the remote. "GRANT GOTHEL!"

No response comes.

I fly into the bedroom and search for any tech to connect me with the outside. The new décor in here matches the colorless palette infecting the rest of the place. Zeli's bed is covered with a black fur comforter. The rocker has disappeared, replaced with a silver anti-gravity chair. The bathroom has black towels with J.T. monogrammed in silver thread.

Frantic to find any sign of Zeli, I shove open the closet to find ten identical Justin Time jumpsuits hanging above a row of black high tops. The bookshelf, now black lacquer instead of white, is empty except for a single Justin Time action figure clad in a black, nylon jumpsuit.

"Where's the chink in your armor, bastard?"

The answer blasts into my head.

The zip line! The very chink that first brought me to Zeli. I'll make a sling with the comforter and shimmy my way across the plaza.

I drag the cover to the window. The bejeweled sword handle, harness, and any other sign of the skyway is gone. The window is sealed shut.

I'm a specimen behind glass.

Tentacles of fear rise in my throat while outside, a searchlight sweeps the grape soda sky.

I smack the glass and holler at the stragglers on the plaza below. No one looks up.

My face burns with a toxic mix of rage and hopelessness. I have no choice but to sing for Gothel.

An idea catches. I'll do what Zeli did the night of "Stars and Fireflies" and leap into the crowd.

That flame sputters. Acting the wild jacklick will only hurt Zeli. *Buzz.*

I check the flatscreen. If it's the last thing I do, I'll make sure

Gothel and Mange spend eternity chipping ash off the devil's boots in hell.

Buzz.

It's not the flatscreen.

Buzz.

The noise is coming from the wall. I lay an ear against the new nailed up while I was unconscious silver wainscotting. The buzz gets louder for a beat then stops.

I run a finger along the top of the silver façade and find a small hole near the place Zeli's sword used to be. Zipping into the kitchen, I grab a knife and use it to pry the top of the wainscotting away from the hole.

Peeking in, I see a weak yellow flare like a dying flashlight. A flicker of light goes off when the buzz starts up again. It's a cell phone.

When Gothel's crew flipped this penthouse at turbo speed, some dolt left their phone behind the new wall.

That phone is my way out. I race back into the kitchen and find a pair of tongs.

"Breathe, MacKenzie. Be a magician. Pull this rabbit out of the hat."

I thread the tongs into the thin opening. When I make contact, the cell buzz sends a vibration up my arm. Inch by inch, I ease the phone up. As I work it closer, its light illuminates a row of pink jewels on the side of the case.

This doesn't belong to one of Gothel's flip crew, it's Zeli's. The dull ache of Gothel's knuckles against my cheekbone brings it all back. While Mange and Gothel focused on me, my brilliant love slipped her phone into the slit where the sword handle used to be.

Only Zeli knows the phone is here. The buzzes grow fainter as the battery trudges toward electronic death.

Closing my eyes, I rely solely on feel and ease Zeli's phone from the wall.

"I freaking love you, Zeli."

The screen has a long crack running high to low. Worse than that, the battery life shows red. I make out the latest text on the homescreen.

J at full dark, open the window or stay away.

Caller ID only says *S.* It's got to be Santino. I frantically poke the screen to call back. The cell takes its final breath.

How much did Santino see from across the plaza? What does he mean by full dark? I rush the window.

Open the window or stay away.

"I can't open the window, Santino."

Stay away.

I hate ominous sans details. All hope is in Santino's hands. My throat aches as if sandpaper rubbed my vocal cords. I must be ready to sing for the devil. It's my only power left to protect Zeli.

"Just in time–"

My pitch is clean, but the words are flat and lifeless. I need Rapunzel's voice wrapping around mine to bring the spark back.

I rip one of the jumpsuits off its hanger and climb in. It's killing me to prep for Gothel's dog and pony show.

Full dark. What happens at full dark?

If I sing, will Zeli be safe? I shake my head. Gothel's word means nothing.

Chatter erupts from the flatscreen as Gothel controls what I see the way he did with Zeli. Reporters surround a man and a woman who cling to one another. "We didn't want our daughter to come home to us this way," says the lady through tears.

The man tightens a protective arm around her shoulder. "Please pray that our Zeli will wake up and sing again for all of you out there who love her as much as we do."

My muscles clench. Our daughter? Who are these clowns? Zeli's folks are dead.

The woman's cheekbones, dimples, and the gentle sweep of her jaw freakishly mimics Zeli's. The man has a head full of blond curls the same color as Zeli's real golden hair.

The twisted fiend sends me a warning.

Gothel fills the screen, sweeping his arms to a sea of microphones. "Zeli is receiving the finest medical care possible. It's a tragedy that during her first duet with Justin Time, criminals impersonating Rampion security attacked our pair of stars."

Un-fucking-believable.

"All you fans in Zeliland, blast her tunes and let the heavens hear your plea for our dear one to come back to us."

Bile surges in my throat. Gothel is using Zeli's absence to boost Tuneful sales of her songs. What has he done to her? His soul isn't charred and rotten. He doesn't have one.

"Tonight, when Justin Time sings his heart out to her in the Summer Number One, I want you all to close your eyes and imagine the day when he and Zeli will make sweet music together."

I will kill Grant Gothel and force-feed pieces of his carcass to Mange.

Zeli and I are two fireflies in a jar without holes in the lid. I lay both palms against the picture window, willing fresh night air to diffuse through the glass into my body. The lights of Hollywood blend into a halo above the city. Two dark spots fall through that amber band. Suddenly black wings like a great raven burst from the spots. I realize what they are.

Parachute canopies.

The figures split, gaining speed as they glide straight toward my window. I've seen them before, on the night my old life disappeared.

They're Singen Mot's jumpers.

When they are less than a hundred meters above me, the searchlight catches them for an instant. Tucked under the arm of a man who can only be Singen Mot is a gun, a nasty big beast.

Open the window or stay away.

I dive across the room to the shelter of a black leather armchair as the window explodes behind me. A storm of glass fragments surges in, breaking around my fortress to lodge sparkling chips into the wall.

There's a *whump* in the center of the room. On the floor just inside the window is a parachute pack.

"Santino, you mad genius."

I spring to my feet, shaking a layer of glass dust from my hair and grab the pack. Out the window, dark angels in wingsuits zip away from the tower to disappear between skyscrapers.

Behind the double doors, the scrape of the spiral stairs goes off like an alarm. I climb into the jump gear like I've done hundreds of times.

Still tugging the rig into place, I lean out the window. I can't check the wind. My altitude sucks. I'm below the limit for even the latest low altitude automatic activation device to trigger.

That means I've got one shot to pull this off, one chute.

The stairs bump into place. I back up to the farthest point from the window for distance. If I eat pavement, what will happen to Zeli? If I don't sing, what will Gothel do to her?

I have to trust Santino. I do trust Santino. He showed up for me. For once, Justin MacKenzie isn't left standing alone while no one looks back.

The double doors creak open.

Crossing the room at a dead run, I leap through the shattered remains of the window into the sky.

I sink like a stone. Instinct takes over, and the pilot chute is on its way. I clench my jaw, praying I've cleared the tower disks. The most beautiful sight in Hollywood blossoms overhead, my chute canopy is a sonnet of obsidian nylon.

Behind me, the roar of Gothel's lions fills the night as my shaking fingers grasp toggles.

The wind jerks me up. In the shadows at the edge of the plaza, the dot of a red laser pointer draws circles on the cement. I shift into jumper mode and site my landing. Another wicked gust throws me backward, away from my target. I work toggles and brakes to force control. The wind bests me, drawing the chute near a tower overhang. I maneuver my feet and kick off the disk, praying the canopy stays free.

A window yawns open. Mange's ugly face appears as he shoves a pole with a wicked hook on the end. It grazes my leg. Inertia is on my side, and he doesn't catch me. The canopy is not as lucky. As I sail away from the tower, a sickening rip of nylon screeches above me.

Falling. Falling. Down from the moon...

I struggle to work the flapping mess that's left of my chute as my altitude goes to hell. The best I can do is aim for the moat. Water beats cement any day.

I barely make out the outline of palm fronds before their spiked points bury themselves in my eyes. White-hot pain bursts through my head. I scream.

More fronds gouge the skin of my neck but slow my fall. I smack into a trunk and blindly throw arms and legs around it. Skidding down ragged bark shreds my suit, then the skin of my chest. I drop like an elephant out of an airplane. Pulpy fangs bite deep into my palms. I throw everything into my death grip on the trunk. Still, I fall, a bleeding, blind mass.

Oh, Zeli, I am fortune's fool. You'll search and find me dead.

The hissing moat fills my ears a split second before water slams into my back. Cold water and chlorine sizzle into shredded flesh. It's nothing compared to the agony in my eyes.

I can't see. I can't breathe. Am I above or below the water?

How long does it take to die?

My head fills with stars like night over the desert. Is this the peace at the end?

A strangling grip on my throat makes me sputter and swallow water. I cry out as my back grates against something unfriendly. Strong arms pull me in.

"I've got you, Justin." Santino's voice is my light. The damn light is not gentle or even a light. It's blackish-gray canvas.

Voices bellow from behind as we run. Every movement sends another burning poker of pain through me. We're Gothel's bloody prey. He'll catch us and eat us raw. Visions of hands blazing with light and emerald-green demon eyes swirl through the pain.

Santino shouts. "Get on."

I manage to eke out three words. "I can't see."

He dumps me onto a seat. The deafening growl of a motorcycle cuts off further conversation. He threads my arms around a slight and thankfully warm body.

"Hold on to Liliana."

"Zeli," I holler. I'm pouring all my energy into not keeling over. I want the stars back, the silence of the sky, and the absence of this bone-snapping pain.

Instead of the relief I crave, we fly. Wind drives nails into my eyes. I press my head into Leeni's back to keep from falling.

She wraps an arm around me as I list to one side. "Hold on," she screams.

Leeni kills the bike and pulls me off the seat. My muscle tone has gone fishing. I slip through her arms and taste pavement.

"Snapper," she screams. Running feet approach.

And then it's truly full dark.

34

THE DARK BEFORE THE DARK

V OICES BREAK THROUGH BLACKNESS FIRST. N EURON-SPLITTING PAIN knifes inside my head. Invisible motion thrusts me forward, and a restraint presses across my tender chest. Both knees jamb into a soft wall in front of me. I grab for my eyes and let loose a death scream.

"Trying to drive here," comes Robbie's voice in front of me.

Santino catches my wrists. "Don't touch your face, Justin."

I strain against him, cursing. I've fallen off a cliff wearing only confusion and pain.

"Tino, calm him down. He's in bad enough shape."

I flail arms in the darkness. "Where are we? Where's Zeli?"

After a beat, Robo Robbie's anguished voice floats back. "I royally screwed up Gothel's GPS trace." He takes in a stuttering breath. "It's my fault you're–"

Santino cuts him off. "We're in Robbie's car, taking you to a hospital."

I spin through a black maw.

Robbie's strained cry doesn't help my anxiety. "New coordinates from the drone."

I find Santino's shirt and grab. "Drone?" The darkness both

literally and figuratively makes me feel like I'm trapped at the bottom of a well.

Santino's voice is close. "Here's the short version. Last night, before you took the zip line over to Zeli–" His voice falters on her name. "Robbie tracked the GPS of Gothel's car instead of his cell."

I wilt against the seat. We weren't even close to saving Z.

"He sorted out the signals and traced Gothel back to the tower. We hacked into the garage security feed and saw Gothel stash Zeli in an SUV. They headed out of L.A. We lost signal about two hours later in the Mojave Desert."

Unspeakable images of Gothel alone in a desert with Zeli flash through my mind.

Santino pats my shoulder. "We're following Robbie's drone as it retraces the route. After we get you to a hospital, we'll follow it to where the signal stopped and go from there."

My entire body pounds, stings, or burns. "Go from there?"

"We make a plan," says Robbie. "There's always a plan."

I trail a finger across my ribs and to my face. Thick padding winds around my head. Matching layers cover my chest. I'm wrapped up like a package.

Every bump in the road is a punch to my face. "My eyes?"

Santino infuses calm into his tone to talk me off the ledge. "Snapper did the best he could, but J, your eyes are shredded." He curses under his breath. "We couldn't take you to a hospital in L.A.. Robbie's hack showed that Gothel's got every ER in the county waiting for you to show."

I wrap arms around my knees and wince at the jolts of pain every movement sets off. Gothel will never call off the hunt.

"Snapper called in a favor from his bud at a hospital north of L.A. near where we lost Gothel's signal. BTW, you need a name change so you don't blip on Gothel's radar. You are now Mackie Diggs, Rand's nephew."

I take a breath and try to assemble fragments into a big picture. "What do you mean, Snapper did the best he could?"

His silence is too long. I hear strain in his breathing.

It's Robbie who has the cojones to answer. "Snapper said he's never seen anything like the way those palms blew your eyes out. You hemorrhaged something wicked. He patched you up and loaded you with antibiotics. His freak out is over infection, not saving your sight."

This gloom is permanent? I'll never see the twinkle of stars or Zeli's eyes again?

How can I fight a freaking fate that hides behind every curve to screw me? It's stolen my family, my sight, and my music dream. It will not steal Zeli from me.

My voice is so quiet I barely hear it. "Ditch the hospital, trace the signal, and find Zeli first."

Santino sounds beyond miserable. "Absolutely not."

I reach inside past the murk and pain to focus on the single point of light in my heart. "She's the priority, not me."

"I told you he wouldn't play nice," says Robbie. His tone darkens as an alarm pings in front of me. "Grab my laptop, Tino. Something's coming in on the link to Justin's cell. Shit, it's Gothel."

"Let me talk to the bastard," I bark.

Santino grabs my upper arm. "Fizz down, Justin. Let it go to voicemail."

I force myself to chill until the playback of Gothel's venom fills the car.

"*Your little game is over, Mr. Time. As long as our contract remains broken, Zeli will scream. I have the means to make her cries grow louder as each hour of your disobedience passes.*"

In the background, Zeli wails. My heart tears down the middle.

The car screeches to a stop. My head snaps back against the seat. Pain upgrades to torture. The only visions in my brain are horrors Zeli could be facing.

"This is the hospital turnoff. Let me call the drone back until we get J checked in," says Robbie.

I holler loud enough to rattle glass. "Keep going." My jacked-up eyes burn. "Follow the drone to where you lost the signal."

Tension in the car tastes like rust at the back of my throat. A rapid-fire series of slaps against glass erupts off to my right. Heat rolls off Santino. I know he's beating himself up whether to save Zeli or me.

Unexpected calm travels through my body. After Gothel's threat, there's only one choice. I find Santino's arm and squeeze. "This is my call." He moans when I say, "Robbie, get me to Zeli."

In the silence, I imagine Robbie looking to Santino for the final word. A voice crackles through what must be a walkie talkie.

"What's the next move, Robbie?" asks a husky voice.

The car pitches back onto the road and speeds up. "We're sticking with the drone, Rand."

Santino lets out a sharp whistle. "Stop, Robbie." The strain in his voice could bend steel. "Nav says we're about to hit military. The Air Force base?"

I hear keys tapping.

"How do I call the drone back before they shoot it out of the sky?"

Robbie doesn't stop. "Can't be the base. We're too far east."

I bite into my thumb callous until I taste blood. Not being able to see sucks more by the second. "What's happening?"

Santino tries to explain. "On the drone's camera feed, I see a complex of buildings along the west boundary of a huge perimeter."

I reach in Santino direction but grab air. His body brushes mine as I assume he leans over the front seat.

"What are those dark lines, Robbie?" asks Santino.

"Agriculture? Crops?" Robbie groans. "Screw that. The fuckers on the left are guard towers."

The car fishtails and the horror show in my head amps up. I grope for Santino. "Zeli said she grew up on a kid singer training camp, Rampion Ranch. Could that be what you see? Maybe he took her there." She never mentioned crops.

I shiver as agitation superheats my body. What's going on in a place with guard towers? If Zeli is there–

"Turn back," says Santino. "We gotta regroup."

I trail a finger across the bandages covering my face. "We don't have time to regroup. You heard Gothel's threat."

Robbie slows. The car bumps onto what I guess is the shoulder. "Let me have the laptop," he says. Keys click like a thousand dog toenails crossing a tile floor. "I'm sending the drone closer. Come on, Gothel, show me a back door."

Santino pipes up and a walkie talkie crackles. "Rand. We've pulled over. Snug up behind us."

Moments later, a roar like jet engines surrounds the car. Santino shouts in my ear. "Rand's leading the cavalry, fifty bikers. As soon as Robbie finds Zeli, we charge in to spring her."

Robbie pants. Fear laces his words. "Tell him about the towers."

I sink into the symphony of revving engines around us, a sweet song of hope. I can't wrap my battered head around the truth that Santino's legions are still on my side, Zeli's side. If I have to trade in my sight for something, I choose this music of family, of belonging.

"What time is it," I yell over the noise of the bikes.

"Almost four," says Robbie. "Middle of the night four."

I find the seat back and pull up to get closer to Robbie. "Gothel won't be expecting us. We have fifty bikers. Let's crash the main gate and get Zeli."

"I see a sign on the drone's camera," says Santino. "Rampion Ranch."

"That's no ranch," says Robbie. "It looks like a flipping prison."

Fear plays a harsh note in Santino's voice. "Robbie how close are we?"

Keys tap again. "Too close."

I sense frantic energy radiating off Robbie. He starts shouting. "Shit! They hacked the drone feed."

The metallic screech that fills the car drives daggers into the nerves of my teeth.

"They took out the drone," cries Robbie.

"Headlights, coming this way," says Santino. "A shit-ton of them." He shrieks, "Rand, abort!"

The car spins. Firecrackers burst across my canvas of runny black ink. Revs and skids scream through the air. We're on the move.

"Can we outrun them?" hollers Santino.

"I'm flooring it," yells Robbie.

Santino growls. "They can't get Justin again. Will they catch us?"

Robbie continues to bellow. "Scramble your people, Rand. Cover us."

Santino outbellows him. "Are. They. Going. To. Catch. Us?"

"I don't know."

Santino's voice is iron as he commands, "Pull over."

Robbie's voice rises three octaves. "You're insane."

Santino is uber-calm. "Do it. Justin, this is going to hurt. Get ready to fly." The pressure from the shoulder strap disappears.

Robbie is full on begging. "No, Tino."

"If they catch Justin, it's over for both Zeli and him. Ditching and hiding is our best option. Trace my cell after you lose them and come back to get us."

I swear the car tilts onto two wheels. A hand pulls me off the seat. I'm airborne with no chute. Grit punishes the part of my face not wrapped in bandages as the car peels away. Santino's hand muffles my scream while he breathes into my ear. "Bite down and shut up. We've gotta run." His arm welds to my back as he drags me along. "Drop."

We lay there breathing in sand, or a pile of bleached bones for all I can tell. I clamp my teeth to keep from crying out as thunder cracks above.

Santino's mouth is on my ear. "Helicopters."

Every noise is gargantuan and adds to the mounting pain

coursing through my head. I can't draw a clear mental image between screeching tires, helicopters, and Santino's ragged breath. Sound without pictures fragment my brain.

"Up." Santino hoists me to my feet, and we run again.

I trip up onto a solid surface. We speak the language of gasps and wheezes. My eyes burn like the pits of hell.

I'll be left behind if I don't have the strength to carry on. I must push through this painscape. I unleash a series of sneezes that split my head. "Smoke?"

"We ducked into a massive stone fireplace on a scorched foundation. Hopefully out of sight."

On cue, gritty wind peppers our faces as Gothel's Air Force circles. New layers of pain rip through my head with every pass. I fight to keep the dark curtain of agony from suffocating me. The roar waxes and wanes for an eternity until finally, it's silent.

Santino leaves my side. His voice comes from a short distance away. "Looks like the choppers gave up."

My heart sinks. Are Robbie and the rest of our rescue squad in Gothel's grip?

Santino's curse disturbs something that skitters over my foot.

"No reception."

I try to stand. The world spins, and I fall, crying out with every new jab of torment.

Santino is next to me in an instant. "I'm going to worm my way back to those fields, and look for a way in." He sucks a ragged breath. "You can't help, stay put."

I'm not going to sit here while he puts his head in the lion's mouth. "If you go without me, I'll follow."

"You are a colossal pain in my ass." Santino slings an arm around my waist. We push through skin-stripping wind that presses the bandages against my eyes like thorny fingers. I yelp.

"Shhh," he hisses. "There are tons of lettuce rows are about fifty feet ahead. Buildings and towers to our left." He grumbles. "We'll never make it across those fields without being spotted."

A familiar scent tickles the edge of my senses. I take a huge sniff. It's there, faint but clear, the aroma of Rampion tea.

"It's not lettuce. That's rampion. This is where Gothel grows the weeds for his vandal tea."

"Vandal tea?"

Fingers flutter to my throat at the memory of drinking his filthy brew. "He insists his singers drink Rampion tea. It squeezes vocal cords to produce his signature sound."

"With tea?"

"The fumes mess with your brain. You can't think straight. Zeli, Gigabyte, Da Da Da Deacon, all the Rampion Record pros–listen to them, their voices reek with variations of the same basic tone."

His voice rumbles. "One that sells a zillion Tuneful downloads." He lets out a low whistle. "Guaranteed formula for success."

"The tea hooks you to Gothel until it ruins your voice." My mind flashes through Rampion's stable of stars. They fly high, launched from Gothel's slingshot, and then burn out early. Former phenoms like Mistress Mango are paraded out at special events. Their performances are never live. The fiend is growing the next string of Rampion stars out here on his ranch. Will they cry magic tears?

"The night we lost her, you heard Zeli's natural voice, not Gothel's packaging."

Santino hums a low note. "She did sound different. Classic."

"Whatever this place is..." I fling my arm toward a strange buzz filling the air. "It's toxic. We've got to bring down Gothel's entire soul-sucking agenda."

A coyote yips nearby.

"It's dawn, J. We lost our edge."

"We can't bail."

I practically hear his gears turn. "We're not. We'll find a way to bust in through the fields tonight. The rampion out this far is wilted. Pray that means this section is off the radar."

His words act as a jinx. Motors hum in the distance, growing louder.

Santino breathes into my ear. "Eight-seater golf carts dropped off about twenty kids. They're walking up and down the rows of rampion."

A single voice breaks the stillness with a song. More join in until a chorus rises to wake the sleeping Earth. They share the melody for several repetitions, and then break into harmonies. Rampion laced air wafts over us.

"Unreal," breathes Santino. "Kids are swaying back and forth between the rows of rampion singing in a freaky trance."

A freaky tea-laced trance. "Do you see Zeli?"

He answers like he's the one in a trance. "The wilted plants are growing."

My heart flutters with every note. Z has to be here. I strain to hear the rich beauty of my love's voice. "Zeli?"

"Not here. The kids are moving farther up the rows. It's wild. Everywhere they sing the plants get bigger."

The tune fades. Swallowing hard, I taste blood and begin to collapse.

Santino's hand catches the side of my face before I hit dirt. "You're burning up."

I use him to stay as upright as I can. "Swear that no matter what happens to me, you'll save her."

He doesn't answer. Short-clipped sniffs tell me he's crying, this brother that's walked into my life.

He clamps his arms around me. "Damn you, Justin. I swear." Suddenly his body goes rigid. "The kids are leaving. Half a dozen small golf carts coming our way."

The putter of engines stops so close, it's hard to believe they haven't seen us. "Any goons or guns?"

"No, adults are harvesting the amped-up rampion into baskets."

"Ask them about Zeli." I'm too loud.

"Get down. There's not one friendly face in the bunch. A tall dude is waving us off."

"Take me to them." I stumble toward the smell of rampion.

Santino leads us toward a brain-squeezing buzz. Suddenly, vibrations make all the hair on my arms stand. The buzz isn't in my head. It's in front of me.

"Stop!" I crook my leg around his and send us both to the ground. The pain nearly chokes me.

"Don't come any closer," calls a deep voice that swirls through my memory. It's familiar.

"Just a quick Q & A, man," says Santino. "We're looking for a friend." He guides us forward.

"Freeze. Can't you see the damn fence? Two more steps and you fry."

Santino pulls up short as I gather a handful of his shirt. "Fence?"

He tenses. "Shit, it's a super thin silver wire fence. Barely visible."

Super thin silver wire, like the vest strapping Zeli's extensions to her head. "I hear it."

A woman's cry cuts through the buzz. "Listen to Deke. You'll get zapped."

Deke? Deacon! As in Da Da Da Deacon the Rampion Records mega-star. I know it's him. I've downloaded everything he ever sang.

"Santino, describe the guy warning us."

"Late sixties, two gray braids, freakishly tall with a scar from the outside corner of his left eye to chin." Santino's squeeze leaves an imprint of pain across my tender ribs as the realization hits him. "My God."

"Hey," I yell. "Da Da Da Deacon."

"Split," he calls out without a hint of acknowledgement.

"It is definitely him," Santino whispers.

I shout over the buzz. "Is Zeli here?"

Deacon sputters. "Figures Zeli fanboys would be the ones to sniff us out."

"I'm Justin Time from the Summer Number One."

"Justin Time!" roars Deacon as fiercely as a lion about to rip into a zebra.

I have to talk him down before he pounces. "I know what Gothel's done to you. He shredded your voices with the Rampion tea and trapped you all on this ranch. Zeli's here, isn't she?"

Santino groans.

Above the pissed off murmur across the boundary, a woman calls out. "You're Zeli's Justin Time?"

"If you are, I'll snap your neck," growls Deacon. "You screwed up her life."

The same woman chimes in. "You have to run. The tower will call out their guards."

Her voice stretches the *ah* in call, sustaining a note. A sound I've heard a thousand times. "Mistress Mango?"

There's a gasp from the field followed by Santino's scream in my ear. "She's walking toward us. There are faded mango tats on her face."

I stretch my arms to them. "I know music. I know you and Da Da Da Deacon. You're both Rampion stars. I've studied all Gothel's talent because I wanted to be one of you."

Deacon's voice, closer now, shifts to red alert. "Justin Time, you need to cease to exist before Gothel grabs you."

The whirr of a cart motor punctuates the end of his sentence. Santino grips my arm. "Mistress Mango grabbed a cart and left. She's whistle blowing."

"Fly, bird. Save your ass and your soul," says Deacon. "Once you're on this side of the fence, you're done."

Currents of ice infuse my blood. "Tell Zeli I've come for her."

"You're too late," says Deacon. "I won't let you shred her into smaller pieces than you already have." He spits out the words. "The gate to Rampion Ranch swings one way. Now go. Any one of us would kill to be on your side of this fence, and you stand there like a jacklick."

Santino pulls me away. My Zeli is close. I can't leave. If there is even a single drop of magic in the universe, I have to tap into it. Using my last energy reserve, I belt our song.

"Just in time. Our stars crossed just in time, to blaze a path across– "

Panic colors Santino's voice. "Shut it. We've got to get out of here." He drags me away from the electrified fence.

I sing like it's my last day on Earth, which it may very well be if we're caught.

"The moon drenched sky. My heart wept–"

"Son of a nightmare," says Da Da Da Deacon as the putter of a golf cart grows louder.

Like an echo from Heaven, Zeli's voice bobs on the morning air. "Destiny–"

Beams burst from my heart, lighting the way to my love.

Deacon's voice rises above the sizzle of the fence. "Mango, what have you done?"

35

WHEELS

Santino aims me toward my angel's voice.

"Zeli," I cry.

A wave of electric burn singes my nostrils. Santino grips me hard enough to cut off circulation. "Zeli's running toward us. The fence sparked when she kicked pebbles into it."

"Let me go, Deke." Zeli's voice is near enough to touch. It sets my nerve endings ablaze.

I reach my arms to her. "Are you okay?" My head whips toward Santino. "Is she hurt?"

Her strangled cry carries across the barrier. "Justin, your eyes? Is that blood?"

Santino whispers. "I'm not gonna lie. She's got wicked red patches and bruises on her face. There's a big ass bandage around her neck."

Gothel's a dead man. "Zeli, I'm sorry I failed you." I flap my hand until it smacks Santino. "Get her out. Now."

Deacon's voice is grave. "Everyone stop! No one is getting out. A life sentence to this ranch is part of the deal when you sign Gothel's contract."

I shake my head but stop when my eye sockets screech in protest. "My contract didn't say a word about Rampion Ranch."

Mistress Mango growls. "Haven't you figured it out? Gothel's got power we can't touch."

"Don't, Mango," growls Deke. "You'll get us all killed."

She isn't deterred. "I guarantee the contract you signed is not the one that exists now. Anyone who tries to break a Gothel contract..." She doesn't finish.

"He goes after people you love," says Deacon with enough acid to wilt rampion. "We sing to his damn weeds, or our families pay the price."

Mango finds her voice. "It's all perfect when you're at the top of his pyramid, love, fame, future, but once the tea blows your voice out, your stage goes dark."

"He's got my grandkids here in his Opus 'training program'," huffs Deacon. "Mango's kids too. Tricked them onto the Ranch once we signed with him."

I stretch my arms toward the sound of their voices. "Zeli, a couple on TV said they were your parents? Did you see them?"

"He makes sure we see all his propaganda," says Deacon. "That's how we know you, Justin Time. You're the echo of our pasts shoved in our faces."

Bitterness crisps the edges of Zeli's words. "Those *parents* were Gothel puppets."

"How can he do this to you, Z? He calls you his angel."

There's a chorus of vinegary laughter. "We were all Gothel's angels once," says Mistress Mango. "Until your wings get buried in the dirt with the rampion."

Zeli sounds frantic. "You have to go, Justin."

"Not without you, Rapunzel." Santino tries to draw me away. I strain against him. I refuse to fail her again.

Deacon is livid. "You shitiots are on borrowed time. Get the hell out of here."

"He's right." All Santino's efforts at gentleness are gone as he yanks me away. "There's nothing we can do right now."

"Attention all personnel." A booming voice from what must be speakers above the fields warbles slightly as it bleeds through the electrified fence.

Deacon's voice is tens shades of pissed. "Dammit, Mango. They must have seen you snatch Zeli."

"Evacuate the fields. We are on immediate lockdown."

Curses from Mango and Deacon slice through the barrier.

"Trespassers, remain where you are."

Panic laces Santino's words. "Vans are coming our way along the perimeter outside the fence."

My heart calcifies. Again, Zeli will take the fall for my screw up.

A familiar voice from the speakers coats the fields with its malevolent purr. "Justin Time. Our stars crossed, Justin Time." Grant Gothel drones his mockery of the lyrics.

Zeli's voice is frayed. "RUN, JUSTIN!"

I stumble toward her, only to pull up when vibrations from the fence grow thick in the air.

"Get her, Santino. Gothel will kill her for this."

Beneath us the ground begins to tremble. A snarl rolls across the desert, drowning out the high-frequency buzz of the fence.

Santino yells. "The boulevard! Rand! Those fabulous fools are off-roading across the desert to cut off the vans."

The soaring decibels from motorcycles make it impossible to follow the threads of screaming voices. Fear drives spikes though my chest. A crack to rival lightning explodes in front of me. The surge of prickly electric heat drives me backward. Charred odor permeates the air.

Deacon is in full rage. "Are you mad, boy? Stop throwing crap at the fence. You'll kill us all."

"I think I can short it out," says Santino. "Stand back."

CRASH!

Scalding winds rips across my face.

"Santino, stop!" There's terror in Zeli's voice.

"That almost did it," Santino yells. "I'm bringing the bastard down. When it blows, everyone run like hell for the bikes."

Licks of energy burst in the air around me. Santino must have seriously screwed up the fence. He grunts like he's bench-pressing a rhino.

Zeli shrieks like the sky is falling, and then it does. A pure animal scream tears out of Santino. A million pinpricks of fire cover my body as the pungent snap of chemical burn saturates the air.

Deacon's voice rises above the chaos. "Fence down."

I send my voice in a thousand directions, hoping they find a target. "Santino! Zeli!"

The smell of burning rampion fills my nostrils. Slender fingers wrap around my upper arm, dragging me through an incoherent melee of ear-splitting pops, screams, and engines.

In the midst of the tumult, hummingbird wings graze my ear. "Come with me, Justin."

It's my Zeli.

Dust coats my windpipe as we stumble toward the monstrous rev of engines. I clutch her to me. Gothel will never rip her from my arms. A wave of sand and rocks crash over us. We fall to our knees. I cradle her head against my chest. My lips move through her hair.

"Zeli."

She kisses the underside of my jaw. "I'm here."

And then she isn't.

A pride of growling beasts surrounds us. A hunk of muscle plucks me up and drops me onto a seat. My calf burns through the jumpsuit as my leg brushes too close to an engine.

A body slides in front of me. A voice shouts in my ear. "It's Snapper." A tight band wraps around my waist, binding me against him. "Hold on. Rand has Zeli."

Beneath us, the bike rears like a stallion. The wail of motorcycle music carries me away from rampion-scented wind.

I'm free.

Zeli's free.

But what about Da Da Da Deacon, Mistress Mango, and their families? My heart hardens to stone, remembering those kids singing to the rampion who will sing for Gothel until he destroys them.

We aren't finished. Gothel must go down.

36

METHINKS, I SEE THEE NOW

DOWNY FEATHERS DUST MY CHEEKBONE. A BIRD CHIRPS MY NAME softly. I'm loath to move and disturb its song. I imagine wings, sun-sizzling yellow in a sky as blue as Zeli's eyes. Beneath my lids, there is no sun, no bird, only gray pain until someone blasts a blowtorch into my right eye.

"Holy fuck," I yell and attempt to shove my assailant away.

"Justin, it's me," says the voice from my dreams.

My Adam's apple trembles beneath a kiss. Lips trace a path along my jaw until they reach the corner of my mouth. In darkness, my fingertips find delicate shoulders and hair as silky as a feather.

Oh, it is my love.

Zeli and I fall into kisses that ache with desperation. I steal blessings from her lips.

Snapper ends the scene. "Did your tears work?"

Zeli's hands cup my jaw. "Justin, I'm going to lift the bandages. Tell me if you can see anything."

The tension in Snapper's voice does nothing for my own anxiety. "Easy! He's breakable."

Gentle fingers brush my cheek as bandages ease away.

"Anything?" asks Snapper.

I move my head, searching for any light in my darkness. "No."

Beside me, Zeli trembles. Her voice breaks with weeping. "Let me try again."

"Try what?" I ask a beat before soggy pressure against my eye explodes into pain. I scream and jerk my head away.

"No more, Zeli," says Snapper in a soothing voice.

"I'm so sorry, Justin," says Zeli. "I've been dabbing your eyes with my tears." Her voice breaks. "I don't understand why they fail me now."

I reach out to pull her into my arms. "I love you for trying. Maybe some broken things aren't meant to be fixed." I attempt to sound philosophical when all I want to do is roll into a ball and give into the pain. That would only add to Zeli's feeling of failure. I won't do that.

Robbie's voice rains from above. "I brought water."

The rim of a bottle settles against my mouth. Cool water bathes my throat. "Where are we?"

"Parking garage under the Rampion Tower," says Robbie.

I sputter. "Have you lost your minds?"

"Relax, we're in a security cam blind spot," says Robbie. "The last place Gothel will look for us is right under his nose."

Zeli's palm rests on the side of my neck. "We're taking Gothel down tonight."

I cover her hand with mine. "Don't go near him. Please."

"Justin, we'll never be free until Gothel is stopped."

She's always been right. We'll be running our whole lives.

"Z, what time is it? What day is it?"

She strokes my hair. "You've been out all day since Rand's people rescued us at dawn. It's evening now, the last night of the Summer Number One."

The night that was supposed to change my life.

I lean against the hard wall at my back. "Did anyone else get away? Deacon? Mistress Mango?"

Zeli rubs my arm. "No."

LESLIE O'SULLIVAN

"Total horror show," says Robbie. "Gothel wanted everyone arrested for trespassing. The cops refused since no one crossed his property line. Folks on the ranch side bolted to the buildings when the fence flamed out."

My fingers search Zeli's face. "How badly are you hurt? Did you heal yourself with tears?"

She dots my temple with a kiss. "People need to see what Gothel did to me."

My heart crumbles. No one else slipped from Gothel's trap.

"Zeli." I start to tremble. "Tell me you're real."

"I am, my love."

My love. My heart. My life.

A horrible thought grabs me. "Where's Santino?"

Off to my right, Leeni busts out in sobs. I whirl toward her, heart racing. Dread punctures my body like a robe of barbed wire. My thumb traces Zeli's cheekbone to find it wet with tears. I croak a single word, "No."

Sorrow stains the edges of Rand's voice as he sits next to me. "The boulder Tino used to short out the fence was mammoth. Momentum pulled him straight into the explosion."

The memory of Santino's final scream careens through my soul. I bury my face into Zeli's shoulder.

"We couldn't get to him through the smoke and Gothel's people. It was too late anyway," says Rand.

Santino, the brother I never knew I needed can't be gone. A moan rumbles through my chest. Gentle kisses teach me how to breathe again.

Rand's voice is glacial. "We gut Gothel tonight."

My voice quavers and then finds strength. "Not just Gothel. We have to destroy everything he controls. Santino saw kids at Rampion Ranch."

Santino.

If I try to process his loss right now, I'll be useless. These people are counting on me. I've got to hold it together and be grateful for the miracle in my arms.

Z speaks low into my ear. "I was one of the babies Gothel tricked away from their parents."

I slide my hands around her waist.

"My whole life I believed his twisted truth." She releases an acid laugh. "Poor Grant Gothel, an orphan just like us, vowed it was his duty to nurture our talent." Her hands fist against my chest. "Talent to serve his cancerous truth." She shudders. "On the way to the ranch, he taunted me with his *real* sick story."

My palm rests over her fluttering heart. "Tell me, love."

She quivers in my arms. "There's a database he calls Gothel's Opus. It's an index of pregnant women with musical gifts. Some are singers. My mother was a violinist." Her fists press harder into my skin. "Gothel targets those families, poisons the fathers, and befriends grieving mothers with offers of contracts and music careers. He tricks them into becoming rampion addicts. When the babies are born, he steals us to raise on the ranch. We're nothing but a crop to him, like the rampion. Even my name, Rapunzel, is just another word for rampion. My mother consumed rampion salads almost to the exclusion of anything else while she carried me. Gothel believes that's why my tears not only have their own power, but also boost his."

Hate fills the hollow space sliced open by Santino's death. "Your mother?"

"Died when I was born." Her voice is barely a whisper. "They all do. Gothel leaves no strings. Mango says even now, he force-feeds expectant mothers massive amounts of rampion to try and duplicate–"

My hand finds hers. "Your gift."

"My curse."

I run fingers through the silky hair that ends at the top of her shoulders. Even though my eyes are broken, I know its color.

Zeli gold.

"You said *boost* his power."

"He uses the heat in his hands to–" Her voice catches. "Discipline us. Mango says singers that lived on the ranch years before she got there spoke of his punishments with those horrible hands." Z is barely loud enough to hear. "I'm afraid his power was weakening when I came along. My tears brought it back." She squeezes my fingers to the point of pain. "It's as if I hurt people through him."

"You can't think like that. He's an evil bastard who takes whatever he wants." I continue to stroke her hair. "Why didn't any of those once upon a time Rampion stars on the ranch get the kids out of there?"

"Deke told me Gothel's threats scared the adults from helping us."

"How long has he been getting away with this?"

Beneath my fingers, her skin turns icy.

"As Grant Gothel, for decades. Robbie hacked into Opus. He found references going back long before the year dear Papa claims to have been born. Gothel has used many names."

The fiend's green glass eyes burn through my darkness. Who or what is this man with his poison weeds, blazing hands, and contract clauses that appear out of thin air? I shudder at the memory of his tea breath and the way it muddled my thinking.

"I'll drive a stake through his heart."

"Grant Gothel has no heart."

We hold each other until she murmurs in my ear. "Snapper, Robbie, Leeni, and others are heading this way." She pulls me in with such force any rib that wasn't bruised before joins their damaged teammates. "Justin, this may be my last chance to say this." Every contact between her lips and my skin raises a spark. "I love you for seeing through the Zeli façade. Gothel's grip on me felt unbreakable until you sang to me. You gave Rapunzel's voice your beautiful music, not Zeli's. I was lost. No matter what happens, I'll love you forever for finding me."

She's kissing me before I have a chance to confess this luminous spirit in my arms saved a heart war torn by abandonment and a life defined by kicks instead of kisses.

When Zeli pulls away, a heavy hand drops onto my shoulder.

Zeli is fierce. "Don't touch him."

"He's cool, Zeli," says Robbie.

"Justin."

I know the voice.

"I've never been so damn glad to see anyone in my life."

Zeli is a she-wolf. "Who are you?"

"Freddie Belarus."

I reach toward him. "Feisty B?"

Arms pull me in. The world spins faster. This can't be real. Freddie, here?

"Forgive me, Justin. I should have fought harder to keep you when your uncle came sniffing around to take you away. I begged Rhona not to let that fucker risk your life to boost his reputation."

Pain like drops of acid prick my ruined tear ducts. "Why'd she let me go?"

He grunts. "The truth, a kid was never supposed to be part of her deal."

Truth blows. My family only saw me as someone to be used or left behind, unavoidable baggage. That's a dark concept to face so I never did. Denying it turned me into a non-trusting prick.

Freddie squeezes my arm. "I was on the plaza that first night of the Summer Number One. I couldn't believe it was you. I've been trying to get in touch ever since, and then Rand called."

I grab a handful of his shirt. "I saw you."

Snapper clears his throat. "Freddie, time to swap in."

Feisty's voice is in my ear. "I swear I will never let you down again, Justin. You're family. Count on me." And then he's gone.

Zeli's voice wraps around me. "He's replacing Gothel's new mix man who just happened to get an emergency call from home."

Bless this insanely interconnected boulevard tapestry. This is what family is supposed to be, people who pull you close and fight for you instead of discarding you. By opening up to trust them, I've begun to see what they see in me, a glimpse of genuine value.

Rand's voice is close. It startles me. "Zeli, help me get the jumper to his feet." Rand and Zeli lift me. "Time to claim our pound of Gothel flesh."

Z's arm locks around my waist. "Justin's not strong enough."

"Forget about me." I raise my hands. "Zeli goes nowhere near Gothel."

Her breath is a torch against my skin. "I'm done with towers and ranches. It's my turn to come out swinging and save the kids damned by his Opus."

The pop queen free of her extensions, turns warrior.

"I know you've both suffered at the hands of that bastard, but tonight is not about you," says Rand, a river of danger coursing through his words. "Tonight is for Santino."

I slide an arm around Zeli's waist. "What's the plan?"

"Turns out," says Robbie, thumping me gently between shoulder blades. "Your woman has a gift in the plan department."

The air around us warms as more gather. Voices bounce and crisscross in this echo chamber, outlining my role in Gothel's finale. Zeli pinches me any time I protest and attempt to distance her from the danger ahead. "This is my fight, Justin."

The ceiling above us rumbles.

Robbie buzzes in my ear. "Stomping from the plaza."

Gothel's voice oozes into the garage from a car radio. "Well-deserved accolades for our number one amateur artist. Take another bow, Cama Rama."

I lock my teeth. "Turn it off."

Zeli lays a finger to my lips.

"And now, sitting on the top rung of Rampion Records' stairway to the stars, is your current number one pro, Gigabyte. Who will soar through the Summer Number One stratosphere into the top spot this year, amateur or professional? Cast your vote, and we'll crown a champion at midnight."

Rand's throaty call to arms ricochets around us. "Gentlemen, to your bikes." Engines snarl to life.

I press my mouth to Zeli's ear. "Paint me a picture."

Her lips grab mine in a kiss filled with rage and fury. Her mouth works against mine as she speaks. "Banners raised. Steeds mounted. Lances pointed. Turn, Gothel, and look upon your destruction."

37

THE SUMMER NUMBER ONE

BLINDNESS IS BRUTAL WITH ITS LACK OF UP, DOWN, OR SIDEWAYS.

"Elevator," says Zeli. I trip over the threshold. "The others are waiting on the plaza. Let's get you changed." Doors hiss closed. The elevator lurches to a stop. Z eases me out of my jumpsuit.

I let her dress me like a paper doll. Everywhere she touches comes alive. I pull her against me, feeling the shape of her, relearning sensations. I will again discover the beauty and perfection of her touch, taste, and every sweet hidden fragrance of her body. Even stricken blind, the precious memory of being twined together with her in passion brightens my gray world.

Z squeezes my hand as the elevator starts up. "Once we step out of here, our goon stand-ins will act like they're hauling us to Gothel."

I hear the swish of a door and the pulse of Gigabyte's music. A muscled arm winds around me.

Zeli growls. "Careful."

The woman knows how to be the boss.

She narrates every move. "Bridge." The moat rushes beneath my feet. "We're hugging the outside of the VIP pavilion."

A goontastic voice whispers in front of us, "Clear."

Z keeps painting the picture. "Now we're between curtains behind the VIP area almost to the mix console. They sealed up the door at the back. We have to climb down the hatch from onstage." She guides my hands shoulder high to the edge of what must be the stage. Gigabyte's drumbeats send vibrations skittering through my bones.

"Stop," I say, hoping she can hear me through the music. "Kiss me. Right now. If anything goes wrong–"

She pushes me against the stage, pressing her mouth hard against mine. My hands slide along her body, and she curls a leg around me, drawing us hip to hip. We kiss with fervor strong enough to leave an imprint on the sky, like our song. If we go down tonight, our passion will haunt the Rampion Plaza forever.

Z breathes in my ear. "This is for reals. Me and you."

With her help, I climb onto the stage. Freddie's rough hands guide me forward. A thumb presses a mic to my hairline.

Zeli whispers, "Did they plant the sneak mic on Gothel?"

Feisty chuckles. "Told him it was a backup so none of his fabulous banter would be lost to technical difficulties." He guides me forward. "Down the hatch, folks."

I visualize my position. I've been here before. The trap door is just upstage of the mix board platform. Zeli and Feisty help me disappear, and she tucks in next to me while the plaza boils over with Gigabyte love.

"What a magical night." Gothel's amplified voice booms across Rampion Plaza. "Fans around the globe, I place the Summer Number One into your hands."

Zeli kisses my ear. "Lights are fading."

The crowd cheers and stomps for the climax of the competition. A single note from a Gigabyte electric guitar rises above the din. One by one the rest of Gigabyte add their instruments. Above us, the audience goes crazy for an encore.

I hear Gothel order the lights back up. Ever the showman, he grabs the opportunity. "You didn't think I'd leave you without one final treat."

The crowd screams their approval.

"I give you GIGABYTE." Gothel takes our bait.

Gigabyte champions every one, amp up their single note and bust into our song.

From under the stage, Zeli and I unleash our voices together. "Just in time..."

By Gothel's second curse, his backup mic is hot. "Where the hell are they? Mange, grab them."

Our song continues to taunt him. My voice is grit, a counterpoint to Zeli's liquid fire.

"I want their asses NOW!"

Feisty directs our voices through hundreds of speakers. Gothel can't pinpoint our nest.

Sweat coats my face as Zeli and I sing, locked in each other's arms. "My heart wept, reaching deep for hope."

"I'll rip the flesh from their bones."

Feisty B. adds reverb to enhance Gothel's demonic overtones.

I find Zeli's lips with my finger.

She's smiling as she sings. "To search beyond the clouds for lover's eyes."

Gothel's ferocity might set the curtains ablaze. "Kill the broadcast!"

A storm of static and squeals crash around us. Gigabyte stops playing backup. Gothel's voice rings clear over the plaza. "I want Justin Time's head with Zeli's next to it." A horrified choke follows on the heels of our death sentence as Gothel realizes he's broadcasting.

Zeli and I nearly crush the bones in each other's hands. From points all around the plaza, engines roar. I envision the bikes converging in front of the stage to bring down a demon.

Gothel sings a different tune: panic. "Mange?"

"Up," says Zeli.

We slam the trap door open. She helps me clamber onto the stage.

"Paint me the picture, Z."

"It's beautiful. Gothel is trying to escape into the audience. Rand's people on their bikes joined the crowd to pin him."

I recognize Kaydance's squawk off to the side. "Cut the feed! All hands to Gothel."

Zeli keeps painting. "We're walking downstage around Gigabyte." She calls out. "Cue the spots."

A blast of heat catches my face. In front of me the plaza has enough juice to lift off.

A chant overrides Gothel's threats and curses.

"ZELI! JUSTIN!"

"They're herding him this way," says Z.

Feisty B. keeps Gothel's mic hot. "Get your fucking paws off me."

I squeeze Zeli's arm. "Stay clear of his hands. Cornered beasts bite."

"How dare you!" Gothel rages.

Zeli hisses. "How dare *you*."

Gothel releases a killing howl. He must have lunged our way because a wave of heat washes over us as hands pull us backward. The rip of tape crackles through the air followed by the glorious tune of Gothel's garbled words.

Zeli shouts in my ear. "They've slapped a fat piece of silver duct tape over his mouth and dunked his hands in ice water just to be safe."

"ZELI! JUSTIN!"

"Hello," says Zeli.

The Summer Number One audience breaks their chant and goes ballistic as their pop queen once again holds court.

"I've got a Summer Number One right here, a Summer Number One vandal. Grant Gothel doesn't make stars. He steals them, twisting our true sound to fit his sick formula for fame. And if you dare to cross him..."

Her fingers slide under the gauze wrapped around my head. "Sorry, love," Zeli whispers as she gently works the bandage away from the pulpy mess I imagine my eyes to be.

"He'll claw you to bits," she says in the coldest tone I've ever heard.

It sounds as if boiling geysers of anger shoot from the crowd. My shredded face must be a horror on the Jumbotrons.

"Once upon a time..." says Zeli. The motorcycle engines rev as one and then purr beneath her voice. She weaves the truth of Gothel's evil. Her banishment in the tower, the Rampion Ranch prison camp, stolen children, tea that destroys a singer's true sound, threats, cruelty.

Her words flay Gothel to the bone.

"Anything I've left out, Papa?" Zeli's voice rings with victory. "Pull the tape."

The cool package that was Grant Gothel disintegrates under Zeli's truths. "You witch. Time, you bastard. You pissasses will not take me down. Keep looking behind. I'll be there. I always am. I always will be." His threats disappear under a buzz of voices.

"Z, his fire fingers?"

Zeli's tone is sharp. "I heard him bellyaching to Mange that he blew himself out when he fried my extensions. He tried to force tears out of me. I fought, and he only got a few. There weren't enough to recharge him."

My mind darts back to the penthouse when he grabbed me. The burn from his grip was missing.

"I hope his power is finally spent without my tears." She threads fingers through mine. "Police took him away in handcuffs. Robo Robbie wrapped up Gothel's Opus files with a big red bow and anonymously leaked them."

It's done. We threw water on the fiend and melted him—me,

Rapunzel, Santino, and the invincible Hollywood Boulevard tapestry.

Zeli is free.

Gothel is history.

But so is Santino.

The rush of victory leaks out. Intense pain takes its place. All the drive and hope that's fueled me since I fell from the tower dissolves as the extent of my brokenness consumes me.

I'm a sandcastle at high tide.

Zeli can't hold me. I crumple to the stage floor. The world siphons away. My name bounces through the crowd as the volume on my hearing fades toward mute.

"Pull the curtain!" screams Zeli. "Justin, stay with me. Baby, stay with me." Her breath floats across my face, a warm current in the snap of cold night air.

I want to touch her. Nothing works, except my lips.

"It's bad, Z."

This isn't passing out. It's beyond that. Cold fear thrills through my veins, freezing the heat of life. Like ice forming over the surface of a pond, my mouth is becoming fixed. Beneath my head is the softness of Zeli's lap. I push words through the frost.

"I'm falling."

"No." She howls.

Warm liquid spills onto my forehead and traces a path down to whatever is left of my eyes.

"I love you, Rapunzel."

My arms manage a last embrace and pull her down to seal my final breath with a kiss.

The liquid stream pools in my ruined eyes. A wildfire blasts through my skull. My back arches, and I scream. Whirlpools of golden sparkles twirl to the core of my bloody sockets. My body convulses. Hands restrain me.

One sweet sound breaks through torment.

"I love you, Justin MacKenzie."

A spike jolts through my head, and I move no more.

A hundred years later, thrumming begins in my skull and flows beneath my eyelids. They flutter down, up, again and again. Each time they open, it grows lighter, until colors and shapes pierce my monochromatic world. There are trusses filled with spotlights and beyond that, the moon.

I see her face.

My Rapunzel.

She leans over me. Her golden miracle tears flow straight from her eyes into mine. They no longer cause pain. These tears are not the tentative daubs she tried to heal me with before or scant amounts that worked for the bruise on her cheek and a slash on Gothel's arm. Rapunzel's river of tears are a gift of love.

"I see you, Zeli."

She presses a thumb to the edge of each eye. "My love."

I grasp Rapunzel's face. "Your tears, they did bring me back."

The light in her crystal blue eyes changes darkness to sunburst.

"Oh, Justin. These tears are a wish made upon my lucky star, a jumper who fell through a Hollywood sky to find me."

Tears drip from my own restored eyes that see nothing but Rapunzel.

"For reals, Rapunzel?"

"For reals," she says. The sweetest sound that ever touched the sky, free from a single drop of Rampion tea, dances from her lips. "Two hearts met, Justin Time, and now our lives entwine."

My eyes awaken fully. I'm alive. There's only music, Rapunzel, and the stars.

Together, we sing. "We banished loneliness found love to stay."

MY ANGEL

F<small>OR ONCE THE AIR IS STILL ON THE ROOF OF THE</small> R<small>AMPION</small> T<small>OWER.</small>
Rows of white chairs fill with Feisty B., Snapper, and the amazing
tapestry of Hollywood Boulevard. Gigabyte, Da Da Da Deacon, and
his collection of grandkids take up an entire section. I wish my
buds from the Slinging Seven were in the ranks. I didn't have the
heart to get in touch and cause shade between Timmer and them.

Zeli and I now steer the ship at Rampion Records. Gothel
forfeited the company by hiding controlling shares under Zeli's
name to avoid tax uglies. Fiend assumed he'd pull her strings
forever. We appreciate the generous, unintentional wedding gift.

We've built space at the label for former Rampion stars now
free from the ranch, and any boulevard folks with a hankering to
work in the music industry. We work with top notch docs to repair
ruined voices, so they'll sing again. Zeli's heart drives our mission.
She's brilliant whether she's in front of a mic or brainstorming the
company's future. Robbie is a kickass head of marketing, and Feisty
B., a mentor from the gods.

As Mistress Mango approaches the mic, Robbie shakes his cell
at me. "Dude, Rampion's *Weekly Number One* just knocked *Kickin' It*

With Midas out of the top spot. Your latest brainchild decimated his numbers."

I sneak a peek at Midas Lear, his three red-headed daughters, and the Holliday brothers, producers of *Kickin' It*. They're all smiles as they chatter with people around them, especially the contingent from Cloudpath Music. Feisty B likes us to play nice with the competition. That's how peeps from our rival labels scored invites to the wedding.

"Keep that on the down-low, Robo. I don't want Midas spilling sour grapes all over Z's day."

Our convo is cut short when Mango fires up the love song that made her a legend. Her voice, recovered from its tea blight, wraps around the guests like a dream. When the same door this cocky jumper walked through all those months ago opens, the rooftop fills with light. Hundreds of crystals that used to adorn Zeli's penthouse ceiling are woven into the brilliant white fabric of her gown. She's a radiant queen to outshine starlight.

My darling steps aside to make way for Leeni to push a wheelchair over the threshold. The tears that began to fill my eyes at the sight of my beautiful bride release in a torrent. From his chair, a battered but on the mend Santino Fedele crooks an elbow for Zeli to slide her hand through.

The sight of him alive and growing stronger every day is better than any platinum hit. I'm so choked up, I hope I recover in time to say my vows.

Freakin' Gothel attempted to hide Santino at the ranch, intending, I'm sure, to use as leverage against us. Snapper and Rand still beat themselves up over leaving him for dead. Ironically, the quick action of the fiend's med team saved Santino's life. He still faces a string of brutal surgeries, but we sprung him from the hospital to give Zeli away.

On Santino's arm, my love makes her way to me. She presses a gentle kiss to our dear friend's cheek. I gently lay a hand on his shoulder.

"We made it here because of you. Thanks, man."

He places his free hand over mine and rasps out a single word. "Brother."

With all three of us and Robbie full-on weeping, Santino places Zeli's hand in mine. I grasp it, never to let go. We vow to love and gift the world with the magic of music. Rapunzel joins me in a kiss filled with pure happiness and the promise of a life forever by her side.

We turn to face our friends, our family. With my wife tucked close to my heart, I reach out and clasp Santino's hand. At the back of the audience, Gigabyte and Da Da Da Deacon pop to their feet and bust out the opening bars of "Just in Time". Everyone rises as if on cue to join them in the song that brought two hearts together under a Hollywood sky.

EPILOGUE

THE HOLLIDAY BROTHER

Zeli and Justin's wedding puts the high in high profile, and not just from the A-lister music folks fanning across the rooftop of the Rampion Records Tower, including their wedding band, who naturally is Gigabyte. The intimidating distance between where I stand and the ground supplies the more concerning high.

The *bonkity bonk* of my heart doesn't imitate the beat of Gigabyte's song. It's the backing track of my terror. I fight the urge to stick my fingers in my mouth and whistle for attention to insist every fool leaning on the railing that surrounds this roof take three giant steps toward the center. Despite the cool evening, there's a distinct possibility I'll nerve sweat right through the jacket of my new Burberry suit. It was a splurge, but a guy wants to fit in at a who's who do.

Slender fingers slide between mine and squeeze. Breath warms my cheek as strands of auburn hair tickle my ear. Chorda Lear whispers. "Are you alright, Adair? Your face is whiter than Zeli's dress."

Leave it to my lifelong bestie to sense I'm about to melt into a pile of phobic goo. I gesticulate with my free hand like the blade of a windmill about to go rogue. "High."

"Hi back," says Chorda, looking adorably baffled.

"Other kind of high: bird – rocket ship – national monument high." My eyes fall to the heels of her bright purple platform shoes that curl into the shape of a music note. How the woman navigates her collection of stilt-high heels without plummeting to the ground bewilders me.

I lie. It usually bewilders me, but today, it totally freaks me out. Up here, a bad spill might send her flying over the edge. I'd relax a smidge if a tether connected Chorda's waist to the railing or if she'd chosen a Justin Time parachute pack as a fashion accessory.

A shriek from behind has the two of us pivoting in unison.

"My phooooooone," hollers Rubata, the middle Lear sister, as she leans over the rail to watch her cell descend thirty stories to the plaza below.

Next to her Glissanda, the oldest sister, aims her cell to be included in a selfie of Rubata's distress.

"Look at me, Ruby. Pout. Now scream." She checks her phone. "I'll tag you."

A tardy evening breeze arrives to whip the silk and gauzy accents of their dresses over the edge. Biting down on my own gut-curdling fear of heights, I try not to imagine the lawsuit our show, *Kickin' It With Midas,* will incur if Rubata's cell phone clocks someone down below. Dropping Chorda's hand, I dash toward her sisters. It's just like the pair of them to put social media hits above fear of death.

I skid to a stop six feet in front of them, unable to get any closer to the rail without passing out and twirl my wrist in a come-hither circle. "Move this way, ladies." If they go over, my future goes with them.

"Adair Holliday, perfect!" says Glissanda, rushing over to hand off her phone. "Get us both and the Hollywood Sign in frame."

My jittery hand is a bad bet to get the money shot they expect. The two sisters strike fashion magazine worthy poses. I snap a series of pictures, hoping there's at least one good one so they move away from the death drop.

Rubata snatches the phone. The two put their heads together and pour over my photographic efforts.

"This one," says Glissanda, tapping the screen.

"No, honey, my lips look better in this one," Rubata insists, imitating the pout I assume she rocks in the shot.

These two will turn my hair grey before my thirtieth birthday. When I take over the executive producer slot on *Kickin' It With Midas* from my father next season, I plan to cope with them the way Dad does now and assign them a keeper. Since the exclusive guest list for this wedding had no leeway for their usual entourage, I inherited the dubious honor of keeping an eye on any and all things Lear tonight.

"We're on," says Chorda, linking arms with Glissanda and Rubata to lead them toward the platform where Gigabyte plays. As they pass me, she bobs her head toward each of her sisters and rolls her eyes. My gaze trails after her. Of all three sisters, Chorda is the grounded one, the generous one, the loveliest...

I ball my hands into fists. Chorda is my friend. Chorda is my colleague. Letting my mind or heart stray in any other direction is shitiocy.

She turns back to me and calls. "Save me a dance."

I throw her my signature doofy thumbs up, complete with wink.

Chorda raises her eyebrows. "Unless you plan on busting out your knee-popping, grasshopper moves."

I flush from neck to face, remembering nights back in college when Chorda attempted to coach me in the art of cool guy dancing. She did not succeed.

She laughs, flipping her hair as she steps up to the mic with her sisters.

With Gigabyte as their backup band, the sisters' voices rise in the lacy love ballad Chorda wrote for Justin and Zeli. The newly-weds circle the dance floor in the center of the roof, seeing only each other. Their obvious adoration bathes the crowd with the magic of honest to goodness true love. Dusk settles over Hollywood, and a thousand twinkle lights brighten the party.

As Chorda sings the solo, she sways to the melody. I imagine her doing the same in my arms as we dance. What would we see if we gazed into each other's eyes on the dance floor?

Oh, I am in trouble.

Thank you for reading! Did you enjoy? Please add your review because nothing helps an author more and encourages readers to take a chance on a book than a review.

And don't miss book two of the *Rockin' Fairy Tales* series coming soon and find more from Leslie O'Sullivan at www.leslieosullivanwrites.com

Until then, find more Mystic Owl books with <u>LOVE AT 20,000 LEAGUES</u> by Lizzy Gayle. Turn the page for a sneak peek!

You can also sign up for the City Owl Press newsletter to receive notice of all book releases!

SNEAK PEEK OF LOVE AT 20,000 LEAGUES

BY LIZZY GAYLE

I'd never felt so vulnerable. The ocean closed above me, swallowing the shuttle into a suffocating vastness that made me itch to claw at the 360-degree windows. Obviously, that would have been useless, but it was hard to turn away from the unending view. So, I hugged myself in an attempt to stifle my panicked urges and found a seat in the circular back-to-back rows of the luxury pod.

Not only were there thousands upon thousands of tons of water pressing in on us, but now that it was too late to change my mind, a million reasons not to go raced through my brain. The faster we accelerated toward the bottom, the less convincing my reasons for coming felt. The engineer in me studied every rivet, weld, and seal and found them flawless—beautifully designed actually—but that did little to sooth my near-panicked emotional state.

The other fifty people onboard crowded close to the impossibly thin AC glass, gawking and chattering like they were viewing the Grand Canyon for the first time and not an endless darkness illuminated by the blue glow that caught the occasional school of silver herring. The new technology that allowed such a thin barrier had been thoroughly tested over the years but that didn't mean I had to like it. Proven or not, I couldn't help but long for the days when glass for underwater vessels had been four to six inches thick. My father and Jackson stood front and center with the other sheeple, smiling like they hadn't a care in the world, like we didn't just leave Mom, weak and battered by chemo, all alone on the surface.

Her unnaturally thin face was all I saw behind her smile, the smooth skin of her scalp visible through the woven texture of her large-brimmed hat.

"I need you to go," she'd said for the fourteenth time, framed by the sun like an angel with a halo.

She'd finally convinced me with her crazy, characteristically unselfish wish that I play nice with Dad and the woman he'd cheated on her with.

"Excuse me, Miss Meadows, but you look a bit peaked."

I stared up into the plastic face of Dr. Candice Lawry, Chief Operating Officer and Artificial Intelligence Guru of Bennet Systems. *Wonderful.*

Candice always looked like she swallowed something horrible but was trying to smile through it and not let on. I suspected it had something to do with being as high-ranking as one can get inside Bennet Systems, yet not being a complete insider, aka literal part of the disfunction that was the Bennet family.

"Thanks," I said, taking the Hydropod she held out to me in the hopes it would be enough to send her on her way.

"Your profile shows you are at an increased risk for DSI," she said, sitting on the edge of the seat beside me and crossing her long legs.

"Depth Sensitivity Illness is a made-up term to excuse the psychological effects of being crushed beneath a million tons of ocean water," I said, taking a sip from the malleable pod she'd handed me. A genius invention, the bubble-shaped object held the perfect amount of electrolyte enhanced water and when it was finished the thin skin remaining could be swallowed as well.

She smirked. "I'll let that comment go, considering the symptoms include lowered inhibitions and heightened anger."

I took another swig, not wanting to feed into it. She leaned in, elbows perched on knees, glassy green eyes unnervingly close as she tapped her thumb and finger together like she had an invisible castanet.

"Let's not have any issues that might spoil this demo trip for anyone. If you feel like you can't control yourself, there's always the option of stasis until it's time to leave."

Did she just threaten to put me to sleep for a month in a box if I didn't behave?

She rose while I remained speechless and cleared her throat to get the attention of the fourteen other families. Bennet Systems, or BS as I lovingly referred to them, was all about family. Frankly, to me, it was more like a cult that kept everyone close enough to monitor. As Candice warned, those who misbehaved were dealt with.

"Welcome!" she chirped in a fake voice that sounded like an animatronic gone wild. "And congratulations on reaching this milestone. You will be the first people to enjoy the new luxury resort, Paradise Atlantis."

She paused for applause.

"We at Bennet Systems are thrilled to be able to offer our very own employees and their families this opportunity before opening our doors to the public. You've worked hard to make this happen, and we extend all the luxury of the finest to each of you in thanks. You will experience AI like never before, as all of your needs are met, and hopefully exceeded, by our artificial staff members. If there's anything you need, just press one of the silver call buttons located throughout the grounds and buildings and you will be showered with assistance. Enjoy the ride, we should be docking in less than an hour."

Everyone erupted into more applause and chatter as Candice waited, clearly not finished.

"One last surprise. We are not the only ones spending a month on Paradise Atlantis."

A hush fell over the shuttle as people began to pay attention.

"The Bennets have decided to join us. Mrs. Bennet wants you to know that you are all part of her extended family."

With this information, Miss C.O.O. disappeared into the crowd, which seemed to swallow her whole.

The entire Bennet clan? For a month? Trapped down beneath the waves with us? My mind immediately went to the only Bennet I'd ever been interested in meeting, Mason. My mouth dried up despite my Hydropod. I'd never been able to string two words together around him. One look at his sparkling eyes or glorious physique and I was destined to become a tongue-tied adolescent all over again.

Pull it together, Sam. I told myself, tightening my ponytail. I needed to focus for shit's sake. I was twenty-six years old and had a master's in engineering in Artificial Intelligence from MIT. I'd be starting work on my doctorate once Mom was healthy again. Not only did I not have time for a man, Adonis-like or not, but I did not have time for frivolities while Mom suffered.

I would simply tour the gallery as often as possible, inspect what I could about the engineering while avoiding certain people, and stay in my room the rest of the time. I closed my eyes and leaned my head back, seeing no reason to keep them open and stare at the dark beyond. Planning would keep me focused on the right things.

"At least somebody here isn't ogling a window with a view of nothing," said a deep voice to my right.

My eyes popped open and took in the face of the dark, handsome stranger. His deep brown eyes reminded me of the woods above land. Thick hair framed his face and carefully trimmed beard.

"Travis Gould." He held out a large hand to shake.

It was warm, but calloused, and he didn't hold back on the strength of the welcome.

"Samantha Meadows," I said. "What department are you in?"

He scoffed. "None. I refused the work study. My parents unfortunately did not. My dad is head of Interior Design, and my mom is the main vital-systems engineer."

I nodded. Bennet Systems notoriously hired females for lead science roles. With the exclusion of my father of course, since he and my mother met Mrs. Bennet back in college. He'd been a fixture since the start, which meant the rest of us were as well.

"Why'd you refuse the work study?" I asked, curiosity getting the better of me.

"I will never work for those assholes."

I smiled despite myself. Maybe we had something in common.

"I don't work for them either," I said. "Dragged here with family, same as you."

The shuttle lurched like it'd been hit by a torpedo, and I froze, clutching the armrests of the seat. My head pounded as my blood pressure skyrocketed.

"You okay?" Travis asked, his thick eyebrows furrowing into one as he stared at my white knuckles.

"What was that?" I breathed.

He grinned and pointed toward a giggling group of girls by the glass. They waved and made silly faces at a dolphin that hovered on the other side. The creature appeared to be smiling ear to ear. I was confused for another moment until one girl put her hand on the glass and the dolphin headbutted it, making the whole vessel seesaw.

"What if it breaks the AC glass? Or it knocks us off course?" I asked, staring at the horrible sight. The engineer in me knew it was a ridiculous fear, but the terrified woman in me disagreed.

Travis laughed, bringing my attention back to him. The rest of my blood rushed to my face and down between my legs when he set his hand on mine. I guess not getting laid in over a year had unfortunate effects on my body.

"It's a dolphin, not an enemy submarine. I'm pretty sure even the assholes could've predicted that. In all seriousness though, are you sure you're okay? If you're afraid of the ocean this is not going to be a pleasant trip."

"Thanks, Captain Obvious. I'm good." I stood up on shaky legs and strode as confidently as possible over to join my father and Jackson. Alyssa was off chatting with Candice, so it was as good a time as any to make a half-assed effort.

"Sammie." Dad held out a hand for me and I took it, forcing a smile. I promised I'd try after all. "Enjoying the view?"

"Jackson sure is," I said, noting my brother's wandering eyes that were locked onto his newest target, a young woman with the body of a super model, too much of which showed beneath her tangerine romper.

My six-foot-two brother bumped me with his hip, making me stagger.

"Are you eight or twenty-eight?" I asked, downing the remainder of my water and popping the rest in my mouth.

My father's smile was worth it though, the way his eyes crinkled when it was genuine always warmed my heart. If only he'd reserved it for our family and not shared it, first with BS and then Alyssa.

"Stand over here, Little Dragon," Dad said, repositioning me with a clear view of the glass. My heartrate sped up, but he held me tightly from behind, grasping my arms for security.

"Dad I'm not twelve anymore," I said, making light of his pet name given because of the way my nostrils flared when I was super angry, like I was about to spit fire.

"You'll always be my baby. Now if you look a bit down and to the left you'll be able to get a first glimpse. It should come into view any minute and this is the prime spot. That's why I've been staking it out."

I bit my lip so as not to make a snarky comment. I promised Mom I'd try. I should at least do so for the first day I supposed.

Within the next thirty seconds or so, a glowing light appeared in the dark waters. As we swooped toward it, the shining bubble seemed to rise from the depths of the Atlantic, revealing a ten-mile-wide snow-globe of something out of a 50's futuristic B movie. Emerald green pastures dotted with bright red and yellow blooms punctuated the circular space. In the center of the maze-like perimeter stood a speckled white statue of some sort. Around it, gleaming silver buildings of rounded glass and metal shone beneath what appeared to be... sunlight.

"How?" I asked, unable to take my eyes off the scene. The cheesy brochure I threw in the recycling can upon receipt didn't do it justice.

"They're called nanosuns," Dad said, reading my thoughts. "I developed them myself. They even dim and wane into a moonlight effect at night that follows the actual cycle of the moon."

It was amazing. But I was not admitting that to him. If that's what started his years of absence from our home—from Mom, then I refused to compliment it.

"Please prepare for docking," Candice chirped.

"Prepare?" I said, unable to control the high-pitched way it came out. "Is it dangerous?"

Jackson laughed, no doubt enjoying torturing his sister. It was like we'd gone back in time to elementary school. I shouldn't have been surprised. We hadn't spoken much since he took the job at BS in our father's department working under him. Better that than in AI with Alyssa. Truthfully speaking, she was closer in age to him than our father. Youngest woman to ever earn a PhD in Artificial Intelligence from Bennet University, she was the logical choice to take over the position from Candice when she was promoted to the equivalent of second in command four years earlier. That's when the affair started and when Mom's first bout of cancer was diagnosed, which made it that much worse. Before that, we'd all gotten quite good at pretending it was normal for Dad to never be around —always working.

I wondered where Alyssa was. It was entirely possible she was avoiding me. That thought brought a big smile to my face.

"You have nothing to worry about, Little Dragon. Just a formality to announce the docking procedure."

I nodded and leaned back into Dad's chest, allowing myself to feel safe for once. It was almost perfect until I heard Alyssa's voice.

"Oh, I'm so glad you two are getting along!"

I pulled away from my dad and hugged myself, stepping far enough away to make a point without saying it. She didn't seem to notice though as she cozied up to him, taking my place in his arms. Her perfect face with her perfect, smooth, dark skin and perfect long lashes, and perfect straight smile lit up as though from within as he rocked her slowly side to side, wrapping his arms around her.

My stomach swam as if the Angelfish outside the closest window had crawled inside it.

"Have you enjoyed the ride, Samantha?" she asked, continuing to beam like a bunch of nanosuns.

"Not really," I said. Dad's crinkle smile faded behind her, and I almost regretted speaking the truth.

Before anyone could say anything else, the shuttle lurched slightly. I tried to convince myself it was another dolphin to slow my heartrate. But I soon realized that was the ship slowing for the docking procedure Candice mentioned.

It looked like we were about to smash straight into the giant glass bubble when we came to a full stop and dropped downward like an elevator until the view was replaced by a bright green door that slid open to admit us. Smooth as silk, the shuttle slipped inside and the door closed. The water around us drained through the grated floor and a second door opened, offering an upward slope festooned with marble mermaid and merman statues lining the glowing path.

"Impressed yet, sis?" Jackson asked as the oohing and ahhing crowd around us pushed their way outside.

"Too gaudy for me," I said, feet stuck to the ground.

Jackson narrowed his hazel eyes at me and drew a hand back through his tawny hair as understanding lit his face.

"Come on. I'll help you."

Heat rushed to my pale cheeks. I'd never been able to hide a blush, so instead of arguing I accepted his offered hand. It was better than being stuck in the shuttle for a month. I scanned ahead and caught sight of Travis at the top of the incline. His sharp gaze bored into me, causing a tingle of anticipation to spread throughout my body. And together with my somewhat estranged brother, I moved forward, focused on possibilities I hadn't originally considered as opposed to the oppressive view.

Don't stop now. Keep reading Mystic Owl books with your copy of <u>LOVE AT 20,000 LEAGUES</u> by Lizzy Gayle.

And don't miss book two of the *Rockin' Fairy Tales* series coming soon!

Don't miss book two of the *Rockin' Fairy Tales* series coming soon and find more from Leslie O'Sullivan at www.leslieosullivanwrites.com

Until then, find more Mystic Owl books with LOVE AT 20,000 LEAGUES by Lizzy Gayle.

Paradise Atlantis: The underwater, high tech vacation destination where utopia awaits.

Not for Sam. Not only is she deathly afraid of being submerged under millions of tons of ocean water, she's stuck for an entire month with the people she blames for her family falling apart. Even with the unexpected attention of two sexy men, including her longtime celebrity infatuation, Sam is sure the trip will be a nightmare.

She's both right and wrong. A type of pressure sickness she was unprepared for hits Sam hard, causing both lowered inhibitions and blackouts. When she gives in to her desires, a passionate romance blossoms.

Unfortunately, even this steamy new relationship can't salvage the trip when a saboteur uses the AI to commit murder – murder timed perfectly with Sam's mysterious blackouts. Now Sam must clear her conscience by finding the truth. But is she prepared for what she'll find? Because either she's a killer or she's setting herself up to be next on the growing list of victims.

Please sign up for the City Owl Press newsletter for chances to win special subscriber-only contests and giveaways as well as receiving information on upcoming releases and special excerpts.

All reviews are **welcome** and **appreciated**. Please consider leaving one on your favorite social media and book buying sites.

Escape Your World. Get Lost in Ours! City Owl Press at www. cityowlpress.com.

ACKNOWLEDGMENTS

I'm so grateful to everyone at Mystic Owl and City Owl Press for the creative, supportive, and collaborative environment they create for artists. The cover by MiblArt took my breath away. There aren't enough words of praise for my talented editors, Lisa Green and Heather McCorkle, for their insights and believing in Justin and Zeli's story. You made this writer's dream come true.

Thank you to the incredible writing and critiquing talents of Lizzy Gayle, Julie Musil, and Sarah Skilton. Your unwavering support is the harmony to enhance my melodies. Our nights at the pub never fail to inspire.

A symphony of thanks to my wonderful mentors, Eric Elfman and Stacey Lee, amazing authors themselves, who will forever be the voices singing in my ear as I craft a story.

A chorus of loving gratitude to my sisters of the heart, Laurie, Diane, and Flo, and the Desmond family, Robert, Tiffany, Tabitha, Gwynneth, and Trillian for encouraging me all – these – years to stay on my writing path.

My dearest, Cameron and Melissa, you are the song of joy in my life and the reason I tell stories. I am constantly in awe of the unique talents and gifts you bring to this world. Rich and John, you are my proof that true love exists. Mom, your belief that my goal to be an author would someday come true is golden, thank you.

To the readers who joined Justin and Zeli on their journey, may your lives be filled with love and music.

ABOUT THE AUTHOR

LESLIE O'SULLIVAN is the author of *Rockin' Fairy Tales*, an adult romance series of Shakespeare/fairy tale mash ups set against the back-drop of Hollywood's music scene. Coming soon is her *Behind the Scenes* contemporary romance series that peeks into the off-camera secrets of a wildly popular television drama. She's a UCLA Bruin with a BA and MFA from their Department of Theater where she also taught for years on the design faculty. Her tenure in the world of television was as the assistant art director on "It's Garry Shandling's Show." Leslie loves to indulge her fangirl side each year at San Diego Comic Con.

www.leslieosullivanwrites.com

 facebook.com/leslie.osullivanauthor
 instagram.com/leslieosullivanwrites
 twitter.com/LeslieSulliRose

ABOUT THE PUBLISHER

City Owl Press is a cutting edge indie publishing company, bringing the world of romance and speculative fiction to discerning readers.

Escape Your World. Get Lost in Ours!

www.cityowlpress.com

Made in the USA
Middletown, DE
26 May 2022

66234578R00177